BAD MOON RISING

Three novellas about despair

The Voice of Rage and Ruin
The end of Alton

Bad Times Today
The sad life of Mary May

Don't Go Round Tonight
Earth's last second

CHRIS HEAL

Published by Chattaway and Spottiswood
Four Marks, Hampshire

candspublishing.org.uk
chrisheal@candspublishing.org.uk

This is a work of fiction, based in part on ideas described in the books of Franz Kafka, Herman Melville, George Orwell, Ivan Turgenev and Kurt Vonnegut. The names, characters and quotes of the principal characters, events and incidents are products of the author's imagination, except where stated otherwise. Opinions about events, characters and organisations are the views of the author.

A catalogue record for this book is available from the British Library.

ISBN 978-1-9161944-5-8

Proofreading: Naomi Aylott MA @naomisproofreadingservices
Design and typeset: Mary Woolley, www.battlefield-design.co.uk
Illustrations: www.radicalcartoons.com
Additional illustrations: 'Don't Go Round Tonight': Ailsa and Murray Heal
Cover design, maps and advertisements: Paul Hewitt, www.battlefield-design.co.uk
Print liaison and website: Andy Severn, www.oxford-ebooks.com

Printed on demand: www.ingramspark.com

I see the bad moon a-risin'
I see troubles on the way
I see earthquakes and lightnin'
I see *bad times today*

Don't go 'round tonight
Well, it's bound to take your life
There's a bad moon on the rise

I hear hurricanes a-blowin'
I know the end is coming soon
I fear rivers overflowin'
I hear *the voice of rage and ruin*

Don't go 'round tonight
Well, it's bound to take your life
There's a bad moon on the rise

Hope you got your things together
Hope you are quite prepared to die
Looks like we're in for nasty weather
One eye is taken for an eye

*Bad Moon Rising**
Creedence Clearwater Revival
Lyrics: John Fogerty, John Cameron
Album: 'Green River', 1969

* Italics show the book and story titles.

CONTENTS

THE VOICE OF RAGE AND RUIN

The end of Alton
(or, perhaps, any British town)

Introduction

We feel a general mood of despair at the pointlessness of existence and arbitrariness of human principles and social institutions. The pointlessness is made worse by the ineptness and venality of all our politicians and leaders. The deeper we sense this, the more life loses its intrinsic value.

The Latin root word 'nihil' means nothing and is used in 'annihilate'.

Despair leads us to deny everything. It is called 'nihilism'.

We do not take any principle on faith, no matter whatever reverence may once have enshrined it. In fact, the more faith there is behind a force that tries to make any of us act in a certain way, the more we fight it.

William Budd
Private diary, 2023

The idea of insurrection in any British town may seem to those who don't follow the news to be unlikely, even impossible. However, reflect on recent spontaneous outbreaks of destruction and mob violence in Bath, Bristol, Cardiff, London and Weymouth. Consider what has happened many times in the past year across France.[1]

Martin Lewis, a popular consumer champion, has suggested that the sharply rising cost of energy and food means civil disorder is 'not far away'.[2] *Just check the internet for growing speculation.*

All an outbreak needs is a determined and skilled leader, sufficient disenchantment and, perhaps, the covert intervention of a malign international actor. When it happens, the forces of order will be far from ready.

Chris Heal
2023

1 *BBC*, 'At least 150 arrests in violent protests over France police killing', bbc.co.uk/news/live/world-europe-66049895, 29/6/2023.

2 *The Economist*, 17/11/2022.

Contents

Illustrations, pictures and maps

1

IT'S THE WAY I FEEL

William Budd joined the army to get out of harm's way. His independent attitude regularly upset rival gangs in Alton, his Hampshire home town, and brought a risk of serious physical injury. His own petty criminal career meant that at each court appearance an impressive dossier sat in front of the prosecuting solicitor. Budd's record was seldom discussed. He was well-known and always pleaded guilty. It was the best way to avoid a non-custodial sentence.

One confident magistrate, a leading local landowner with much experience of young lads employed on his estates, knew what was best for working class types like Budd. He pronounced a third, three-month probation order that was to be managed by a case officer too busy to attend court. The magistrate leaned forward across his bench in a semi-paternal way.

'Budd,' he said bluntly, 'you're going the wrong way. It's not looking good for you. You need to get a grip. Have you thought about the army? It might prove your salvation and make a man of you.'

Budd looked mildly appreciative.

'What does it matter?' he mused.

He could think of no creed or organisation he had met in his short life that made him feel like he belonged, that he was valued. On this, the last day of his teens, he was hardened against power from wherever it came. Without heavy prejudices or any strong beliefs, he was not accustomed to yield to anything. He respected nothing. No arm of authority that sought to control him, school, employers, police, courts, social workers, were worthy of a second thought. When Budd chose not to obey, he often found ready rewards in comfort and pleasure.

Two years later, almost to the day, Budd's comrades had different ideas. They scrabbled for cover against a loose rock wall or tried to dig deep into matted sand. Each soldier knew in his heart that there was no real advantage whichever choice he made. From the loud protestations, a few wanted to be at home with their mothers. Many declared true faith in a divine spirit, usually Jesus, but occasionally Jehovah or Allah. They called out their preferred name with strength and regularity. These shouts were strangely intermingled with others declaring a futile commitment to sexual activity. A handful more of the desperate and emasculated platoon expressed a longing to kill an attacker, immediately and without remorse.

To his surprise, Budd made a good infantryman. Good-looking, wiry and of above average height, he was tough, enjoyed testing his endurance, had an aptitude for tactics in the field and was readily at home with the army's weaponry and equipment. While never at the centre of any group, being a good listener and usually available to help made him popular. His problems, as could have been prophesised, came from his interactions with those in charge, especially when the orders came from a fresh-faced, well-schooled officer who had been taught from birth to claim his place as a leader of men.

Budd's current lieutenant half recognised the challenge. Budd was usually ready with sharp and deliberate insolence, but it was always just on the right side of insubordination. The officer was too inexperienced to understand the depths of Budd's disassociation. Budd cared about officers just enough to get by and that meant that his own lieutenant, not far off his own age, was rarely worthy of attention.

Budd gazed around. Possibly five men were either dead or would be shortly if there was no rescue. Morphine, drips and bandages were not likely to appear in time. His section sergeant was lying on top of a pilot and alongside the patrol's two medics, their supplies ripped apart and scattered. The sergeant had tried a brave but useless rescue. One hundred metres away lay the remains of their transport, its sophisticated self-defence equipment surprisingly breached. The ageing and burning Chinook helicopter, on its side with both sets of rotor blades snapped, spat overheated ammunition. The intermediate tracers from its machine gun showed the paths of the shells, wavering thankfully away into the characterless, sparse scrub. A thick column of black smoke rose carelessly into the dry night air, gradually fading as the last of the light began to ebb.

At this moment, Budd could think of nothing useful to do so he hunkered down. Time sometimes flies like a bird, right now it crawled like a worm. He contemplated his prospects. He decided he should not place too much trust in the British armed forces, support from Uncle Sam, the efficiency of his own equipment, so often found wanting, or the sympathy of a determined and increasingly accurate enemy. It was their desert homeland, after all.

As if to prove Budd's reasoning, a rocket propelled grenade hit just far enough away to leave him untouched, but covered in fragments and dust. A piece of the wall collapsed and killed the corporal he had met for the first time only yesterday. The body was badly broken and could never be put back together, not even for the mother who had been the last thing on the boy's mind. Two short, controlled bursts raked the stones above his head. Their rattles identified Russian and American-made automatic weapons. A sliver of granite lodged in Budd's cheek underneath his right eye. He pulled it out and bright blood ran freely over the grey grime smearing his face. He inspected the shard. Another inch and he would have been blinded and in great pain.

Perhaps he should worship luck? He already knew from the last few months that, statistically, chance was more likely to save his life than any decision taken by his superiors, especially his lieutenant. A shadow blocked part of his view of the Chinook.

'Why aren't you firing, Budd?'

'Sir, because I have no targets, Sir. Thought my ammunition would be better with me than peppering the mud wall of a hut, Sir.'

He patted the stock of his assault rifle, a weapon with over fifty 'appalling' faults when its first models were introduced in 1986.[1]

'If you fire, Budd, they'll think twice about charging us.'

'Sir, never known them to charge, only ambush. Then they melt away before our support arrives, Sir.'

'They'll probably be no support till morning, Budd.'

Lieutenant John Claggart was interrupted by the unmistakable thump of an Apache attack helicopter coming low from behind the wreck. The nearest two

1 Standard assault rifle: A much-modified, British-made L85A3 issued around 2018, with 5.56x45mm cartridges and an effective range up to six hundred metres.

huts disappeared in a flare of black and crimson. The combined smell of high explosive and unwashed sand was unmistakable, even welcoming. Behind, a replacement Chinook lumbered in to collect the wounded.

'Lucky, that, Sir.'

'Budd, your corporal's dead. Take those three men over there and clear the village. The rest of the platoon will supply backup. If the bandits have now melted away as you suggest, you won't be in much danger.'

The accusation of fear was unnecessary and deeply insulting to Budd. There was a brief pause as the two men, each from a different planet, exchanged looks of irreconcilable dislike. It was typical of this boy-man, thought Budd, to use the word *bandit* to try to promote an idea of world-weary experience. Another petty insult followed.

'That's an order, Private.'

It was the first time that Budd had led men into combat and the selected soldiers from his section knew this. If Budd was bothered, it didn't show. He was in his element. He was also freed from most constraints. If his luck continued, he realised in a surge of adrenalin and joy, then there was a possibility that he would kill.

'Leave your packs,' he ordered. 'Load with clips. Ten metres apart, lads, zigzag, make for the hut with the flagpole. One man always on the ground. Communicate. Quicker the run, safer we'll be.'

Budd ordered two other watching men to drop red phosphorus grenades into the attack zone to make smoke and to nullify any visual or night-vision devices that might be waiting.

The lieutenant heard the crisp commands, the voice of leadership under stress. His own fear and indecisiveness drove his dislike into something much worse.

The dash took less than two minutes. The four men grouped, panting, against a wall.

'No time for weaklings,' teased Budd. 'Straight in, lads, before they've all hopped it. Remember your house-to-house training. Watch for wires and IEDs.[2] Free to shoot. Take a prisoner if we can. On me.'

With that, Budd ran down an alley, checking each second doorway and trusting his men to follow and do likewise. He reached the main street without

2 IED: Improvised explosive device.

incident. There was no sign of life. Any villagers unable to escape would be cowering in their main room protecting children with their own bodies. Three men began working the houses, another always outside to supply cover and to watch for any sign of flight. There were, perhaps, thirty dingy homes, innocuous and dangerous. The soldiers approached the last block when a short burst of automatic fire from a doorway sailed over their heads. It meant, probably, an inexperienced shooter. One of the first things to be learned with an automatic weapon was its tendency to force the barrel upwards when the trigger was pressed and held.

Budd didn't hesitate. He pulled the black safety clip from a hand grenade and lobbed it into the space. Its high explosive had an effective casualty radius of fifteen metres, devastating in a normal room. As the echoes from the blast died away, he charged through the shattered entrance. Inside was a bloody mess of women and children. One young girl was screaming. Half of the back door hung on broken hinges. Instinct drove Budd through it. He caught sight of the familiar shape of an AK-47, held by an arm robed in dirty white, as it disappeared around a corner.[3] He gave chase. Within a few seconds, he had a fleeting view of a full figure and fired. He reached the body, kicked it over and looked down on the face of a boy, maybe twelve years old. The boy twitched and Budd loosed a despatching round.

'What the hell are you doing, Budd? You just shot an unarmed child. I told you to wait once you made the main street.'

Lieutenant Claggart had caught up and moved into the fire zone without calling a warning.

Budd did not glance at the officer, but kept his eyes on where snipers might be hiding.

'Sir, he was armed. I didn't know if he was incapacitated. There's his gun by his side ready for use. I had no idea it was a boy, not that it would have made any difference.'

Budd looked the lieutenant full in the eye as two of his men caught up and heard the end of the conversation.

'And you, Sir, are a lying piece of shit.'

---

3 AK-47: A Russian-designed, gas-operated Kalashnikov assault rifle still, after seventy years, one of the most popular and widely-used shoulder weapons in the world.

Two more shots came from behind the village well on the far side of the small square. Budd and his men turned and ran, providing cross cover, and took up separated positions. The lieutenant was left screaming at Budd to hold his ground. The second attacker disappeared and was never found. There was, however, a final single crack. The body of the lieutenant was discovered with a bullet hole in his forehead. Across the street, Budd stood by a remnant of long-forgotten wars, a Lee Enfield rifle with a broken stock which leant discarded like a broom against the wall of the well.[4]

4 Lee Enfield: A bolt-action, magazine-fed repeating rifle that served as the standard weapon of British infantrymen from 1895 until 1957.

'The remnant of long-forgotten wars, a Lee Enfield rifle with a broken stock, leant discarded like a broom against the village well.'

Radical Cartoons

2

GUILT AND FAIR PLAY

Safely returned to base, William Budd, as a matter of course, was ordered to complete a patrol report. Budd declined. It was not deliberate disobedience, he explained. He had lost any memory of what had happened.

This was difficult for many of the regiment's officers to swallow. A brother lieutenant had been shot dead. For members of an organisation that prided itself on its modern, enlightened standards, officers with little experience too readily saw guilt and became putative persecutors. Greater values than simple fair play must be upheld; a direct assault on the honour of the corps needed to be met with firmness. These leaders talked glibly about placing Budd in a cell without a key. If guilt could not be proved, at best he should be sent packing in a disgrace so bad that he would be unemployable. There was wild discussion about instigating a drumhead court-martial.[1] A preliminary investigation was hastily improvised and tentatively begun without formal authority.

A glimmer of common sense, the rule book and a dose of political savvy soon put paid to all these ideas.

The military police quickly took over. They were confident that Budd had killed his officer, but had no direct proof. The indirect evidence, all with witnesses, showed hostility, proximity and means. The lead investigating officer

1 Drumhead court-martial: Held in time of war to hear urgent charges of offences committed in action. The term is said to originate from the use of a drum as an improvised writing table.

was incensed by the claimed loss of memory and, as a result, normal attempts at impartiality were in short supply.

Budd was seen to be evading any personal enquiry. He functioned and interacted normally, carried on everyday conversations, followed orders grudgingly and relaxed with his fellow soldiers. There were no outward signs of illness. It was only when questions were asked about what had happened in the desert from the time of the crash of the Chinook that his face went blank and he struggled for words. Budd could not, or would not, offer any help to find a resolution. Because Budd neither admitted nor denied, his attitude brought into play a legal minefield of disobeying orders. Doing and saying what you are told is the bedrock of any army.

Doctors, one flown in especially from Cyprus, were divided: on the one hand, Budd was in a genuine catatonic shock, on the other he was faking. The condition might be a front for either guilt or innocence. Deception, it was decided, would be proof of murder.

As a result, Budd's case, poorly managed from the start, became a catalogue of petty errors. He was never formally charged with any crime. The defence advice offered to him was incompetent, uncommitted and inconsistent.

Within the week, it was decided that Budd could not continue on tour. There was a danger to general discipline as he became a celebrity in the garrison. There were crude and little disguised jokes about how to handle young and obnoxious lieutenants. He was recalled to England. However, in Winchester, separated from his regiment and held in loose confinement, he did face trials of military and public opinion that later threatened to tear away at the army's hard-won self-confidence.

A parliamentary enquiry, held many months later into the far greater horrors that were to come, declared that Budd's treatment at this time was abusive and unjust.

'What was the evidence against this soldier?' queried a Labour firebrand. 'Were the rights of this man upheld? Can anyone provide a joined-up argument that merits his defamation? What blame do the army command face for what followed? Has anyone been disciplined?'

At the core of the question was the necessarily admirable Claggart, killed while standing alone in the middle of an impoverished and unimportant village, in a, perhaps, foolhardy search and destroy mission that he had chosen not to lead. The attack was in retaliation for a successful ambush which downed an expensive helicopter and left seven other soldiers and airmen dead or dying from wounds. Nine women and children, including an armed boy insurgent, had been killed or injured, all by Budd. The officer had died from a single, well-aimed bullet from an old rifle which had been left nearby and discovered by Budd. Discarding a valuable and serviceable, even if damaged weapon, in flight would never have happened, said some. No perpetrator was seen. There were no witnesses to the death.

From the start, thought the police, the treatment of Budd stemmed from his public disagreement with the officer. Fellow soldiers, unwillingly and under threats, admitted that Budd had called his superior 'a lying piece of shit'. No one heard what led to Budd's accusation, but it was clear that it followed an argument. There was no suggestion that Budd had made a personal threat. Indeed, if anything, his insult had been made with grudging soldierly respect for rank.

Three other matters added confusion and, depending on personal leanings, could have been taken to support one side or the other.

Budd was a courageous young man, given a sudden and dangerous field command, which based on experience alone should have been led by another. He had conducted his task in a highly professional manner, safeguarding his men as best he could. These men all stood by him. He was right to throw the grenade and had killed a terrorist who had fired on him. He deserved a medal. Alternatively, thought others, he was a depraved thug, operating in blood lust, who had wantonly disobeyed an order, pointlessly killed eight non-combatants without offering them a chance to surrender and then executed a boy soldier who was already seriously wounded.

The accusers might have wished for better material for the dead lieutenant. Claggart was not popular, on his first tour and proving to be a weak leader who was impossible to lionise. Had he lived, he would soon have been moved to a less onerous rear position. The difficulty was that he was the offspring of a much admired, much decorated, colonel whose lacklustre son was his one overwhelming blind spot. Sentiment moved to the fore as the officer corps looked to protect their own.

Finally, there was Budd himself. He was one of three sons and a daughter of a truly dysfunctional family. His own drunken father was long gone; other fathers of his siblings, equally sodden, appeared only from time to time. Budd was typical of young men from broken homes who had been in and out of courts of various hues since they first learned to steal and fight. In his home town of Alton, a sleepy and declining centre surrounded by an ever-growing commuter dormitory, many people who knew of him were pleased he had left. To a hard core of miscreants, Budd was a hero for standing against rival, out-of-town gangs and for his refusal to give in to the civic organisations which, they felt, persecuted him.

When his local supporters realised Budd was confined to barracks and not allowed to chose his own legal help, all hell broke loose. The *Hampshire Chronicle* took up his case and that brought the matter to national attention. Budd became a left-wing cause at a time when there were few other emotional sticks to beat an increasingly unpopular government. Here was the establishment denying fundamental democratic rights to one of its own soldiers in order to protect its officer caste.

Budd's far-flung and dissolute family, a short drive from the county capital, smelled easy money. They quickly warmed to their task and learned how to negotiate story and picture fees from newspapers and the foreign press. Professional agitators moved in to help with the organisation of protests. A semi-permanent small city of tents appeared overnight on the green opposite the two Napoleonic-era gate towers of a city barracks. Eggs and tomatoes, although in short supply with the short-term collapse of supermarket supply chains, landed all to readily on staff cars, in fact on any vehicle entering the garrison. The police declared there was insufficient or unclear legislation for them to act and they defaulted to protecting the protestors and ensuring they had sufficient bottles of drinking water.

It was, suggested one of Winchester's senior politicians in an unguarded moment and when under great stress, 'a complete and absolute fuck up'. The comment was overheard by the BBC and gleefully broadcast, with a modesty bleep in place, to a nation that was taking sides with enthusiasm. Social media was everywhere agog and, fanned by suspected Russian state disinformation units, was full with conspiracies, falsehoods and personal threats. As one of the prime minster's senior advisers admitted privately, the situation could well undermine civil order. COBRA, the Civil Contingencies Committee that handles matters of national emergency or major disruption, was given a regular update.

What continued to stick in his command's craw was that Budd refused to say a word about what had happened. Further investigations and more experts in mental health reached an impasse with a lack of proof or any consensus. The affair dragged on with the army indecisive, not wishing to give up on a prosecution. A trial was wishfully pencilled in for six months later at the military court at Bulford on Salisbury Plain.

The army, of course, hated the situation. With the collapse in the esteem over the past fifty years of most of the professions – lawyers, teachers, the civil service, politicians, journalists, the police, the established church and the NHS – the army had assumed the mantle of the country's most respected organisation. Now, here was that essential faith being cast to the winds.

Politicians ordered the army to find a quick solution. Careers were in the balance, honours might be lost, and pensions and knighthoods threatened. Finally, the obvious decision was made. There was insufficient evidence for a trial. If that was so, went the logic, then Budd was a casualty of war. The only remaining route was to give him a medical discharge.

Today, the whole world knows that Budd's loss of memory was faked. No one knows, contrary to accepted opinion at the time, whether this proved he had pulled the trigger.

Budd later explained that he had withdrawn simply because of the lack of belief, the total loss of respect, that had always rested inside him. His reasoning as he leant against the brick wall and heard the bullets flying was now integral to his character. He knew the powers in the army were lined against him, but that was not what concerned him. What mattered was, he realised, that these people were without merit. Officers held no value or interest to him. If anything, he had a personal duty to ignore them and, if roused from his casual state, it would probably be to kill them, indiscriminately and with a modicum of pleasure.

He was content in his newly-concreted freedom. He was secure in himself and, for all the tantrums and coercion around him, he was undisturbed.

His discharge when it came was surprisingly simple. A senior military policeman explained the decision to Budd. For the first time, Budd raised his head and replied.

'Thank you, Sir. I would like to leave the army as soon as possible. I would like to never again have any contact with it.'

'Do you have any other requests?'

'What does it matter?'

Budd signed a letter saying that he accepted he was to leave with immediate effect because of a mental condition brought about by combat. He had been offered and declined unspecified psychiatric treatment. He was not given a reference. The army press office issued the briefest of statements.

'We can confirm that Private William Budd has left the army. The circumstances are personal and confidential. There are no outstanding matters between Mr. Budd and the army. There will be no further comment.'

Within two days and without notice to the outside world, Budd was deposited from an unmarked car at his shabby, terraced erstwhile home in Victoria Road in Alton. He had a thousand pounds in his pocket and a note of a draft for £15,342.73 to his bank account in lieu of six months pay, compensation and an agreed and terminated pension.

No one was ready to greet him as none of his family or friends knew that he was coming.

3

CARE IN THE HOME

As news of Budd's arrival spread through the town, his wider family made for his home. When people at large also heard that their great friend Billy had money in his pocket, the number of well-wishers grew quickly. Youngsters were sent out for bottles and by late afternoon an exuberant party spilled into nearby houses and, as it was a mildly sunny day, into Victoria Road blocking traffic.

By early evening, the police had received more than a dozen complaints. Two hours later, when all hope of an amicable resolution was lost, a spare patrol car was found. The two officers were roundly insulted and quickly embroiled in several scuffles. Half-full bottles flew and hit their targets. Windows were smashed in the houses where unpopular residents lived. A taser was fired in desperation and without proper warning. Two barbs lodged in the skin of Budd's baby brother, Den, aged fifteen, and he lay writhing on a pavement. The youngsters in the crowd were infuriated and surrounded the constables who fought back-to-back with their batons to defend themselves. Their vehicle was overturned and set on fire. The flames spread quickly to the street's nose-to-tail parked white vans and ageing family cars. Den was unhooked and spirited away. The taser was taken as a trophy.

Emboldened, the throng moved the short distance down Littlefields Road and turned right into Normandy Street, part of Alton's depleted shopping thoroughfare. The despised primary school where some had received their only taste of discipline quickly lost its front windows. Many of these ex-pupils were ghost children, lost to education after Covid-19 and no longer recorded on any system.[1] A splinter group lunged away, smashed in a casement, entered and began to pile children's books for a bonfire.

The riot was an unusual incident for local law enforcement both in its severity and in the number of participants. Alton, though, was no haven of peace; it was firmly established in the top ten most dangerous small towns in the county. Recorded crime, more than a hundred incidents a month, far less than reality, concentrated on sexual assaults, break-ins, drunkenness, violence and anti-social behaviour, shoplifting and drugs. Some parts of the town were recognised as no-go areas in the dark hours. The municipal gardens and green spaces generally, car parks, especially by the railway station, and the several narrow lanes running north off the main street were avoided, particularly by females and those walking alone. The lack of patrols forced the town's politicians to band together to criticise publicly and in writing the lowering levels of protection.

The pack, about fifty strong, passed the long-closed police station and lawcourts, now flats and entry homes, and made for the town's shops to start an aimless looting. The few first police to arrive were used to backchat and the occasional push and shove, but this was a mob swelling with drunken inconsistency.

Budd's other brother, Charlie, and their sister were cavorting openly with little thought of consequences. Budd was there on the edge of the crowd, but took little direct part in what went on. He kept an eye on the many night surveillance cameras and made a few suggestions for targets. He also made sure that his jacket hood kept his face in shadow. Having only just that day been set free, Budd was wary of coming under renewed scrutiny.

Besides, what was happening around him was small beer. At the end of the next day, the forces in power would try to downplay everything to a minor if embarrassing inconvenience. Budd was convinced that, with his disdain for authority, he held a power that would not be easy to thwart if it was carefully unleashed. He wanted to strike a telling blow against those who directed his life and kept his family in poverty. If he had his way, what followed would be something never to be forgotten.

---

1 Covid-19: Coronavirus disease 2019 is a contagious disease caused by a virus, the severe acute respiratory syndrome coronavirus 2. The first known case was identified in Wuhan, China, 12/2019. The disease quickly spread worldwide, resulting in a pandemic. Hereinafter abbreviated to 'Covid'.

It took another thirty minutes before backup police vehicles arrived from the local headquarters in Aldershot. By the time the seriousness of what was happening had been realised and further reinforcements called from Winchester, excitement among the participants had begun to pall.

Anyone with knowledge of Alton's shopping area will know that it is a supermarket town. Private shops have gradually been forced out by high business rates and dwindling visitors. Smaller premises were reduced to the standard collection of estate agents, betting outlets, bank branches with limited hours, charity shops, a few fast-changing low price stores and several fast food joints easily found by the pungent oil vapours that permeate from their deep fat fryers.

It is a characteristic of mobs, especially those comprised mainly of an area's poor and unemployed youth, that their attention turns to the businesses that are most likely to provide them with help in desperate times. A special distaste is shown to places whose presence highlights dependency and failure. Alton's Town Hall stands alone in the centre of Market Square. Two sides have arcaded shop windows and doors which house *Citizens Advice* and the town's foodbank and *Energy Advice Cafe*. All glass was systematically shattered and the rudimentary furniture broken. Files and publicity material were scattered. Some well-visited pubs that supplied the cheapest alcohol were invaded and crates of beer and spirits snaked back to the Anstey Park area. All the while, the occasional jeweller with toughened glass windows received only a passing kick or brick.

When the police finally lined up in force, there was little to be seen except for debris. Commanders were anxious to show some results to cover for their tardiness. A few arrests were made among the stragglers who were too drunk to run. Among them was Budd's loudmouth sister, Annabella, known to all as *Belly*, partly for the rhyming of *Billy* and *Belly*, but mostly to recognise that she was grossly overweight as befitted her devotion to supermarket salt and sugar-laden ready meals. It was said that, for her, the kitchen was just a place where plates were left unwashed. She lived her life to her tummy's content.

The next morning, Budd cadged a lift to Aldershot to see how bad matters were. He went alone in order, he hoped, to reduce any ill will that might come from his history. He was quickly recognised and quizzed for an hour by officers smarting from the previous night's humiliation. Little came from it apart from

Alton's Town Hall stands alone in the centre of Market Square. Two sides have arcaded shop windows and doors which house *Citizens Advice* and the town's foodbank and *Energy Advice Cafe*. 'All glass was systematically shattered and the rudimentary furniture broken. Files and publicity material were scattered.'

clear antagonism from his interviewers. They looked for any chance to prove him one of the leaders.

There had been few arrests, but, already, the police were anxious to be rid of Belly. She had been charged with urinating in a public place and with assaulting an officer. The last offence was unlikely to stick, pointed out Budd, as she was still incapable of coherent speech or movement. He made a deal. Belly was given a caution on admittance of guilt, something she later, of course, denied had happened, if Budd would take her away immediately wrapped in a old blanket to allow for her cell to be hosed.

Back home in Victoria Road, the dregs of the family and friends drifted in to sympathise with Belly and to wash her as best they could and put her to bed. Billy first spent time with his mother who had stayed at home throughout, befuddled with a cocktail of pills of many colours. Since Billy had left for the army, she had lost touch with any coherent reality. She did not understand that there had been a riot in the High Street. Slouched in a chair in a loosely-gathered dressing gown without a chord, a cigarette dangling precariously from her lips and with her hair bedraggled, she was alternatively angry and crying. Everyone was called foul names, even her Billy who she loved the most. Billy gazed sadly and recognised there was little he could do for her. She needed to be in rehab for a long time, maybe for ever.

He scoured the table tops and drawers for invoices and card statements and made notes to pay them off. It would be like pouring water into a leaky bucket.

The rest of the morning was spent assimilating all the bad news that was the standard repertoire of the Budd clan: illnesses, drug dependencies, welfare demands, job dismissals, lack of employment opportunities, maxed out credit cards, petty gang fights, loan sharks, broken household equipment, mounting debts at the corner shop, the pubs and the bookies, pending court cases and probationary hearings, the lack of hand-outs.

None of the mishaps was anyone's fault. It was all bad luck. No matter where the Budds turned, they knew the system was against them. Even the few local social workers seemed to have given up; no one rushed to advise the clients from hell.

What surprised the family was their Billy's seeming equanimity as he heard their tales.

As each new calamity unfolded, it was met with a repeated refrain, 'What does it matter?' Even as Budd said the words, he paid close attention to the differing reactions he received.

Early in the afternoon, Billy walked to a bank and made arrangements to cash his army draft. He then went to *The Bakers Arms* where he waited in the small space to the right of the entrance. The wall had half a dozen prints of old Alton. The pub was a surprise, refurbished while he was away with painted wood and fresh plastic-backed seating. The number of TVs increased the deeper one looked. The loudspeaker rap was deafening. Billy asked for it to be turned down and was left alone when the sole bartender went out into the street to smoke and chat with a girlfriend.

The money had arrived. Billy left his half-finished drink to stake a claim to his table. The large sum was given grudgingly by the bank clerk who took to himself some unwarranted responsibility. His instinct was that the banks had the moral ownership of all money and part of his work was to make it difficult for people he did not trust to access what was wholly theirs. One look at Billy Budd told him that the cash would be wasted and not respected.

Billy returned to *The Bakers Arms* and set up court. He sent instructions to close family and to those acquaintances who had caught his eye the night before to visit him alone and in turn. He was looking for those tearaways of both sexes who had been wantonly destructive, had given up on their future and showed no respect for authority. Few of them could articulate what Budd was after, but by his questions they readily understood they were being invited into a dark pit.

'How did you feel last night? Did you hurt anyone? How much do you hate the police? The landlords? The loan sharks? Priests? Bank managers? Lawyers? Social workers? Probation officers? Would you take on a job which meant that, if you survived, you would never be able to come back to this place?

'Would you hurt someone badly if I told you to?'

Some backed off, accepted a little money to soften their problems and left Budd's inner circle forever. Then, again, others listened carefully, still high on their success the previous evening. They whetted their lips and glanced at the diminishing pile of banknotes. Their eyes hardened as they followed the questions, nodded slowly, recognised the leader they desperately needed and offered themselves. They felt hope, not for luxury, but for a chance to get their own back on the people who controlled their awful world. Budd put his hand on the neck of those he selected and pulled their ear close to his mouth. Commitments were exchanged and secrets guaranteed that were much deeper than promises to magistrates or any religious vows.

'The church and the courts aren't the centre of things although they like to think they are,' Budd told them. 'They're not what we measure ourselves against. We don't believe anyone has the right to tell us what to do especially if they are trying to protect what they've stolen from us and their parents stole from our parents. If they try to boss us, treat us as if we are nothing, we will destroy them.

'We are like that sailor in the film who wanted only one thing, to kill that great whale whatever the cost. He took his ship everywhere for many years to get what he wanted. We believe in killing that whale.'

Most of Budd's money crossed the table until he had very little left. Souls were bought.

If the men felt they had found a trailblazer, most of the women were enraptured. Billy was handsome, had killed an army officer so it was said and he had money. He had several offers for his bedroom. Budd selected two girls without remembering their names or ages and they followed him. He didn't make love. He had sex, determined, lengthy and automatic. The girls felt a part of something important. After the immediate enjoyment, he felt nothing at all.

4
GETTING FUNDS

Billy's lumpy sofa acted as his soap box. Three intense faces hung on his every word.

'I don't believe there is a God,' he began. His inner circle nodded. This was hardly controversial.

'Nor do I believe in a government full of toffs and landowners and rich bastards,' he continued. 'They don't care about people like us. They think we're dirt. They just put rules in place so that they can protect their own good life. There's no advantage for us in all the things they make us do.

'We all die, them and us, and then we are gone and anything we've done which hurts or upsets anyone has gone, too. So, the rich people have everything they want and screw everybody and they never really have to pay for it. It's just a case of what you can get away with today and not get caught.'

Billy drew a deep breath and took a pull from his can of strong lager, a present from the riot. He realised what he wanted to say was important, the key to what he wanted to do, but he was not practised at explaining his ideas. He needed to think a bit so that he could share more easily what was on his mind.

'That means I'm against anyone or any organisation that puffs itself up and tells us what to do,' he added.

He tried a bit of emotion to check the response.

'They cramp my style, man. I just want to take them down. I just want to hurt them and if anyone else gets hurt then it's not the best, but at the end of the day it doesn't matter because it's less important. Yes, I just want to take them all down until there's nothing but rubble and all the rules and all the places and all the people in them that make the rules are broken, smashed in pieces and there's nothing left.'

Well, that worked, he thought. His listeners yelped and slapped their thighs.

His brother, Charlie, slowly worked through what it all meant to him.

'You mean,' he asked, 'that when you've pulled everything down, that you don't want to stick anything in its place? You're pulling everything down? Everything? But surely we've got to build something as well? What are you going to do about building afterwards?'

'Nothing.'

'Nothing at all?'

'It's not our job to replace things. It's our job to show how rotten everything is and to tear it down. We smash things because we are a force. A force doesn't bother about anything. It just does.'

A tall, red haired lad called Sam watched a lot of television. Missing some of his favourite programmes worried him.

'What about the blasted TV and radio? Do they have no value?' he queried.

'None at all,' shot back Billy. 'What it seems is that they're run by the rich bastards and the politicians.'

'What about if the programmes are made by people like us and people like me love watching them?'

'It doesn't matter. We condemn everything. Others can build up again if they want, but they'll probably want to build the old things they knew before. It's not for us to do. First, we have to clear the ground.'

Sam tried again.

'If we clear the ground and someone builds back, then we'll have wasted our time?'

'No. If they build, everything can be pulled down again.'

Sam's best mate was Alex, his complete opposite, short, curly black locks, stout, fond of a bag of chips with lots of vinegar. He had even finished school in one piece, without being suspended and with a couple of GCSEs in his satchel.

'You're right, Billy,' he threw in. 'Even the clever ones on social media, the so-called leaders and experts are no good. They're busy talking a lot of nonsense, fussing about with this and that when the real business is about getting one's daily bread and not being bossed about.'

He paused then explained his personal worry.

'If we are going to start this revolution, we need money and we haven't got any. We need cash for our food because we'll need time and space to plan.

'And, of course, we'll want guns and explosives.'

Just then, in one of life's coincidences, there was a lazy knocking at the door. The bell, of course, was broken. It was a courier. Billy came back into the room with an envelope marked 'Private' and 'Only for the attention of Mr. William Budd'. Inside the envelope was £500 in £20 notes. With the money was a sheet of paper with, written in pencil, the number of a storage unit on the road to Selborne, some directions and a padlock key. Another piece of paper was tucked into the pack of notes. It carried a personal message, 'Might be best to collect when it's dark.'

'Can you do that trick again, Billy?' asked his brother.

'I think someone up there likes us,' offered Sam.

'Probably,' mused Billy, 'or at least there's someone very private who wants something done that isn't legal and thinks that we're the lads.'

'There'll be cameras,' said Alex. 'Always are at these storage places. We'd better go hooded. And we'll need a van as we don't know what we'll be picking up.'

'And as that's all true,' finished Billy, 'we'd better change the number plates. Something said during my army training has always stuck in my mind: these cameras 'have turned citizens', you and me, 'into walking ID cards'.' He emphasised to his team the need to be careful and to protect the identity of each member of their band.

The UK is one of the most watched countries in the world with an estimated six million CCTV cameras across the nation – one camera for every ten people.[1] London is the most watched city outside China.

Cameras, some costing as little as £100, can be seen in every public building and private business and on every High Street. The low prices are fuelling rapid growth. Over 180,000 CCTVs are connected to the public internet including stores active in Alton like Costa Coffee, Dominos Pizza, Iceland and Southern

1 CCTV: Closed-Circuit Television. 'The Ministry of Truth. The secretive government units spying on your speech', *Big Brother Watch*, 2023.

Aftermath of a small town street riot: 'The UK is one of the most watched countries in the world with an estimated six million CCTV cameras across the nation – one camera for every ten people. London is the most watched city outside China.'

Radical Cartoons

Co-operative. Many companies never admit the full purpose of their electronic watchdogs.

The variety of surveillance capabilities is breathtaking. Checking for specified physical items is standard: types of clothing, glasses, baggage, umbrellas, bicycles, masks, hard hats, vehicles, queue counting and, of course, weapons. Most members of the general public now know that these cameras can also recognise types of facial hair, gender and age to within five years and even the amount of heat in a space to check how many and how long people stay.

The big advances in facial recognition are less well known. Targeted people can be recognised in a crowd and instantly flagged. Their emotions can be scanned to check for, for example, anger, calm, happiness, sadness, disgust, surprise, confusion and fear.

The military and security services make increasing use of surveillance cameras which explained Billy's inside, if limited, knowledge. Cameras were placed covertly in general thoroughfares and busy places, like festivals and sports grounds. When discovered, the practice was often proved illegal, but that doesn't stop constant attempts by the police to evade questions about the extent of their camera use. Nor does the government seem to be in any hurry to place restrictions that would curtail the police's ability to spy on the voters who placed them in power.

Billy sent Sam and Alex to Barn Store at Hartley Park Farm in an old and nondescript van. They were back within the hour and quickly offloaded a chunky wooden box. The van was driven to where it came from with only its dangling ignition wiring to show that it had been borrowed.

'It was all easy,' reported Alex. 'Maybe you'll remember the storage space as a lavender farm. Most of it is now an industrial park with lots of small businesses for pets and lawnmowers and the like. Barn Store has loads of these blue containers under a large roof. We went straight to it. There was no one about, but you were right about the cameras. They're hanging everywhere. Inside the unit, in the middle of the floor, there was another five hundred smackers.'

Sam threw the notes onto the mug rings that covered the coffee table. He followed it with an A4 brown envelope.

'We didn't open that or the box.'

Charlie picked up a knife from a dirty plate of unfinished food and levered the nailed lid open.

'Fuck me,' said Billy. 'These have never been used. They're bang up to date.'

One by one and with some respect he unwrapped and laid out four semi-automatic pistols.

'These are Glock 17s,' he explained. 'Two months ago, I had one on my belt when I was on patrol. They're for use in close combat. This magazine holds seventeen rounds.'

He picked up a cardboard box and tipped some of its contents onto the table.

'And these little babies are 9mm bullets.'

With practised hands, he removed the empty magazine from the stock and passed it round for inspection.

'Perhaps we should have a look in the envelope,' suggested Alex, 'to see where all of this is going? Then I guess we take these lovely guns out into the woods and learn how to use them?'

Billy tore open the package and put two sheets of paper on the table. They were the floor plans of two Turkish barber shops across the road from each other in Alton High Street. The doors, chairs and tills were marked.

'Someone really is pulling our strings,' he said. 'They know who I am and I think they know what I want to do. How would they know that? They've given us a thousand quid, some top guns, and here are our targets to get some more loot.'

'I get it,' added Sam. 'These barbers are cash only. I went a few weeks ago. It's £15-20 a time. They cut the sides clean and then fade up – like you see on me. These two places each have maybe seven chairs, takes around twenty minutes, pay at the door on the way out. That's, err …'

'… about £400 an hour in readies waiting for us to walk in with our Glocks and take it all,' finished Alex.

Billy laid out the plan. Sam was to travel to Aldershot the next morning to buy a good banger and false plates for cash. It would be hidden after the robbery. Training and target practice would be held the following day in Ackender Wood. Alex and Charlie would get their hair cut so that they could suss out how the places worked. That evening, they would meet together to compare notes, sort out the details and develop an escape plan.

And that's how it went. Billy recruited Ben Smith, a noted local stock car driver, so that the team could hit each barber with two masked and gloved men at the same time while the tuned, two-tone Ford Escort waited outside. Smith was paid in advance and left for Spain for a two-week holiday with his girlfriend within hours of the raid.

It almost went as intended. The money collection was easy. Billy warned that they had to be prepared for opposition. If there was a fight they had three simple choices: run, fight back and risk capture or shoot. In one shop was Ahmet Thakur, twenty-five, newly-arrived from Ankara and a first-time customer. He was also in debt to his uncle Toni for a loan to set up a new business in England. Thakur was quick to temper and seldom thought before action. With a roar, he made for Charlie who pressed his trigger once knowing that was all that would be needed. Thakur lurched in mid stride and fell face down on the floor. Alex scooped money into his rucksack while Charlie pointed his Glock in turn at each of the staff and seated customers. As instructed by Billy, he said nothing. All eyes went to the body and its spreading red pool. No one called out. No one moved.

The four men waited to make sure that they exited together. They strolled to the car and drove to a lock up at the back of houses in Lipscombe Rise for which a few notes had changed hands. They left the vehicle with, in the boot, the guns and money, a little under £5,000. Ben Smith left for his lift to Gatwick.

There was little discussion and no recriminations, as all had decided beforehand. A defining line had been crossed. If any of them wanted out, they had agreed that this was the time when they would take a share and disappear.

They made their way separately to their own homes without celebration to wait for another day.

5
CHINESE RAINBOW

Billy and his three apprentices met less than normal during the next few weeks. They laid low, continued their unemployment routines and spent no unusual amounts of money in public. True, some family debts were paid with used £20 notes, but these were all private affairs and under the radar.

There is nothing like a good murder to engage any police force and Hampshire was no exception. A brazen armed daylight robbery committed by a clearly professional team of five men co-ordinated across two establishments had them salivating. Even hate crimes took a back seat, as rows of constables combed the High Street on hands and knees for evidence. It took five wasted days to reopen the road. The amount stolen varied up to £10,000 depending on insurance claims and stories of bulging plastic bags shedding notes as the robbers ran to their souped-up SUV.[1]

The investigating team knew better, of course. The area was awash inside and out with CCTVs. They noted the masks, gloves and nondescript clothes. All they could deduce were the heights, assuming no platform shoes, and, from the way they moved, that they were probably young men.

The thieves clearly knew the working practices and the layouts of the two businesses. The guns were Glock 17s, newish and loaded. The men were trained marksmen, comfortable with their weapons and prepared to use them.

---

1 SUV: Sports Utility Vehicle.

No one spoke at any time even after the murder, which was defensive, but premediated and deliberate. The escape went like clockwork even allowing for the shooting. The car with the fifth man wearing a cap and scarf drove away in a steady manner. The vehicle had false number plates and was nowhere to be found. There was no panic; the robbery was so well planned that it could almost be described as casual. None of Alton's known villains was spending money unwisely, but then again, none of them were thought to have the brains to have organised the raid.

Other matters interested the detectives. The proceeds, as best they could determine, could be no more than £5,000, hardly enough return for all the effort and risk. Where had four Glocks come from? These were not street firearms for provincial Hampshire. The men's knowledge of the shops suggested they had at least visited and that meant they would likely have gone inside as customers. Specialists began the task of reviewing internal CCTV and identifying all visitors for the past month, a task that found hundreds of young men who all had the same fashionable haircut. And where had the Escort gone and so quickly? It must be nearby and that suggested that the villains were local.

'One would almost think they were soldiers,' offered DCI Terence Stamp.

He recalled the street riot of a few days before. The wayward drunkenness of the one could surely not be associated with the preparedness for murder of the other? He reviewed the paperwork and found a local ex-soldier with a chequered background who may have killed his officer in cold blood in combat. William Budd's house had been at the start of the riot, but Budd was not known to have played a major part. Budd was not one of the barbers' customers, but there was a family link. A younger brother, Charlie, had been a customer and was part of the riot crowd. Was this an important connection or just coincidence?

The two brothers were picked up separately but at the same time and driven in unmarked police cars for interrogation in Winchester and Basingstoke. Both worried where they might have gone wrong. Billy kept his counsel and his cool, offered nothing and asked repeatedly for a solicitor. He eventually worked out how he had been caught in the net. It was simply a fishing trip. He then began to worry about Charlie's stamina when unpleasant and experienced officers sought to trip him up.

Charlie admitted to have been frightened when he met Billy later at *The Bakers Arms*.

'But, I always remembered what you kept saying, Billy,' he shared. 'If I got picked up, I was to ask for a brief and keep my mouth shut so that's what I did.[2] For two bloody hours. They never did me for the riot and you can't get arrested for 'aving no bleedin' 'aircut.'

Billy bought another pair of lagers.

'Don't worry, my son, they would have to be really useless if they hadn't got round to us. They've got nothing on us that counts.'

As Budd left the pub, he noticed a new bookstore nearby called Goldfinch. After a moment's hesitation, he went in. It was not like any shop he had been in before. He ordered a Triple fff craft ale, browsed and selected a handful of books to take with him to a quiet table.[3] He felt comfortable and at home. When he left an hour later, he took a small parcel with him.

DCI Stamp shared almost the same conclusion as Budd with his superintendent later that day.

'We've kept a discreet watch on both men, Sir, and we are building up a contact profile. But I just don't see it. Billy Budd is a dark one. He is strong. Charlie's a lot more lightweight. How could Budd have got kitted up, made the plan, found a team and whipped them into shape all within a couple of weeks of his unceremonious departure from the army?'

Some unexpected information helped sway Stamp. Even as the flowers, Turkish Delight boxes and teddy bears mounted on the pavement near the fatal barber's shop inviting the rats, reports arrived that Thakur was no innocent. He had a long record in his home city for drugs and violence and should never have been let into the country on a student work permit. A few days later, his uncle Toni was killed by a bomb attached to the starter of his car in his garage. Toni was head of a leading criminal family.

Perhaps the two deaths were connected and Alton was just an innocent host? Stamp moved resources to checking the backgrounds of Alton's small Turkish community.

In the investigation by the independent office for police conduct which later followed, Stamp's assessment and its acceptance was seen as a key part of the police's failure to anticipate the subsequent mayhem. The wider Budd family was not placed on any watch list; the shadowy organs of the UK state that

---

2 Brief: criminal slang for solicitor.

3 Triple fff is a brewery based in Four Marks, near Alton.

spied on its own citizens were not alerted. Many felt privately that it was harsh and unreasonable that Stamp and his boss both later lost their jobs and were forced into early retirement. In any great failure, great injustice can often be found as leaders and the guilty seek to protect themselves.

If word had reached the Research, Intelligence and Communications Unit (RICU), a part of the Home Office, or 77 Brigade within the Ministry of Defence, some pieces of the jigsaw might have been joined together earlier and saved lives and reputations. RICU, in particular, pushes official lines that support counter-extremism, sometimes using domestic front organisations to publish propaganda. These included dozens of campaigns and products from Google advertisements to leaflets. For instance, RICU tried to squash and belittle the hypothesis that the Covid virus originated in a Chinese laboratory, labelling it a conspiracy theory. 77 Brigade undertakes modern warfare on the internet by seeking to adapt behaviours of opposing forces like the Chinese Communist Party. Its operations regularly caught up people living in the UK. The government deployed soldiers to monitor its own citizens time and time again, especially perceptions of the Conservative administration during Covid.[4] This was, of course, officially denied.

In addition, the Rapid Response Unit (RRU), part of the Cabinet Office, was originally asked to tackle a range of online stories thought harmful during the pandemic. There was a rapid and covert increase in its functions. The unit began working with national security to monitor anyone contradicting official guidance. Dissent was treated as disinformation. Soon, RRU was tracking political opponents.

The Counter Disinformation Unit (CDU) originally monitored only deliberately false information often spread with malicious intent. Its orbit widened rapidly: the pandemic, then the Ukraine war, Northern Ireland Assembly elections, UK local elections and COP-26.[5] Quickly, the work included large-scale monitoring of discussions on social media including on Islamic terror groups and child abuse. The on-screen thoughts of writers, journalists, politicians and activists in general were collected.

Charlie described his interrogation in Aldershot to Sam when they met at Alton's *The Railway Arms*. They both had a leaning towards Triple fff *Moondance*.

---

4 *Big Brother Watch*, 'Ministry of Truth, The secretive government units spying on your speech', 2023.

5 26th UN Climate Change Conference held in Glasgow in 2021.

'Believe me, Charlie, the first time your brother said to me that there was no need to believe in authorities,' announced Sam, 'I knew I had found a real man. I felt such excitement it was literally as if I had seen a vision. We are going to do great damage together and pay all the bastards back. Whatever the cost to us.'

Billy Budd felt no pressure and waited patiently for the contact that he knew must come. The group had money in the 'bank'. They had automatic pistols and a car safely hidden. He would have a growing underworld reputation if he cared to announce himself and to call on it.

Three weeks after the robbery with Alton almost back to normal, and with automatic cash registers newly-installed in a panic in almost all the town's retail businesses, another courier called at Victoria Road. The delivery had been illegally intercepted by the police, but the letter's origin was untraceable. The contents were brief and carefully imprecise to a casual reader. Budd was asked, if he was comfortable with the earlier request, to meet at the usual place. One of his friends would confirm the detail. Alex called by that afternoon and said he had been passed a message in the street: 'Lunch at 1200 on Thursday at *The Greyfriar* in Chawton'.

'All very cloak and dagger,' shared Alex. 'I'm to place a white stone on an upstairs window sill if you accept. We are to destroy both notes. You are to go alone and to take a roundabout route as there are 'people of bad faith interested in your movements'.

Two days' later, Billy looked up from his beef burger, onion and pickle falling on to his plate, and stared at his host.

'We've established that you know my name and that you won't tell me yours,' he stated. 'What shall I call you, then?'

'You can call me Caihong. It means a rainbow. You know there is supposed to be a pot of gold at the end of a rainbow.'

She sipped at her glass of water and picked up a battered calamari ring with two delicate fingers.

'I'm not sure how to take that. What are you offering me?'

'Nothing personal at the moment. When we have finished here I shall soon be on a plane. It is unlikely that you will ever see or hear from me again.'

There was a pause as they ate, one hungry, the other carefully choosing. Billy took a long draught of Dark Star *Hophead.*

'Where are you from?' he asked. 'When I first saw you sitting here with your long, dark hair and oval eyes, I thought maybe you were Chinese. Now, I'm not so sure. Your English is perfect.'

'I was born in London, but where my parents are from isn't important. I shall be heading east.'

'Why are you bothered with me?'

'I, and all my friends, are very interested to know a man who has the boldness not to believe in anything.'

'And how do you know that about me?'

'We don't, for sure. But we noticed how the army treated you. We kept an eye on you. Then we saw you at work during the riot in Alton. You were discreet, but you were the man in charge. You gave orders clearly and well. You were respected although most of your hooligans were drunk and mindless.

'We decided to test you. We offered you some gifts. You took them and used them. You were efficient. Now is the time to know if you want to go to the next step, the whole hog, as you say.'

'You've obviously been watching me closely. How have you done that?'

'Guess. You are a resourceful man.'

Billy explained that everywhere he looked, there was a CCTV camera. The great majority, he had been told, were made by two Chinese state-controlled companies called Hikvision and Dahua. Many more Chinese CCTVs were rebranded and sold by Honeywell and Toshiba.[6]

'Very good,' said Caihong.

'I did some research,' continued Billy. 'These companies had combined revenues a couple of years ago of over £10 billion. They are ultimately controlled by the CCP, the Chinese Communist Party. Both were placed on a US list of firms that are thought to pose a threat to American national security. Their equipment is blacklisted there, but not here. The bad news for you is that anyone who checks knows that these cameras enable human rights abuses, security risks and a truly dystopian surveillance state.'[7]

---

6 Big Brother Watch, 'Who's Watching You? The dominance of Chinese state-owned CCTV in the UK', 2022.

7 The Chinese government uses CCTV to target ethnic minorities like the Muslim Uyghurs in the north-western Chinese province of Xinjiang. The Uyghurs are subject to a brutal campaign of persecution and repression with thousands of their people placed in detention camps called 'anti-extremism education centres'.

'Does that matter to you?'

'Yes, it does, but not if it gets me to where I want to go.'

Billy waved for another pint.

'So, to answer your first question,' he continued, 'hundreds of thousands of these cameras are internet-connected. These links allow record keeping and maintenance to be transferred live by satellite to China. Embedded microphones can turn on illicit listening devices. You've screwed up from time to time like when hundreds of airport CCTVs suddenly switched to an unknown internet address.

'In short, you captured my face. You followed and recorded me down Alton High Street and many of the places I've been since. You probably have microphones installed at my home and, possibly, *The Bakers Arms*.'[8]

'You forget,' added Caihong with a slow smile, 'you also have these systems in army bases and a third of your police stations.'[9]

'This meeting suggests you want to help me to go further along the road I have chosen,' said Billy. 'You must explain the paradox. I want to destroy the local powers and their symbols. You are offering to help me do that. Yet your people have about the most controlling government in all the world. If I was active in your country, you would snuff me out without thinking.'

'You are right, but you know this answer also,' replied Caihong. 'You can easily see that our objectives within this country overlap. Any serious disturbances here will work to our advantage. We wish to see the weakening of authority in this country, so do you. What does it matter if we have different reasons for wanting this? I could as easily turn the question. How do you rationalise using our gifts to undermine 'power' in your own country?'

'People are saying openly that China has successfully penetrated every sector of the UK's economy,' countered Billy.[10] 'But, It doesn't matter where the tools come from,' he mused. 'What matters is that power is taken away from the old orders.'

8 *BBC*, Panorama, 'Is China Watching You?', 26/6/2023.

9 Three out of five UK schools and further education colleges use CCP-linked surveillance, including in toilets. Over half of NHS Trusts use CCTV implicated in human rights abuses.

10 *BBC*, news/uk-66189243, 'UK approach to China spy threat inadequate, ISC report warns'; 'Failure to develop an effective strategy for dealing with national security threats from China has allowed their intelligence to aggressively target the UK', 13/7/2023.

'We think you are ready to take the next and more serious step. We are prepared to help you do this as long as who we are and our links with you are never disclosed, not even to your closest followers. We would, of course, deny everything. There would be severe consequences for you.

'Do you want to take the next step?'

Billy looked deep into her eyes and saw no immediate warmth, but he did see intensity and commitment. And, of course, great personal danger. When he was no longer of any use and if he survived, they would probably kill him. He paused for effect.

'Yes,' he said.

For the next half an hour, Caihong discussed Billy's requirements and how and when they would be delivered: weapons, including RPGs, a considerable amount of explosives, personal communications systems, vehicles and a lot more money.[11] Caihong took no notes. Billy realised he had passed any point of return in several ways. He assumed everything that had been said had been recorded.

Caihong stood abruptly.

'It was interesting meeting you, Mr. Budd. As I said, we will probably never meet again, certainly not in this country. Never try to contact anyone here who you think may be connected to us. If need be, we will contact you. If you are forced overseas, you can go to any of our embassies and tell them who you are. Mention 'caihong'.

'You, I suggest, should have another pint. Do not attempt under any circumstances to leave for fifteen minutes.

'Goodbye. It was a pleasure to meet you face to face and to know you like red meat.'

'Whatever, Caihong. You are a beautiful rainbow. I hope one day to find my pot of gold. I might even live to tell the tale.'

11 RPGs: Rocket-propelled grenades.

6

SEVENTH BATTLE OF ALTON

William Budd decided he would have made a good officer. He had a taste for organisation. He enjoyed being in charge, but he also knew how to delegate. He was a natural leader with a message that his disciples were happy to follow. As his confidence grew so did his ability to enthuse a group of men with simple arguments and slogans. He was also, without knowing it, a fatalist. He could take problems in his stride. He quietly welcomed the adventurous turn in his affairs which offered novel scenes and martial excitements. He felt sure that he could live with the consequences.

It was easy before the fighting started for the boys under his command to offer excited and blind commitment. The big unknown was, when it came to the crunch and his men were asked to risk death, which of them could he trust to do what they were told without argument. He worried that he commanded so few proven lieutenants. If his plans went awry and he lost those he could most rely on, he could be left with a rabble of headless chickens.

His broad plan was to rip out the heart of Alton, his home. The place was complacent; its leaders felt no threat and therefore practised no security. However, the readiness and enthusiasm of his recruits suggested that beneath the surface of the town bubbled a lava flow of discontent.

Services, like health and the hospitals in Basingstoke and Winchester, had long since delivered declining support. The extent of near collapse could be measured in the rise of black humour. Trains, buses and taxis were beyond the pockets of many. Starter homes for those who wanted to escape the strictures of squabbling parents were limited and expensive. The streets became more dangerous with each influx of cheap drugs. Respect for authority, for age or for females was long past. The war in Ukraine meant prices climbed inexorably. The Government's headlong drive for net-zero energy meant the cost of keeping warm was artificially high and unaffordable for the poorest. Debt came in an unending spiral. Drink and gambling was the ready solution. Gangs of children ran wild at night; street violence and sexual assault the norm. Beggars lived in cardboard boxes in shop doorways. There was a ready joke that the way to find a cash terminal was to follow the trail of blood. All the while, the local councils sought to do the government's bidding and to fill the remaining empty green spaces. More and more houses were built on soulless estates available only to those who could afford a mortgage and the part-paid, shiny car necessary to reach the burgeoning supermarkets.

For a significant number of the town's underclass, there was no hope. Dependency was cemented into their lives. Decreasing community lived alongside limited charity. When hope had left, the choice was between despair and anger. Alton's managers and business owners failed to heed the signs. What they never contemplated was that they had introduced the seed bed for the thirsty shoots that welcomed William Budd's brand of revenge. There had been bad times before. What was different now was that Budd in secret provided assured leadership. He had also been given the tools to make his plan a reality.

Budd's suppliers proved true to their promises. Goods moved silently into the area and were collected with scarcely a hiccup. The day of the first attack was set for two months after the barber shop murder. Thakur was mostly forgotten. The shop's owners ran a steady business with their cut-throat razors now underpinned by a frisson of remembered violence. Their shop frontage was mostly cleared of tributes. Shoppers walked by without a sideways glance.

Budd expanded his inner cadre to twelve individuals. Another twelve formed an outer group where commitment was not quite proved. A young woman who talked too freely disappeared one night on her way home. Discipline improved. Two isolated and uncherished farm houses were rented ostensibly with a view to assessing 'development potential'. Apart from their size, both had two distinguishing features: the proximity of woodland without public paths to provide an area for covert weapons training and a large number of outhouses which could be used to hide vehicles and armaments.

It was late evening the day before Alton's world changed forever. Belly, a mindless convert to the cause and member of the outer group, was proud of her association with her brother. After closing time, she led a large, loud- and foul-mouthed hen party out of the *The White Horse*. They staggered, singing and buffooning, down the centre of the length of the High Street. The road quickly emptied of the few remaining late night pedestrians, all anxious not to get caught up in the embarrassment. A police patrol disappeared. A few of the tottering ladies moved from time to time to the doorways of the various shops and premises to urinate or to harass sleeping beggars, or both.

Eight of the women carried four 500 gram packets of PE7 plastic explosive in their copious handbags. The other revellers were too drunk to spot that there was anything unusual underway. PE7 is the army's latest front-line bomb material offering much improved adhesiveness and higher detonation velocity.[1] It is completely safe to handle. On reaching a secluded alcove, each lady took a white slab and moulded it within seconds to the doorway handle and stuck in a plunger, a pre-set, state-of-the-art electronic detonator which the army believed was still a well-kept secret.

The party sashayed down the street. They left behind twenty-four deadly packages.

At seven the next morning, a white van stopped in the no parking area outside Alton Assembly Rooms in Crown Close. A man got out and gently forced the door. The alarm sounded immediately. To the left in the office, he checked the four CCTV security screens standing on a wooden desk. There was no sign of activity. He turned off the strident bell. Three other men carried in several boxes of equipment and two of them left soon afterwards, locking the door and sticking over it several wraps of tape which declared, 'Police aware. Do not enter'. The van was driven away.

Outside and near the High Street, a single transmitter button was pressed and triggered signals to the detonators. The slabs were strong enough to rip

---

1 PE7 is the army's recent replacement for the long-serving PE4 plastic explosive. Blocks of PE7 are much more malleable than PE4 and stick even in cold conditions. PE7 also replaced American C4 and Czech Semtex. The material was developed from Hexomax explosive manufactured by the French company, Eurenco. One of the main reasons for PE7's development was to meet an obligation to include a taggant, a chemical identifier which also allows various forms of testing.

out the doorways and to destroy the ground floors of the twenty-four buildings. Eighteen of their fronts collapsed completely, leaving rooves dripping tiles on to the pavement. It was, as they say, like a war zone.

Many well-known stores, Boots, Café Nero, Clarks Shoes, Co-op Food, Coral, Costa Coffee, Greggs, Iceland, Leightons, M&S, Specsavers, Superdrug and Vodaphone were in ruins in company with their neighbours, banks and building societies like HSBC, Nationwide, NatWest and TSB. They were joined by established local firms like the Joyce and Lucas delicatessen, Mike Frost carpets and accountants Wettone Matthews. The Swan Hotel and Weatherspoon's *The Ivy House* and charity shops and estate agents were wiped out. It was a street of small fires in black, gaping tooth sockets.

The body count of early employees and passers by, agreed much later, comprised twenty-three dead and forty injured.

Despite the mayhem and, presumably, continuing danger, a swarm of human locusts carrying empty bags descended as if by plan. It was an orgy of looting with little rationale. If an item could be moved, whatever its value or usefulness, it was lifted.

At the Assembly Rooms, the two men, Sam and Alex, stuck their slabs of PE7 into place and added sensory detonators. They carried their assault rifles with underslung grenade launchers up the stairs to the second smaller function room used by the judo section, and set the weapons ready for use. Then, they settled down and poured coffee as they waited for the second wail of police sirens.

'It's all a bit of mess in here, ain't it,' commented Sam. 'I've never been inside before. That main hall with the stage and the big mirror is all right, but the rest of it is a bit higgledy-piggledy with little spaces and windy passages and messy gear left all about.'

'I was reading up on this place,' replied Alex. 'You know over a hundred years ago it was a hospital, then a cinema and after that a skating rink. Now anyone can use it.'

A short distance away amidst the devastation, the looters melted into the High Street's passages as DCI Stamp found himself the earliest senior officer on the scene. The police, of course, were completely ill-equipped for what they found. There were procedures for extreme events, but they were little practised and mostly lay at the bottom of untidy filing cabinets. Despatchers had difficulty believing the scale of the demands made on them. All available

The Victorian Assembly Rooms in Crown Close, Alton: 'Two men stuck slabs of explosives into place and added sensory detonators. They carried their assault rifles with underslung grenade launchers up the stairs to the second smaller function room. Then, they settled down and poured coffee as they waited.'

ambulances and fire appliances across three counties were called out. Every hospital in Hampshire and Surrey was placed on alert and called in what staff they could. Two armed police response units were on their way within thirty minutes. Ministry of Defence military police at Oakhanger who guarded the satellite communications facility, the nearest military base to Alton, and at Gosport were on stand by.

Sam and Alex listened to the chatter on their Bowman VHF radios. It was time to make their presence known. They broke windows and began firing grenades into random targets. Sam's position overlooked the High Street. He fired into the sitting duck businesses across the road just a few yards away. In quick succession, the solicitors Bookers and Bolton, Beech Tree Dog Grooming, the Italian restaurant *Cucina Dei Sapori* and the *Crown Hotel* were demolished. Alex's window gave him a view of the whole of Crown Close. One grenade reduced the war memorial to a pile of rubble. He then worked his way along the facing side wall of the Curtis Museum destroying many of Alton's historical artefacts.

The Assembly Rooms main phone rang.

Alex went down the stairs and answered.

'Hello, Assembly Rooms here. How can I help?'

'We have the place surrounded,' began Stamp. 'You could start by stopping shooting. Then, you could surrender before you kill anyone else.'

'No surrender, Sir,' replied Alex.

'At least think twice before you fire into the old people's home to your right. That's the large building at the end of the close. It's called Inwood Court. It's retirement housing. There's about thirty flats.'

'Yes, I know. But don't try to kid me that the place is full of poor, cuddly, old people. They're all smelly rich bastards who pay lots of money to live there. What's your name?'

'We'll swap names. I'm DCI Stamp.'

'I think you're taking me for an idiot, Stamp.'

To make Alex's point, Sam fired a grenade into the top floor of Inwood Court and made a large hole in the upper façade.

'All right, Stamp. That was just so that you know who has the big guns until your special forces guys arrive. I will give you something though. At the end of this building facing your retirement home, there's an upstairs flat with Ukrainians living in it. If you move now, now I mean, I won't fire and you can get the women and kids out. Don't want them to have a bad impression of Alton hospitality.'

'Promise?'

'You'd better go now. Remember, no sign of firearms.'

A couple of uniformed police ran around the High Street corner, picking their way through the rocks from the war memorial. Two minutes later they were back, shepherding half a dozen dazed young people who thought they had left all this violence behind.

Sam's personal radio crackled.

'Twenty-four. Repeat twenty-four. Confirm.'

Sam acknowledged and confirmed.

'Time to go, Alex.'

Behind the Assembly Rooms in the Drayman's Way car park, a convoy of three Land Rovers, one marked with a Red Cross, pulled past the Majestic Wine store and stopped by an army observation post. A major in camouflage gear stepped out of the first vehicle and called for an officer.

'Major Melville,' he offered along with his hand. 'We've just been ordered to go straight in. The terrorists have started potting grenades into the retirement home and none of the occupiers have been evacuated, all old people. We also believe that there is a hostage or two. No time for a proper recce. Have you seen any movement?'

The young lieutenant shook his head. Melville waved his men up the chalk and gravel slope.

'We're going in through that shack on the back, the one that was used by Wey Valley Radio. We hear it's empty. Keep your heads down.'

'I've had no notice …' started the lieutenant, but he was already talking to thin air.

Melville's men were efficient. With two minutes, there was a dull explosion and an emergency exit blown in. There was muffled shouting. Automatic fire was heard in three distinct phases, then two single pistol shots. Two soldiers emerged supporting a third who had a bloodied bandage on a thigh. They were followed by Melville and the rest of his men. A small team escorted a pale-faced and shaken civilian to the second Land Rover. The lieutenant was still trying to get orders from anyone in his command who knew what was going on.

'All yours, lieutenant,' reported Melville. 'There was only one hostage, that's him, and we're taking him straight to the field hospital. One of my men was wounded. There were only two bandits. They're both dead and I've left them for the clear up unit.'

The three Land Rovers roared off and were never seen again.

Thirty minutes later, the lieutenant received backup and twelve men entered the building through the blast hole. They reached the stairs by the entrance, confused by the lack of damage and with no sign of the two bodies. There was an almighty roar and a characteristic smell of burned electricity as the plastic explosives placed around the external walls by Sam and Alex detonated. The whole of the Victorian Assembly Rooms quivered, seemed to rise a few inches, and then collapsed inward. The dust from the old brickwork took time to settle. When it did, there was nothing of consequence left, just a mass grave.

As Melville explained later to his men over some cold cans of lager, 'embarrassing the army was always an important part of the plan'.

7

INDECISION, PANIC AND POLITICIANS

Anyone who writes a history book likely has an agenda, even if unrealised, that involves making one group look better than another. Until recently, only a few people were able to publish and be widely read. That was certainly true in the mid-twentieth century: only governments and government-supported businesses had the money to publish textbooks and determine what was in them. These textbooks were just about the only way a high school student could learn anything about the past. Today, with the internet, lots of people publish many different opinions, some honest, some malicious, many incorrect. Even more so now, questions should be asked about what we read. Who is behind the information? Who wishes to manipulate us?

When it came to the debacle of Alton, the British government's secretive Ministry of Truth was quickly into action knowing they needed to beat the enemies of democracy on to the virtual front pages of the global social media.

'Who controls the past, controls the future: who controls the present, controls the past.'[1]

Gainsayers loved that they lived in a world of half-truths and conspiracies and had the space in which to operate. Events that had just happened had no

1 Orwell, George, *1984*.

objective existence, but survived only in hastily-written records and in faulty human memories. Later, the past was whatever the records and the memories said it was. The first influencer to fill a space is often in control of the records and is therefore in control of the minds of its readers. It follows that the past is whatever the early reporters choose to make it. Once this version of reality is taken up by susceptible minds, the tendency is for them to fight tooth and nail rather than admit a mistake might have been made.

Billy Budd made it a little easier for the government. He said nothing. His group had no name. His objectives gained nothing by stating them, he thought, especially in a form that Middle England might understand. He had no particular wish to stir up a storm of supporters to do similar things. If anyone felt the same way, then they were free to follow their own path, if they could find the explosives and weapons to do so. Budd's purpose was laid clear, he felt, in the piles of rubble in what use to be Alton's town centre.

Despite the government's early publicity lead, national politicians were, as usual, confused in thought and weak in direction. Because of the enormity of what had happened, its extent was difficult for them to grasp. The first instinct was to try to play things down. 'Town centre ruined in concerted attack by well-organised and well-armed terrorists' was reduced to 'A series of possibly connected explosions'.

This quickly became laughable as news agency drones flew over Alton High Street and beamed their pictures into every television set in every country in the world. This was Ukraine and Sudan and Yemen in Europe's back yard. Many rejoiced in the humiliation. There were well over one hundred dead and injured.

Below the radar, Britain's European security partners fed back what information they had which was almost nothing. The British at least had a suspect, Billy Budd, which he had given them on a plate when there was no need. DCI Stamp immediately recognised Melville, the name given by the rogue major, as that of the twentieth century American writer Herman Melville and author of *Billy Budd, Sailor.*[2] In Melville's story, Billy, tongue-tied at a false accusation of mutiny, strikes out and kills his accuser, a master-at-arms of higher rank. The ship's captain, Vere, recognises Billy's lack of intent, but claims the law, especially in a time of war, requires him to convene a drumhead

2 Among many other works, Melville also wrote *Moby-Dick; or, The Whale*, first published in 1851.

court-martial. To everyone's chagrin, a much-admired Billy is inevitably found guilty and hanged.

'It seems our Billy is seeking to improve himself,' suggested Stamp. 'He's reading classical literature. Maybe he sees himself as a popular hero who is doomed by the system? Can he be saying that his motive is revenge?'

Stamp raised the link with his fellow investigators and set off a flurry of reading. Some saw a parallel between a levelled Alton and the pathetic killing of an ostensibly innocent sailor. Others recognised the cold-bloodied obstinacy displayed by Captain Ahab, another of Melville's great characters, in his maniacal pursuit of the great whale Moby-Dick.

Now Stamp had a name, he soon had confirmation of a likeness as Budd's photograph was identified by the lieutenant at the Assembly Rooms observation post. The find did Stamp little good, except diverting some heat from his superiors. Budd's disclosure had been calculated for he was nowhere to be found. Stamp saw it as less of a taunt, but more of a great confidence which he hoped would stray into the arrogance that would make Budd vulnerable.

The list of Budd's acquaintances, previously drawn up, also identified several other Alton men who had not been seen for a couple of days. They included Budd's brother Charlie, and Alex Redhill and Sam Player. These three, and a couple of others, had disappeared.

Stamp was convinced that the men were holed up with their vehicles and what remained of their weaponry somewhere that was both local and discreet. He began a search of large, rented properties.

It was the weaponry that caused almost as much panic as the damage done. PE7 was traceable due to its unique taggant and yet the evidence that came from Alton High Street and from the Assembly Rooms was confused. There was no record of thefts or missing stores. The assault rifles, grenade launchers and pistols were all state-of-the-art army stock and should not have been available. Where had three army Land Rovers come from? And how much money must have been spent? Who had provided the impressive planning and organisation?

Stamp forwarded a number of theories in a written report, one of which raised the possibility of the involvement of a foreign power. This did not help the fevered brows in Downing Street and Whitehall who were daily dealing with tongue-in-cheek offers from distant governments of help to guard British towns by lending troops. These offers were mixed with little concealed delight from hostile states. Iran, Russia, China, North Korea all pointed out that the 'insurrection' was not surprising given the repressive nature of the British government, the failure of weak Western democracies and the hidden poverty of much of their population. These accusations captured the headlines everywhere and other erstwhile neutral nations like India, Argentina and Scotland sought to deflect attention from their own problems.

It was only a few weeks before there were copycat explosions in widely separated English towns. These incidents in Peterlee, Toxteth in Liverpool, Gloucester and Bridgwater were all minor in comparison with Alton, lacked any serious explosives and were quickly tracked to known dissidents. However, all of those arrested, expressed similar ambition, to tear down the government and social order which had continuously failed their families and their towns.

Parliamentary opposition seemed interested only in attacking the government. They offered no serious debate on a new contract for the protection of the poor. A few outliers did raise questions about the general societal decline and lack of self-restraint. But, came the reply, what had really changed apart from scale since the coalminers' strikes of 1984-5, the race riots of 1919 and the enclosure disturbances in the centuries before? Hampshire, and England in general, was still largely owned and managed by landowners who had their own best interests at heart.

A local historian chipped in and claimed that the extensive destruction in Alton in 2023 was actually its seventh major battle. It followed two Viking invasions met by local Saxon resistance, the internecine Norman struggle for supremacy in 1101, two street slaughters in the Civil War in 1643 and the abrupt hop-pickers' wage uprising of 1830.[3]

Two opportunist European Union politicians sought to rub British noses further into the rubble for the temerity of Brexit. Suddenly the temperature changed. Without warning, there were two large car bombs in the centre of these politicians' home towns in Dendermonde in Belgium and in Mulhouse in France which together left thirty dead.

Budd listened to the news in bemusement. Statements had been issued by the car bombers, who claimed to be associated with the atrocities in Alton. The European politicians were castigated for their rude intrusion and the crassness

3 Vikings v Saxons, 1000 and 1001, Heal, *Four Marks Murders*, p. 292. Henry 1 v brother Robert Curthose, 1101, Heal, *Winchester Tales*, pp. 173-5. Royalists v Cavaliers, twice in 1643, Heal, *Four Marks Murders*, p. 144. Wage riots, 1830, Heal, *Four Marks Murders*, p. 128.

of their arguments. A similar punishment would follow any more second-rate 'idiots in Brussels' who intervened only to raise their public profile. Budd suspected an increasingly confident Chinese hand on the tiller.

Eventually he gave an inward shrug. He decided to say nothing.

'What does it matter?' he thought.

Hysteria followed with breast-thumping demands for results. However, those dozens taken into custody across the country were a blind collection of known loud mouths and wannabe terrorists. All were back on the street within forty-eight hours.

Was the mayhem now over? Would the killers be back? Where? When? The army didn't know where to put their stretched resources: in Alton? Ports? Centres of government? How did one guard the country against seemingly indiscriminate attacks against unimportant towns?

Unaccountable civil servants served their own careers and barely-concealed political biases. Disinformation and guesswork became the norm and filled the BBC's one-sided and censorious reportage. Scraps of knowledge were repurposed and became weapons in febrile political debates designed to discredit rhetoric, delegitimise opponents and to suppress and censor their arguments. False websites abounded, many funded from overseas. The government's arms of illegitimate influence began to contradict each other. The Rapid Response Unit moved to monitoring and silencing critics. Lawful speech was identified for potential censorship. Online discussions were adulterated. Dissent from policy was treated as disinformation and tracked, whatever the source. The Counter Disinformation Unit directly influenced the suppression of content on social media companies and collected information on writers, journalists, politicians and activists in general. The Government Information Cell decided that Russia was the bogeyman and had targeted Alton as apart of the Kremlin's war in the Ukraine. They would accept no alternative thesis. The 77th Brigade continued to allow soldiers to monitor the general population for signs of further discontent.

8

EIGHTH AND NINTH BATTLES OF ALTON

DCI Stamp's search for large, rented buildings around Alton that could house the terrorists' arsenal and vehicles eventually paid off. The frustrating delay was simply explained: most of the estate agents' offices in the town were destroyed. Identifying likely properties often depended on unfamiliar staff working with sketchy, computerised files in distant centres.

Stamp received a telephone call just before noon. A dilapidated farm on the edge of Bushy Leaze Wood across the Medstead Road in the village of Beech had been taken with a view to demolition and the building of three luxury homes. The hirer was the Honourable Edward Fairfax Vere, a young bachelor from London whose references had not been checked deeply as a three-month deposit had been paid in cash and insurance settled privately. Stamp's heart missed a beat. He recognised the name Vere as that of the ship's captain who hanged Billy Budd for mutiny.

Despite the devastation, or maybe because of it, Budd had undeclared friends in the remaining local community. The call to Stamp was not the innocent disclosure it purported to be. Within the half hour, the chief inspector, busy gaining authority for a raiding party, received another call. It came from one of the army patrols that constantly weaved around Alton's country roads. A Land Rover with a large red cross on its side had been spotted driving on a little used track near Bushy Leaze Wood. A military drone confirmed the Land Rover was parked near a farmhouse. There was evidence of heat given out by several life forms within the sheds, half-protected by substantial metal roofing.

This sighting was all the confirmation Stamp needed and he requested an army operation to surround and take the hideout. It was also the final nail in the coffin of his career.

The raid was smartly executed. A platoon of heavily armed soldiers, carrying weaponry identical to that used by Budd and his men, entered the farm and captured, with little struggle, a herd of thirty Friesians all bellowing loudly to be milked. Among the food waste were signs of recent extensive human occupation. The search took some time as the men were mindful of the sabotage that followed the putative clear up at the Assembly Rooms.

The Land Rover was found well hidden under bales of straw and taken away for thorough analysis. Under the driver's footwell mat was seeming gold dust. A number of detailed maps showed that the town's remaining big supermarkets – Aldi, Lidl, Sainsbury's and Waitrose – were all to be targeted on the following night with explosives left at their customer entrances. Iceland and M&S Food had already disappeared in the High Street debacle.

The supermarket companies anticipated that they might be attacked and had advanced plans in place to safeguard their property. Three of them were already on the verge of closing their Alton businesses 'in order to protect our staff and customers who are our major priority'. Within hours of being alerted to the upcoming attack, lorries that normally brought food deliveries began arriving empty and taking away what goods they could without arousing suspicion. Outwardly, the next evening, the stores seemed open for business. An observer may have noticed fewer cars than usual, but there were figures, in fact mannequins, standing near shelves with their shopping baskets. All the premises were ringed by sharp shooters. Two builders' trucks contained heavily-armed soldiers. A substantial force of infantrymen and a handful of police stayed well back in various car parks.

The appointed hour came and went. A general nervousness descended on the waiting men. One of Stamp's officers commented, a little too loudly, that it always seemed that Budd was one, or even two, steps ahead.

The tense atmosphere broke in an unpleasant manner. The sequence of events was later pieced together. A Land Rover, marked on each side with a red cross, pulled up in a parking bay on the A31, Alton's by-pass, and near to

'The raid was smartly executed. A platoon of heavily armed soldiers entered the farm and captured, with little struggle, a herd of thirty Friesians all bellowing loudly to be milked.'

Radical Cartoons

the town's sewage treatment works. The works served Alton and the nearby villages of Farringdon, Holybourne and Four Marks and discharged its cleaned effluent into the River Wey. Treatment involved passing the sewage through primary and secondary settlement tanks. The tanks lay between the waiting forces outside the Aldi and Lidl stores on Mill Lane and the parked vehicle on the by-pass.

Three men unveiled an 81mm mortar mounted in the back of the Land Rover. What the ambushers heard behind them were six rapid, but dull, explosions as rounds landed in the two primary settlement tanks, those full of the rawest and most dense sewage. The brown sludge exploded upwards and, helped by a slight breeze from the south-west, settled messily over the waiting ambushers.

Apocryphal stories suggested that the unified cries of disgust could be heard sixteen kilometres away in the town of Farnham.

As Budd was reported to have said later to his men over some cold cans of lager, 'embarrassing the army was always an important part of the plan'.

With the army shown as unable to protect property even with warning, Alton's supermarkets activated part two of their joint plan. More lorries arrived and took away all the goods that could safely be resold elsewhere. The store entrances were left open for two days and townspeople invited to take whatever they wanted from what was left. The shelves were cleared, down to the last cabbage, within two hours.

Budd had dealt a deadly blow to Alton's economy without a serious shot fired in anger. The town became the butt of comedy shows around the world. DCI Stamp was moved to somewhere in Cumberland while his failures were investigated.

Budd felt he was close to achieving his objectives, but he sought one last battle.

There were five large recent housing developments tucked in and around Alton. The new homeowners were now suffering from a collapse in local shopping. Even when they did eat, the difficulties in dealing with household sewage made life unpleasant. It was hard to calculate, but the combined effect of these new estates, when added to smaller ancillary projects, had been to almost double the town's population within five years. A commensurate doubling of the town's facilities and infrastructure to make the growth palatable was unlikely, indeed laughable. If Alton was to die, one final push to make life intolerable on the new estates might win the day.

The answer was car bombs, ten of them, two for each estate. Using all but one final stash of PE7, unwanted Land Rovers and stolen cars were driven into position one morning just after the commuter exodus, now much smaller than usual.

It was a noted change of tactic by Budd when he contacted the police and alerted them to what he had organised. Some speculation saw a sign of a new-found weakness, perhaps brought about by the numbers who had already died unnecessarily. The inspector who took the call got over-excited and tried too hard to pressure Budd.

'Inspector, may I call you Frank … ? began Budd.'

He was interrupted by a flurry of questions and orders.

'Inspector, you are not allowing …'

He was cut short again.

'Inspector, if you don't shut up, I will detonate some car bombs.'

At last, Budd had the floor. He explained where the bombs were. He said that the vehicles were booby trapped by experts.

'I want you to be very clear about this, Frank. If you try to disarm the bombs you will set them off. People will die. It will be your fault. Are you listening, Frank?'

Budd got confirmation.

'Now, Frank, the time is currently 1000 hours. The bombs will go off, set by timers, at 1800. Anyone within two hundred metres will be in danger of their lives. Anyone within one hundred metres will probably die. Your job, Frank, is to clear these estates before 1800. This is all that you have to do and there is nothing else that you can do. Do you understand?'

Budd got a second confirmation.

'Right, Frank. I have nothing more to tell you except that this is a burner phone and when I hang up I will immediately destroy the SIM card.[1] And, oh yes, say 'hi' to Terence Stamp for me, will you?'

It took longer than one might imagine to get the job done: a dozen road blocks to stop people getting in; door-to-door calls on several thousand homes;

1 SIM card: A subscriber identity module, widely known as a SIM card, intended to securely store an international mobile number and its related key which are used to identify and authenticate subscribers on mobile phones.

persuasion; children kept at schools until collected; helping those who had cars to load; buses and accommodation for those without transport. The police and soldiers were at work until fifteen minutes before the deadline.

At 1800, without further warning, the bombs detonated. The devastation was immense, far more than Budd and his team anticipated. Some of the houses and apartments were closely packed with three-story walls and narrow streets. They acted as wind funnels. When the blast from one bomb met that from another, both travelling at high speed, the cumulative effect was considerable. In the development on the old Bass site off Draymans Way where building was still under way, there was an unexpected side effect. Part of the underground passage of the River Wey was deeply cratered. A large lake formed in the middle of the estate as Kings Pond emptied and the water reversed its course.

To other inhabitants, even before news of the devastation reached them, there was no question of ever returning. Budd's gamble had paid off and, in that five minutes, Alton was no longer a community.

At six o'clock, the last part of Budd's plan and the last part of Alton's ninth and final battle was put onto action. A large white van with windowless panelled sides pulled up hard against the pot plants at the town hall entrance. The hall stood alone in the middle of Market Square. The van door was rolled open and the building's two locks forced. Four men stepped straight from the van into the small lobby where stairs led to the council chamber and offices. The ground floor offices and associated charity shops, still unrepaired from the street riot that greeted Budd's return, could not be reached from this side.

The chair lift was pressed into service to take armaments to the first floor. Sadly, the carefully renovated wooden handrails and balustrades were damaged by the large boxes. A surprise waited in the small council chamber, not grand with tiered seating, but holding half a dozen wooden tables set in a hollow square with Windsor chairs placed about. Seated on the chairs were four members of Alton's town council who had volunteered for telephone service in the complex relocation of the home owners on the new estates.

'Well, well,' chuckled Sam, 'what have we here?'

'I recognise a face or two from the *Alton Gazette*,' answered Alex. 'These are some of the important people who run this town.'

'It looks like an unfortunate day for these noble people,' announced Billy.

There was loud indignation and protest which finished immediately Billy loosed off a few rounds into the expensive cornices. Within a few minutes, the four large sash windows overlooking the square and Market Street were knocked out. Tables were shunted beneath them and the unlucky dignitaries tied spread-eagled across the gaps with their hands roped to the ornate brass curtain rails and their feet to radiators.

'There, a little bit of horror for onlookers, a little bit of dread for participants, and a little bit of protection for us terrorists. My name is Billy by the way. Have you heard of me? And this is brother Charlie, and these are Sam and Alex.'

Billy explained that his men were now going to use the grenade launchers that underslung their assault rifles to destroy surrounding buildings.

'If you are good, we will fire past your waists,' Billy added. 'If you are naughty, then we will be firing through your legs. Your choice.'

He also explained that there was an added excitement for him in the destruction that would shorty follow.

'When I was a boy, that building there,' he said as he pointed towards Mifta's recently opened Indian restaurant, 'was called Budd's Bakery. I always thought they were family. One day, I popped in and asked if they had a cake for a young relative. They told me to go away. They were rude. I think I may have suffered long-term damage as a result. No one offered me counselling.'

With that, he fired a grenade through the legs of a stout lady councillor. Two others rounds, carefully spaced, followed and the old bakery subsided like dough behind a prematurely opened oven door.

'Did you know,' Billy added, 'that there used to be a cage, stocks and a whipping post down there so that people like you lot could keep poor boys like us in order?'

In a corner of the chamber, Charlie found a locked glass case containing four large bottles of Bass commemorative beers, presented to the council in 1982 by the town's long-standing brewer.

'There's one for each of us,' he explained breaking the glass with his rifle butt. He worked off the waxed cork tops.

Billy tasted a King's Ale for the first time.

'Forty-years-old and still very drinkable,' he opined.

A senior councilman of many years' service finally found his voice.

'Why are you destroying our town?' he pleaded.

Billy loosed a grenade at the Salvation Army Hall, while his comrades leisurely destroyed the *Market Hotel*, the closed *Kings Head* so that it no longer needed to be raised for development, and into Pizza Express.

'I'll tell you,' he answered. 'We have lost all faith in the worth of institutions including your council and your town. It's not particularly Alton, it could be any town, but Alton is our town. You and your kind have failed us and people like us. We believe there is no hope. Our only way for a better future for those who will follow us is to tear down everything that smells of authority. We no longer believe in anything. Others can do the rebuilding if they can be bothered.

'We want our rage to be felt by the whole world through what we are doing to Alton. We want its ruins to be our monument and our thanks for our wasted lives.'

Sam chanted 'Hear, hear, old chap' and took a long swig from his Ratcliff Ale, touted as Bass's number one strong beer. He raised the bottle mockingly to the councillor in a toast.

The last six grenades flew towards final targets.

'But, don't you think you wasting your time now that the army has pulled back?'

'What?' said Billy, nonplussed for the first time in a long while.

'Didn't you know? The army command ordered everyone out late this afternoon after your damn car bombs. There's just some men on the estates checking for bodies. There's no one here in the town centre to watch your futile victory. No one wanted to give you excuses for more useless destruction. You can just walk out and leave if you want.'

Billy and his three pals had agreed that taking the town hall would be their final act of defiance. They were out of explosives and grenades and had only personal arms left. There was no sensible escape route from the building. In their various ways, they had imagined it would be their coffin. Their last hurray had been stolen from them.

The four men slumped on their chairs and pulled on their quart beer bottles.

'Would you esteemed councillors like to prove what you've said?' asked Billy of the crucified public figures hanging from the walls. 'What would you say if I let you all walk out to see if there's any army out there? You can take Sam with you and, if it's all OK, he can come back and let us know. If there's any firing, it'll be your last walk.'

A deal was quickly struck. Sam and his four hostages worked their way through the van and out of the driver's door. Billy and the others took positions in the upstairs windows in order to provide covering fire. Ten minutes later,

Sam was back walking down the centre of Market Street waving his arms and then giving a double thumbs-up.

'Dead as a dodo,' he reported. 'There's not a soul about.'

'As we've won and Alton is ours, we'll leave them their precious town hall,' announced Billy. 'I could do with a rest.'

He reflected for a second.

'What I do feel sorry about is that we've done nothing to hit the pockets of all the fat cats in their big houses with electric gates in the countryside all around. They've still got their money piled in their trust funds. Still, perhaps, next time?'

The four friends climbed into the van and drove off down Amery Street so that they could park near to *The Bakers Arms*. They had decided on a farewell drink before they went their separate ways. Robbed of death, they now had to go into hiding. At the end of the gloomy alley, they found the pub's front door ajar. They paused to look up the High Street and to admire their recent handiwork.

Billy saw Sam staring confused at the bright red dot which moved slowly over his chest.

'What the hell?' said Alex staring at his own copy.

'Snipers,' yelled Billy as two high velocity cracks split the air, killing his two men instantly. The bullets had ripped through them and exploded out of their backs. Billy grabbed a bemused Charlie and dragged him to the pub's door.

'While they reload,' Billy shouted, but the next two shots arrived before they reached cover. He realised these were not highly-trained marksmen as both shots only just hit Charlie's moving target, one low on the shoulder, the other high on his thigh cutting his femoral artery. By the time he had dragged his brother behind some of the pub's seating, the blood was spurting deep red. The leg wound was too high to consider a tourniquet and Billy had to make do with sticking his thumb deep into the damaged flesh. Charlie's face was white with shock, but he was fully conscious.

'Jesus,' he offered. 'Do you think those damned councillors did for us?'

'Possible,' said Billy, 'but it was all organised a bit quickly if they did. More likely these lads were always waiting here because someone told them this was our local. The withdrawal was a ruse.'

'I'm killed, aren't I, Billy?'

'You are Charlie. They've killed you and Alex and Sam.'

'When Budd reached the tombstones at St Lawrence church, he dropped behind the perimeter wall, like a musketeer from another bloody battle of long ago, caught his breath and waited. Dim forms move slowly forward in the dusk.'

Radical Cartoons

A large tear fell down Billy's cheek to disappear in the pool of blood. Billy had never cried before even as a boy.

'You're my brother, Charlie, and I love you. I am proud of you.'

'We done good, didn't we, Billy. We showed 'em.'

'I think we showed 'em, Charlie. It may not matter, but I hope it does.'

Charlie coughed, long and deep.

'Can I have a last lager?'

There were steady footsteps from the street. Billy removed his thumb and Charlie's blood pulsed out. There wasn't even time to fetch his drink.

Billy grabbed his rifle and moved quickly to the back of the pub where locked doors led to the outside. He forced his way out and ran for his life. When he reached the tombstones at St Lawrence church, he dropped behind the old perimeter wall, like a musketeer from another bloody battle of long ago, caught his breath and waited. Dim forms moved slowly forward in the dusk. He fired carefully from long practice and three bodies fell to the cold pavement.

Billy remembered a fight a world away in a fading desert light. He pulled his electronic detonator from his pocket and flicked its switch.

The roar from the town hall provided revenge, but no satisfaction. The old building never had any foundations. Years ago, surprised renovators found it was erected on river gravel. Its walls grew straight up from a third of a metre below ground and needed to be underpinned during restoration. As a result, much of the blast flew sideways and flattened the square's remaining structures.

It was the last shout in the rage and ruin of Billy Budd.

9

AN IDYLLIC VILLAGE AND AN AMUSEMENT PARK

Vang Vieng might be the world's most beautiful village, much quieted by government edict since its hippy party days and much cleared of ordnance since Laos became the most bombed country on the planet. In a covert Cold War operation over fifty years ago, the CIA attempted to wrest power from the communist Pathet Lao.[1] American bombers dropped over two million tons of cluster bombs, more than all the bombs dropped in WWII.

Today, towering karst mountains still rise around seas of rippling paddies where conical hats bob above the crops.[2] Stilted huts sprout along the banks of the determined Nam Song. Women set traps for freshwater prawns and some fish for *khai phun*, 'moss', from the streams and throw it on hot stones to dry. The older children walk slowly home from school, one arm weighted with books, the other pulling the family buffalo from where it had grazed while they studied. Younger siblings catch lizards and rice rats to carry to the leisurely evening market.

---

1 Civil war in Laos: 1964-1973. CIA: Central Intelligence Agency, a civilian foreign intelligence service of the USA. Pathet Lao: Officially the Lao People's Liberation Army, a communist political movement and organisation formed in the mid-20th century, which assumed political power in 1975.

2 Karst: A land of limestone, a soft rock that dissolves in water. As rainwater seeps in, it slowly erodes. Above ground, there are steep, rocky cliffs and, beneath, caves, streams and sinkholes.

'Vang Vieng might be the world's most beautiful village, much cleared of ordnance since Laos became the most bombed country on the planet. Karst mountains rise around seas of rippling paddies where conical hats bob above the crops … Younger siblings catch lizards and rice rats to carry to the leisurely evening market.'

Radical Cartoons

Vang Vieng had been Billy Budd's home for the past four years. Waiting for Caihong, he sat in that calm half-hour before twilight with a pre-dinner gin. A copy of the first volume of Proust's *In Search of Lost Time* lay open on a side table. The veranda breeze was just brisk enough to keep the mosquitoes at bay as he soaked in the view of fishing canoes and children splashing at the water's edge. A slight rainbow remembered a late afternoon shower.

Billy was morose as he reviewed, yet again, the results of his infamous achievement from all that time ago. He tried to be honest in his assessment and to strip out his personal feelings. His mind flew like a migrating bird, never heeding when it crossed a frontier.

The British had lost their lion's heart since the razing of Alton, capitulated to appeasers, and so Europe had lost its martial guide. The Chinese had landed in Taiwan. The Pacific Rim democracies stood alone against the communist forces. United States' isolationists turned further inward and questioned why more of their boys should die in yet another foreign war. The West lacked moral leadership as the world boiled to a great catastrophe.

Despite fearful losses, the Taiwanese defenders clung to a large slice of the north of their main island. There was no sign that the Communist Party would stop rattling its carefree sabres, continuing confident in its destiny and oblivious to failure. The stalemate looked to become entrenched and might well turn Taiwan into another divided Korea or Vietnam.

Caihong came home from her work at the party's educational and monitoring centre where she was in charge of the distribution of prosthetic limbs, mostly legs, for the latest victims of uncleared explosives. She brought a kiss and a newspaper.

The main story discussed a railway accident with many dead. The line was Laos's first ever to connect the sleepy capital, Vientiane, to Boten and the Yuxi-Mohan railway on the Chinese border. It had been opened as Billy arrived. The ambition of the six-billion-dollar project, begun in 2016, was breathtaking. A link in the south crossed a new bridge connecting Thanaleng to Nong Khai and the high-speed rail network in Thailand. The route north to the Chinese system had thirty-two stations spread over 250 miles with 167 bridges and viaducts and with almost a half of its length inside seventy-five tunnels.

'I despair,' mused Billy out loud. 'The total railway is a one-thousand-kilometre dagger driven south into Laos. Because of it, the Chinese will overrun this country whenever they choose. Every time the Chinese offer the

Laotian government some piece of infrastructure, they add crippling loans which mean they will soon become the majority owners. They always bring their own workers to do the construction. When it is all done, the workers stay. It is the new colonial capitalism.'

'You need to be careful what you say, Billy,' Caihong admonished him. 'Buffalos have ears and the Party usually knows best. Anyway, that's not why I brought you the newspaper. Look inside.'

A three-year review, grandly called 'Ideas for the Future of Alton', had reported to almost universal indifference, but was gleefully translated by the Chinese and their acolytes. The town's devastated areas had been made safe and the rubble cleared. The costs of resurrecting the High Street and rebuilding municipal buildings was astronomical and beyond the capacity of the declining economy. Barely a thousand people stayed in their houses, all of them in the older part of the town. It was still dangerous at night as the police no longer made patrols. One of the few places to survive was *The Bakers Arms*. To the Government's annoyance, the pub had become a raucous shrine for the cult that surrounded Billy Budd. Many drinkers hoped that Billy would return from beyond the grave and be a leader again. A rough blue plaque commemorating his vision had been placed on the the ruins of the old war memorial alongside the graves of Sam, Charlie and Alex, murdered by the state. The many soldiers and townspeople who died were mentioned as an aside.

Budd was sighted almost every month in some part of the globe, most recently running a cannabis bar in Amsterdam.

Alton's new estates, developed in the last dozen years by official edict, were deserted. The government was forced to pay compensation for the discarded homes. Despite incentives and a comprehensive publicity programme, there was no appetite for a return to living in the town. The sewage works was still only half repaired, its projected budget running at six hundred per cent of target and delayed for another three years. South Western Railway now terminated at Farnham. Alton's surrounding villages had dwindled. Their limited infrastructure and the lack of shopping in the destroyed town meant long drives for supplies.

The report's great idea called for turning the remains of Alton into a large amusement park. Guides, carrying aloft specially designed lollipops emblazoned with the Budd emblem, would lead parties of tourists, bussed in for the day, to the sites of Billy's battles. Suitable, none to subtle, slogans would

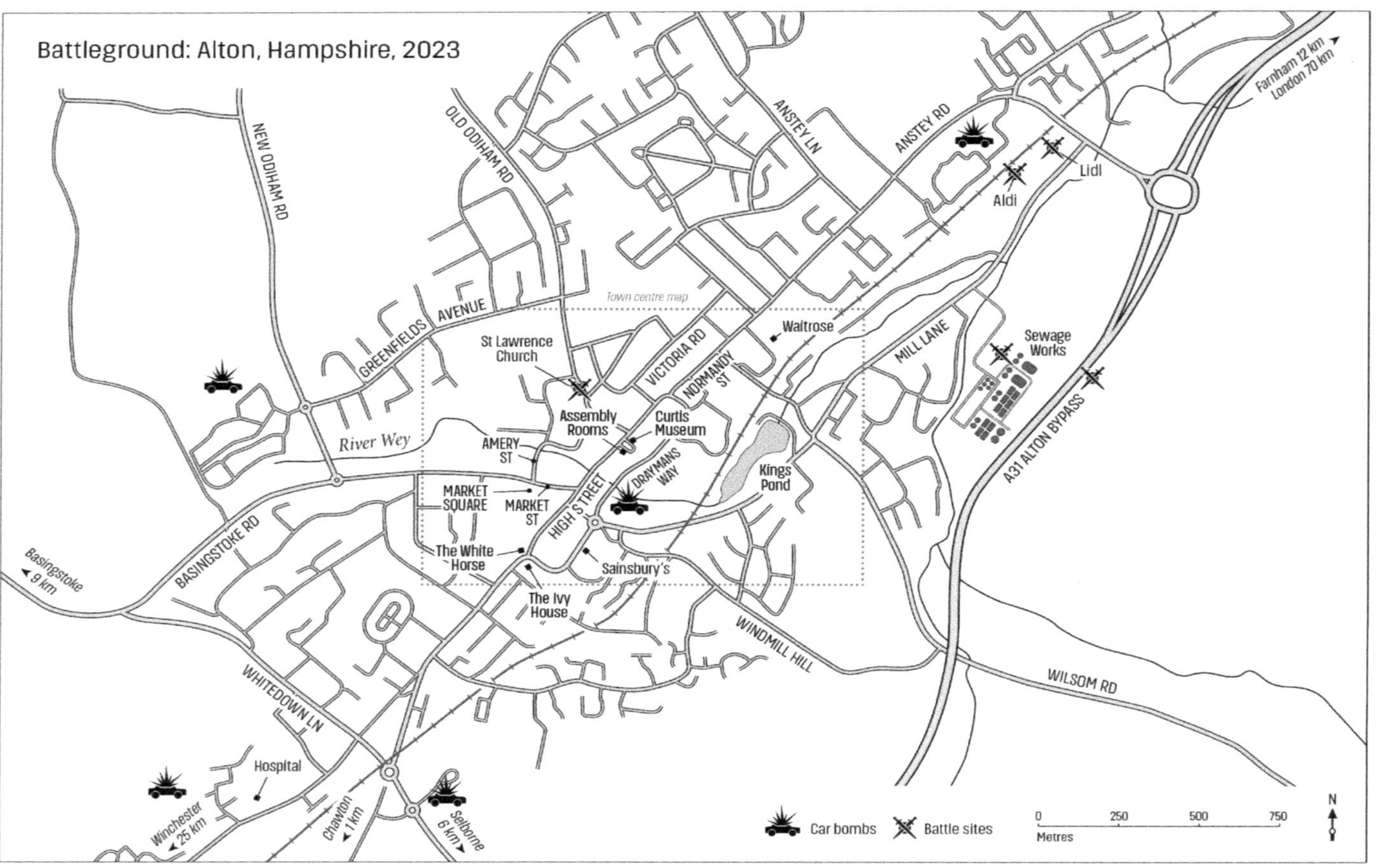

Battlefield Design

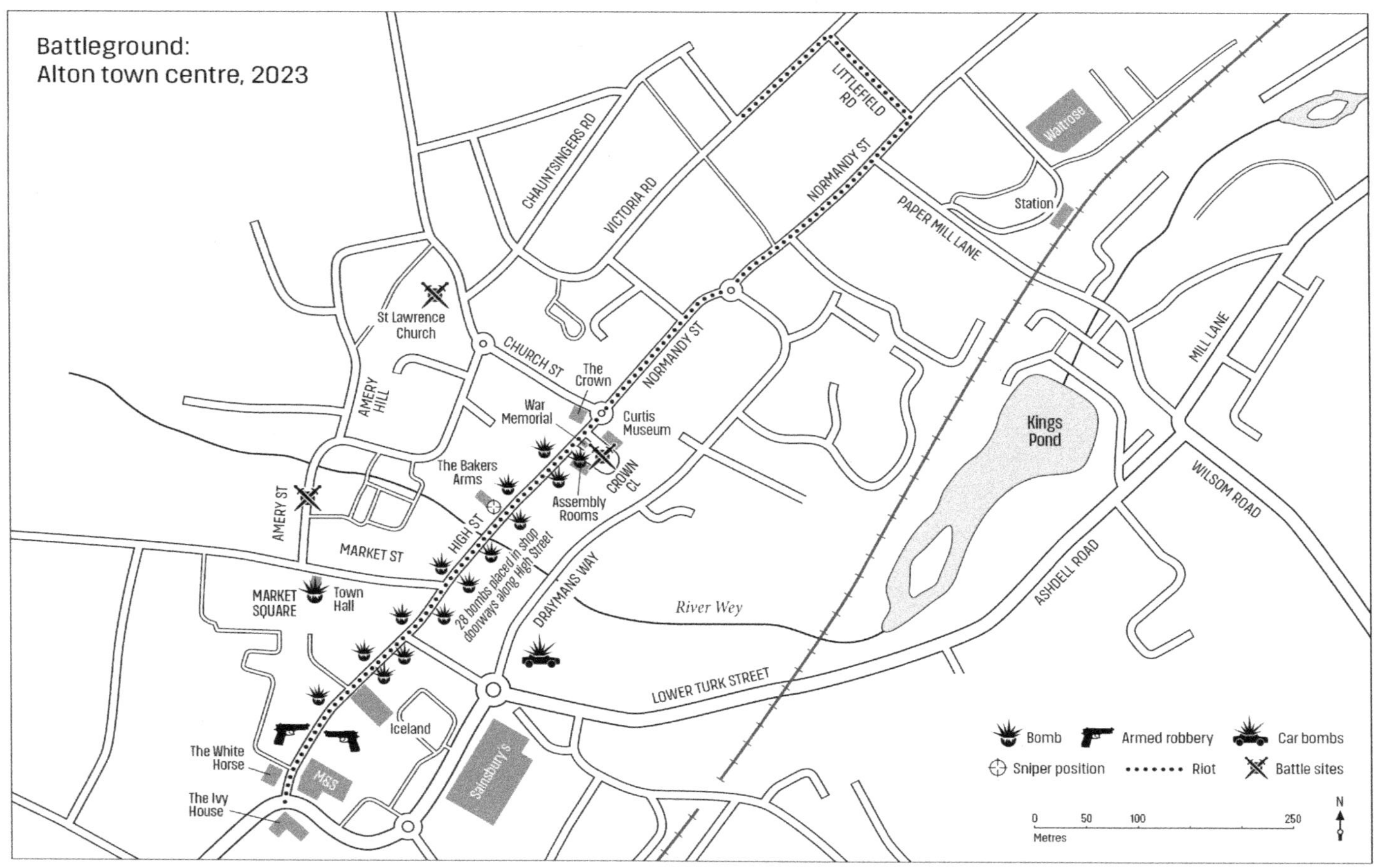

Battlefield Design

dull the minds of the visitors.[3] Given a slogan to chant, they would not have to think about the implications. Tourists could just chant.

Every site would have a large flashing neon sign, each with one of Billy's most famous sayings:

Honesty is just a feeling.

I like being negative. It's the way my brain works.

Once you've decided to mow everything down, you might as well knock yourself off your feet as well.

A real man shouldn't be bothered what people think about him. A real man is one you don't think about, but one you've got to obey or detest.

And, above the entrance to *The Bakers Arms*:

The tiny little space which I occupy is so small in relation to the rest of space where I am not living and which is none of my business; and the amount of time which I shall succeed in living is so insignificant by comparison with the eternity where I haven't been and never will be … and, yet, here I am, my blood circulates, the brain works and even has desires.

The Bakers Arms, its apostrophe long lost, already offered 'Budd Vegetarian Burgers', his reputed favourite meal. Strolling players would re-enact authentic scenes from the struggle.

The report concluded with its clarion calls:

We have to accept the implications of human curiosity. Some of what people say will be wrong. Some of it may even be harmful. But we cannot discover truth without accommodating error. It is the price we pay for allowing knowledge and understanding to develop and human civilisation to progress.[4]

3 Orwell, George, *1984:* 'War is peace', 'Freedom is slavery' and 'Ignorance is strength'.

4 *The Spectator*, Sumption, Jonathan, 'The Hidden Harms in the Online Safety Bill', 20/8/2022.

Billy put down the newspaper, heaved a sigh that came from his very depths, and fell quiet. Caihong leaned over for another kiss and then replenished his gin. The rain began to fall again without any great purpose and the bamboo drainpipes played soft tunes.

'What do you think?' she asked. 'Do you think it was all worth it?'

He sipped his drink and thought for a while.

'What does it matter?'

The End

Suggested reading

Big Brother Watch, 'Who's Watching You? The dominance of Chinese state-owned CCTV in the UK', 2022; 'The Ministry of Truth. The secretive government units spying on your speech', 2023

Brassier, Ray, *Nihil Unbound: Enlightenment and Extinction* (Palgrave Macmillan, New York 2007)

Buddha, 'Doctrine of Nihilism', Apannake Sutta (c. 500 BC)

Ladyman, James, and Ross, Don, *Every Thing Must Go: Metaphysics Naturalized* (Oxford University Press 2009)

Melville, Herman, *Moby-Dick; or, The Whale* (1851, Penguin, London, 2003); *Billy Budd, Sailor* (1891; Penguin, London 1967)

Orwell, James, *1984* (Penguin, London)

Rosenberg, Alex, *Atheist's Guide to Reality: Enjoying Life Without Illusions* (Norton, New York 2011)

Scruton, Roger, *The Uses of Pessimism and the Danger of False Hope* (Atlantic Books, London 2010); *The Disappeared* (Bloomsbury Reader, London 2015); *On Human Nature* (Princeton University Press 2018)

Turgenev, Ivan, translated Freeborn, Richard, *Fathers and Sons* (1862; Oxford University Press, 2008)

BAD TIMES TODAY

The sad story of Mary May

Introduction

This story takes place in Alton during three weeks of March and April 2023. It concerns Mary May, a pensioner and recent widow who, for a variety of reasons, slips through the cracks of decent care. I wrote the story to query the wholesale move of welfare information and contact processes away from the coal face and onto the internet. As a result, Mary May faces a series of challenges that, I hope, would not be possible in real life.

Most of the places described are real places in the town. None of the actors, including Mary, are real people. They are all inventions and, if you are reminded of someone you know, then it is a literary accident. However, all the incidents and conversations that happen to Mary are true in that either I witnessed them experienced by others or they were reported to me in thirty-three separate interviews with pensioners and practitioners in the district.

I have been inundated by people with their own horror stories. I expect that the 'The Sad Life of Mary May' will strike a chord with many of you.

It was never my intent to criticise volunteers' and professionals' hard work and dedication. However, every organisation falls below its own high standards from time to time.

I expect there are errors of fact and description in the story for which I apologise and take ownership. Again, however, I did contact nineteen organisations concerned with welfare in Alton and asked for their help through a short interview. Ten of these busy organisations never replied, even after three attempts that were often accompanied by the offer of a useful donation.

It set me to thinking how near to collapse our welfare system is and how susceptible it is to an occasional lack of humanity. I hope the story upsets you and makes you angry enough to reach for your purse.

Chris Heal
September 2023

Illustrations

March 2023

Mary May lay half-dazed with her cheek pressed hard against the cold wall where her head had come to rest. The wall was yellow and smelled of disinfectant. She gazed with mild interest at a long, grey smear from a casually-used cloth. There was no comfort in the colour or the smell or the smear.

Mary had moved little for more than ten hours, her legs now refusing to answer her call and her arms too weak to take any weight. She had long since given up trying to control her bladder and she was ashamed. Her urine had puddled onto an underlying plastic sheet and was gradually soaking into her blanket making her cold. Occasionally, she shivered violently. She thought of happier times when her Tom was alive. He would have rescued her from this unending embarrassment.

A foreign voice, female, flustered, routine, shouted briefly, close above her head.

'You all right, lovie? Anything you want? Can you remember what your name is? Don't worry. We'll get to you soon.'

The words came too fast. It took Mary time to decipher them and by then it was too late. The nurse had moved away from the stretcher and down the long corridor, pausing and shouting every now and again, to where the bright lights showed a batch of drunken, swearing young men, newly-arrived, pushing each other as they carried a red-haired youth in a sodden football shirt. He cried in pain as his twisted leg, pointing in the wrong direction, hit the door.

In the reception area, mothers sat on rows of red, plastic chairs, resigned and dozing. Some had brought sandwiches and packets of biscuits as they were well-versed in the humdrum of regular visits. Their children played around them or screamed or slept in their clothes on the floor, some already packaged in gay pyjamas or nightdresses covered in film characters.

It was a Tuesday in late March, three o'clock on a bitter morning with the rain lashing down.[1] There were no beds free, most still blocked by patients not released from a busy weekend and the workings of a glacial pharmacy. Administrators with the power to lubricate the admission process would not arrive at work in large numbers for another five hours. Medical staff laboured within a managerial regime that saw patients' needs as just one of a number of competing factors.

Outside the accident and emergency department, five ambulances waited in a line, docile, doors shut and engines running for warmth. Two frustrated crews argued with a triage nurse that their occupants were victims of a three-car pile up and needed urgent assessment. Some had suspected head injuries and possible internal bleeding. A disturbed elderly man lurched into the middle of the debate and vomited.

A young doctor, on duty without a break since Mary's arrival, paused at her trolley.

'Good lord! Are you still here? Has no one been to see you?'

Mary tried to say 'no one', but managed only a muted grunt.

The doctor, aged twenty-six, and in his first month on the front line, looked down at a badly bruised face. The redness was turning yellow indicating the time for applying the most effective treatment had already passed. This old lady had been failed and he was a part of the system that had failed her. He lifted her blanket with trepidation. Perhaps a broken limb had been missed or, worse, not even looked for. He recoiled involuntarily before regaining control. The stench of many hours of neglect turned his stomach.

'Nurse. Get me a nurse,' he shouted.

'You're not the only one with a problem,' came a response.

'Nurse, this just isn't good enough. She needs to be cleaned before I can examine her.'

'You shouldn't even be looking at her. It's not her turn.'

'She must have been lying here for a half a day. Look at the state she's in.'

The nurse went stone-faced, about turned and marched to her rest area and called her union representative. She had been insulted, she reported, was

1 *Daily Telegraph*, 'Six-hour delays make Tuesday morning the worst time to visit A&E', 8/4/2023.

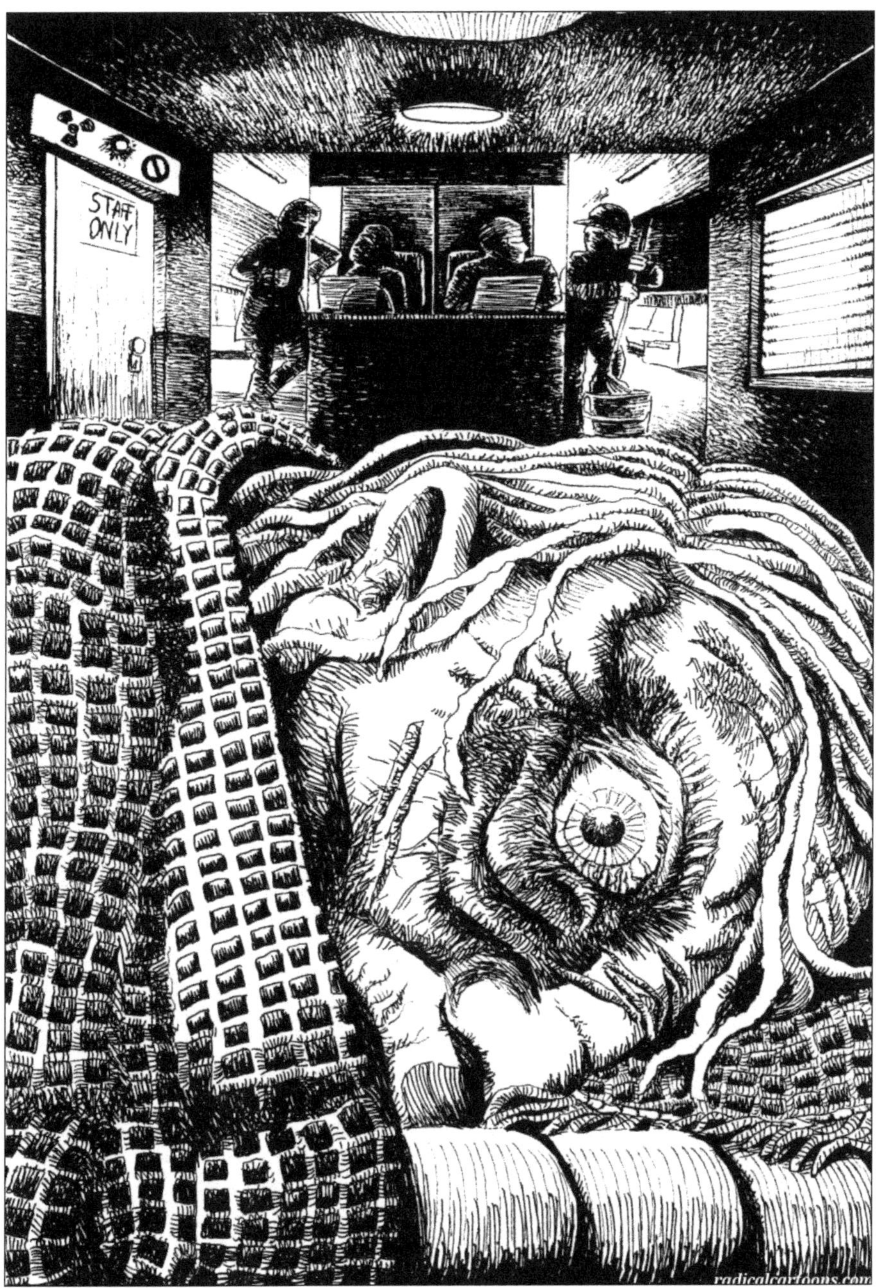

'You all right, lovie? Anything you want? Can you remember what your name is? Don't worry. We'll get to you soon.'

Radical Cartoons

deeply upset and, with all her other problems, felt unable to work from mental stress. The official agreed that she should stay off duty until a manager was found and permission obtained for her to go home sick.

A young police constable arrived having spent time walking up and down the corridors looking for Mary. There was no record of her arrival as no one knew her name.

'Is this Mary May? Is she well enough to be interviewed?'

'Why do you want to interview her?' asked the doctor. He had arranged some blankets on a table.

'I need to lift her off the stretcher so that I can clean her and get the bedding changed. Will you help?'

Together, the two men placed Mary on the table. The doctor replaced the sheets and blankets and set to work wiping Mary.

'She was attacked in her home in Alton some time on Monday evening,' explained the officer.[2] 'It took at least five hours before she was found by a neighbour and then another three hours for the ambulance to arrive. Do you mean she's not had any treatment for over a day since she was beaten up?

'This is awful. I came back on duty tonight and found no one had been to interview her so I came over myself. I saw in the newspapers that we, the police that is, failed to solve 100,000 burglaries last year despite promising to send an officer to every break-in. I'm embarrassed. I thought I should come and do my bit.'[3]

'I think we are all lucky that she's not died,' said the doctor quietly, almost to himself.

The constable turned to Mary.

'Can you speak, love? Can you tell me what happened?'

Mary strained to speak, but could only open her cracked lips. She began to cry.

'Can you get her some water,' said the doctor. 'I'm not sure that she has even been offered any food or drink.'

---

2 *The Sun*, 'Man charged with murder after 'tied-up' pensioner, 78, found dead in his home in attempted robbery', 21/11/2021. *The Times*, 'Wife, 86, killed and husband, 88, severely injured in attempted burglary', 16/1/2022. *Express*, 'Teenagers, 14 and 15, arrested after 82-year-old robbed and killed for her pension money', 30/3/2023.

3 *Daily Telegraph*, data from freedom of information requests, 8/4/2023. Also, many more stories, like 'Police criticised for failing to solve one million thefts and burglaries', 28/12/2022.

'OK. Of course. She's not fit now to tell me what happened. This is horrible. I'll come back tomorrow. My name's Jason, Jason Smith.'

Three days later

It was three days before the constable returned. His headquarters in Aldershot was short-staffed and lacked sergeants with the time or inclination to make decisions about travelling to interview low priority burglary victims. Smith was assigned to other matters including checking on expired shotgun licences and following up complaints about potential hate crimes. After calling the hospital each afternoon and getting vague responses, he decided to visit Mary in his own time while off duty that evening.

After half an hour of fruitless searching in A&E and in several likely wards, Smith spotted the doctor who had looked after Mary walking down a corridor. He hailed him.

'Hello. Do you remember me, Jason Smith? I'm looking for the old lady, Mary May, to see if I could get that interview about her burglary. Do you know where I can find her?'

'I could have done with you here this morning,' came the answer. 'I'm still waiting for X-ray results. She discharged herself this morning, far too early in my opinion, but she insisted she wanted to go home. Some of the staff had taken against her and everybody wanted the bed so they seized the opportunity. No bones broken that I found so that was a Godsend.'

'Good Lord'.

'To make matters worse, there was no ambulance spare and they couldn't find a voluntary driver either so they drove her down to the bus station to catch the next service to Alton.'

'Good Lord. I wish someone had told me. I could have taken her home or at least saved myself the trip. No one here seems to have heard of her.'

'You'll soon get to learn about the NHS in your job,' he was told.

'OK, OK. What did you mean when you said that you could have done with me this morning?'

'Just a bit a cynicism. You could have attended my disciplinary hearing. The nurse who wouldn't help me with Mary and hadn't checked her properly all shift complained that I had been rude to her. She was no longer able to work.

The complaint was upheld. She's been given a week to recover with stress counselling. I have a black mark on my disciplinary record for bullying.'

'Good Lord.'

'Don't worry about me. I've seen enough of the way things are in this benighted health service. I applied yesterday through friends for a job in Australia. They almost bit my hand off. Hopefully, I'll hand in my notice by the end of the month.

'Best of luck with your burglary interview. I hope you catch the bastards.'

He paused. 'By the way, her medicines hadn't arrived by the time she left. I've got them in my cubicle. Would you mind taking them to her? They will help relieve any pain.'

A few hours later, a member of the team responsible for ensuring adequate home care arrived at Mary's recent bedside to check on her condition. Finding, instead, an incontinent old man, she sent an email to social services to alert them to Mary's departure. Because of the mugging, she suggested that an early home visit might be necessary.

Friday morning, Day 1

Mary May had an uncomfortable journey home as the bus jolted over the potholes. She had bruising across most of her face, neck and trunk where she had been punched by both of her attackers. They were young men, both masked and wearing gloves, but one in particular seemed to enjoy the power.

Mary found them ransacking her living room when she returned from the local shop with a small loaf, a tin of baked beans and, a big treat, an orange. One man took the orange and scattered the bread slices over the kitchen floor. He did it, he told her, 'because she was a useless, lying bitch' and had only a £5 note and a few coins in her purse. They took the money and the purse which contained her bus pass, house key and her favourite, and last, picture of Tom, her husband, who had died only a few weeks before. She had nursed him alone for two years after a sudden and debilitating stroke.

Mary, wrapped in her thin coat against the north-east wind, told the bus driver her story and, grudgingly, after several moans, and because of her obvious age and condition, he let her ride for free. She was, despite or because of all her troubles, a tough lady, white-haired, brown-eyed, with deep facial lines, but not heavily wrinkled. She looked kindly, perhaps a favourite grandma, except she had no children after her Billy had gone to the army.

She often pulled out his picture, taken as he stood proud in his sharp uniform, and wept inside. He had died in Afghanistan as a result of American friendly fire. The truth was kept from her and was never publicised. It was a traffic accident, they said. Fortunately, considering her lot in life, Mary's strongest trait was her perseverance. She kept going with little obvious complaint.

'This will cost me my job,' the driver reminded her several times as she sat close behind him. She all but welcomed the harping as it was the first real company she had had in the last few days. Light rain came on at Alton railway station as she waved goodbye and mouthed thanks. The driver ignored her, pleased to see her go as he took his break and made for a warm café and a bacon sandwich with a large cup of strong tea.

It was a painful ten minute walk to Mary's small, terraced house. She crabbed along as the pain grew in her left leg. Some passing youths jeered at her for her ungainly posture. Mary reached her front door which opened onto the street and froze in fear at her memories. Ten minutes later, she still stood motionless as the aftershock of her attack hit home. She started to shake. Who might be waiting inside to harm her? Her coat was now heavy from the rain. She had to move.

Her house was one of a set of eight identical homes built just after the war by local businessmen full of hope and intent to aid the local community with cheap accommodation to replace that destroyed by the *Luftwaffe*. Time had run its course. The entrepreneurs had become a local housing association and the original trustees were all dead. Several of the properties had been sold. Management had fallen by default to an elderly solicitor who, in truth, neither knew nor cared how to do the job. The rent remained low, but that was because most requests for repairs were placed in the pending tray. The communal roof leaked, condensation clung to the walls and the paper was peeling. Nothing had been painted for decades. The tiny back garden was unkempt, especially since Tom had had his attack. Mice abounded outside and silverfish, woodlice and cockroaches slid within.

Mary remembered her key was lost with her purse. She shuffled to the house next door belonging to the only neighbour she knew. John Christophers was a man of her own age, a widower, and they occasionally helped each other out with shopping and chatted on the pavement. The six other houses were

'Mary, wrapped in her thin coat against the north-east wind, told the bus driver her story. 'This will cost me my job,' the driver reminded her several times as she sat close behind him.'

Radical Cartoons

occupied by single mothers and their strings of boyfriends. The music was always loud and her greetings, when noticed, were ignored. Who needed a fussy neighbour who wanted favours and would poke their nose in where it was not wanted?

All John's windows were dark. She knocked, but there was no answer.

Steeling herself, she walked down a side alley, unlit and smelling of urine. She saw a syringe on the ground and what she thought was a used condom. Her gate was hanging open. She felt her way to her back door. Its single pane was smashed and she guessed this was how her burglars had broken in. Covering what broken glass remained was the side of a cardboard box held in place by masking tape which was already beginning to lift. She inched sideways to a solitary plastic flowerpot, long since unused. Underneath was her spare key.

Getting inside took another five minutes and the last of her courage. The kitchen was cold and smelled of damp. There was no central heating in common with the homes of over sixty thousand pensioners in England and Wales.[4] She thanked God that the electric light still worked. Her loaf had been picked up from the floor and placed on the kitchen table, she assumed by John, but the mould and the mice had been at work. There was a small patch of dried blood next to her chair. She measured a cup of water into the kettle, checked and threw away the half bottle of curdled milk, and made a pot of black tea. It had been a long time since she could afford sugar.

Mary hung up her wet coat, dried her hair, found a jersey and sat sipping her drink in front of her television. The whirling in her head gradually slowed down, but never left entirely. Ten minutes of a forty-year-old comedy show did not raise a smile.

As she moved to her bedroom, Mary passed a small pile of letters on the mat inside the front door not yet knowing, nor later understanding, that a television licence that used to be free for pensioners before 2020 would now cost her £159 a year.[5] A summons to attend a magistrates' court lurked among the envelopes.

Mary climbed the stairs backwards sitting on her bottom, made a quick visit to the toilet and crawled under a blanket with no energy to undress. She

4 Great British Life, *PA News Agency*, '66,000 pensioners live without central heating', analysis of 2021 census, 14/4/2023. *Daily Telegraph*, 'Pensioner fearful of high bills dies of hypothermia', 3/4/2023; *The Guardian*, 3/4/2023.

5 gov.uk/tv-licence, 23/6/2022. bbc.co.uk/news/entertainment-arts-55754914, 21/1/2021.

thought she would never sleep as she tried to stay alert for noises downstairs. A fitful unconsciousness claimed her within a few minutes and she began a whirlwind of dreams which always returned to a repeated bus journey.

The bus had plenty of empty seats but, whenever she moved to take one, someone pushed past her to stake their claim. No one spoke to her. She was too shy to argue and so moved from seat to seat. Everyone was in uniform, but none she recognised. She became hungry. The other passengers had all brought picnics which were shared, but not with Mary. She needed to go to the toilet. There was a facility on the bus, but she was always at the back of the queue. When the bus came to her destination it did not stop, but went round again and again. Finally, when everyone had left the bus, it came to a halt in the middle of a muddy, empty field. There was no driver. She opened the door and there stood two hooded men with baseball bats. She turned back, but the door had closed behind her.

Sunday morning, Day 3

It was late morning when Mary was woken by loud banging. With a heavy head and shaky legs, she slid down the stairs to open her door, fearful of what she might find.

PC Jason Smith was relieved when Mary finally stood before him.

'I'm sorry to have banged so much, Mrs. May, but I was worried about you, having to come home on your own from the hospital in your condition. Was it very uncomfortable?'

'I managed all right, officer,' Mary said, 'but who are you? I don't recognise you. Is there something else wrong?'

'No, there's nothing to worry about. I called to see you in hospital, but you weren't too chipper. Then you were released before I could get back to see you. I wanted to take a statement from you about the louts who broke into your house and stole your purse. Can I come in for a cuppa?'

The house felt colder inside than out. The officer handed over the small parcel of medicines sent by the doctor. He checked the contents.

'There's some *Paracetamol* in there is case you have any pain,' he told her. 'Remember, no more than two at a time.'

The two were hardly settled at the kitchen table when there was another clattering at the door. Smith went to answer and found a colleague from Aldershot. He was not looking for Mrs. May in particular, but for any neighbour of John Christophers. This second constable was a blundering man who probably dozed during the training course on the giving of sensitive information.

'Mrs. May, I am PC Budd. The man who lived next door, John Christophers, was involved in a road traffic accident last night. He was knocked down by a stolen car driven by two young tearaways. Mr Christophers died before the ambulance arrived.'

And, then, almost as an afterthought, 'Did you know the deceased well? Do you know who his relations were?'

PC Smith was appalled and tried to help Mary.

'Mrs. May just got home yesterday from a stay in hospital after being mugged and burgled in this room.'

Mary looked around as if her assailants were still there.

'Doesn't help me much, mate. Different case.'

Mary fought through her shock and gathered her thoughts.

'I was the nearest person that John had to family. We were friends and looked after each other. Neither of us had any family. He was poor like me.'

She started to sob quietly for, she realised, she was now truly alone for the first time in her life.

Budd gave a long and audible sigh.

'There'll be paperwork as someone will have to decide about his things.'

'I have a key to his back door if that helps?'

Budd took the key, kept in an empty tea caddy.

'I'll have a look round. I've also got some things he was carrying when he, err, was hit. Just his wallet and groceries. I'll need to put some of them in his fridge.'

'His fridge doesn't work, but you can put the things in mine. If they are mostly vegetables they were probably for me anyway for when I got back from hospital. He was kind like that.'

Budd made a point of removing the wallet from the carrier bag and putting it in his own pocket.

'Needs to be part of the estate,' he said. 'I'll add it to any money that I find in his house. All needs to go through the official channels. If there's no will and no relatives, then everything belongs to the Crown. Can't upset Charles and Camilla.'

PC Smith finished his brief interview with Mary. He was just leaving when Budd quit next door after his search of Christophers' house. Budd didn't say anything and his hands were empty. The policemen walked off in opposite directions. Smith returned a few minutes later and handed Mary her purse.

'We're lucky,' he said. 'I just checked the gardens a little way along and I found this under a hedge. The money's gone, but everything else seems to be there.'

Mary gave him a huge smile, grateful for the return and the key, but also for all the queuing for the replacement documents that would no longer be needed.

When PC Smith arrived five minutes late to start work, he found an immediate summons from his sergeant.

'Have you been working in uniform while you're off duty? I hear you've been to a hospital and to someone's home.'

'Just helping an old lady out, Sarge. She'd been mugged in her own home.'

'Have you got her statement written up?'

'Well, I …'

'Thought not, Smith. How many times do you have to be told that you're not a bloody social worker? You're not supposed to get personal and involved. Hands off at all times. I'm putting you on report. This is a warning. Do your job, not everyone else's.'

Thursday morning, Day 7

Toothache always starts towards the end of the week. Mary used a finger to check along her gums where she had been hit on her left cheek. One tooth was loose but, worse, part of its inside was missing. The phone in the house had long since been disconnected, too expensive to maintain and never needed for that foreign country called 'online'. Up to one million people cancelled their internet in the UK in 2022 because of the high cost of living.[6] 'People who

6 *BBC*, Citizens Advice survey, 'One million cancel broadband as living costs rise', 17/5/2023.

really need the internet to access help schemes are being priced out of the service,' claimed a welfare chief.[7]

The phone company bombarded Tom and Mary with letters about better, more expensive two-year deals which required a bank account. Tom had once gone into a bank to inquire about an account, but had quickly learned that as they only had their monthly pensions there was little enthusiasm in providing a service. He was frightened away by threats of overdraft charges and the complexities of a credit card. Immediate access to £2,000 seemed attractive, but interest rates that could reach forty per cent did not.

The dentist, unvisited by Mary in several years, was a fifteen minute walk away. The premises had changed beyond recognition, no longer homely with shabby if scuffed wallpaper, but now plastic bright with expensive toothbrushes and large wallcharts with the costs of treatment. The receptionist was polite, but firm. They no longer took NHS customers. Mary's lack of visits meant she had lost her rights as a customer. The minimum charge for an inspection was £40 and they could not possibly estimate the full charge beforehand. It could be several hundred pounds. She waved at the wallchart.

'See for yourself,' she instructed.

With an air of dismissal, Mary was given a list of Alton's remaining NHS practitioners.[8]

'You'll find that most of them won't take new patients over eighteen years unless they are referred by another dentist,' she was told. 'We don't do referrals. You'll also find some of these NHS dentists don't take new patients who are entitled to free medical care.'

'That's me both times,' said Mary. She left mouthing her polite thank you to a lady who had already picked up the phone to a paying customer.

Mary decided to try Citizens Advice which had its offices in the archways on the ground floor under the town hall. She sat on a hard chair by the front door and waited her turn. Gusts of sleet washed over her as the door opened every few minutes with some newcomers not caring to close it behind them.

The lady who finally called Mary was, maybe, not ten years younger than her. She looked tired, harassed, perhaps a little defeated. She heard Mary's

7 Citizens Advice, Dame Claire Moriarty, chief executive. *BBC*, 'Cut low-cost broadband VAT to help more online, peers say', bbc.co.uk/news/technology-66033209, 29/6/2023.

8 *BBC*, bbc.co.uk/news/health-66167563, 'NHS dentists: Driving hundreds of miles unacceptable', 14/7/2023.

story, tut-tutting at first, then her lined face creased in concern as the details registered. After a few minutes, she reached across the desk piled high with paper and held Mary's hand.

She called up the NHS website and checked their dentists in Alton who were taking new patients.[9] She released a sigh.

'There are currently no NHS dentists taking new patients in Alton,' she reported. The closest NHS dentist to Alton which might take Mary was in Aldershot, eleven miles away; the next six miles further in Camberley. Then, there were two in Slough and one in Feltham. If they failed, there were possibly three available in London.

'And it will cost you £25.80 for an examination and at least another £70 for basic treatment unless you have an NHS HC2 exemption certificate under the LIS, the low income scheme. Do you live in a care home?'[10]

Mary shook her head, confused and in pain.

'My husband did all that, but he died a few weeks ago. I have to find out about all these things now.'

'Let's see what I can do on the phone.'

The woman was interrupted and called to one side. Mary heard a reprimand for hand holding. 'Never get involved.' The conversation, while hushed, was heated. The woman broke away in clear irritation.

'Come with me, please, Mary.'

Mary was ushered into a car and taken to a private practice on the other side of town.

'Wait for me, please.'

The woman was gone for five minutes. Out of Mary's earshot, she explained Mary's predicament, the mugging, the lack of hospital care, the absence of any NHS dentist, the pain. She pleaded. She then went back for Mary who was led inside. When the treatment was over, the dentist took Mary to one side.

'You had an impressive advocate, Mrs. May. There is no charge. Here are some painkillers, but you do need further treatment. I have called a colleague who takes NHS patients. She has agreed to see you. Here is her address and the appointment I have made.

---

9 www.nhs.uk/service-search/find-a-dentist/results/Alton, 1/4/2023.

10 www.nhs-services/help-with-health-costs, 1/4/2023. Costs increased by 8.5 per cent, 24/4/2023. 'One in four patients delaying or avoiding treatment', *British Dental Association*, press release, same date.

'Now, if you will excuse me, I must get back to my regular patients.'

Her Samaritan was gone The receptionist handed her a note.

'Come and see me again when you feel a bit better. I normally work in the mornings Tuesday to Thursday.'

Thursday afternoon, Day 7

Mary's thoughts turned to food. She had not eaten a proper meal since she left hospital.[11] She hoped the work on her teeth would at least enable her to do some mild chewing. She remembered seeing the Alton Foodbank next door to Citizens Advice in Market Square and so made her way back into town. The Foodbank was closed. She pressed her nose to the glass pane. It opened next on Saturday morning at half past ten.[12] Another sign said the bank had too many tinned tomatoes, pasta, baked beans and soup. Mary took comfort. She could easily get by on any of those items. The bank had a shortage of other tinned items: vegetables, rice pudding, custard, spaghetti and any meat. Equally, thought Mary, she could get by without any of those.

Market Square is one of the places in Alton where fast food outlets congregate. The aromas from an Indian, pizza restaurant and the pubs began to tug at Mary's stomach. She remembered her poor neighbour, her only friend, Christophers, who was dead and the house next to her which now lay empty. The listing of tinned vegetables reminded her of what was being stored in her fridge to stop it going off. She was sure dear John had bought the items for her and may have died because of it. She would go home and eat some of them. She had just enough money to buy some bread. She rose from the bench where she had enjoyed the first warmth from a pale yellow sun to make her way to Greggs in the High Street.

A memory made Mary stop. Last year, when Tom retired and was given money from a cash collection, he had taken her for a rare treat to Mifta's, an Indian restaurant which had recently opened. Cheaper introductory meals were on offer.[13] They had taken a seat in a corner, safe and alone, in an almost empty

---

11 *Age UK*, 'Tackling the cost of living crisis for older people: What the Government must do', July 2023.

12 www.alton.foodbank.org.uk.

13 www.miftas.com.

'I wondered,' said Mary, looking up, hesitating as her words dribbled out in small bursts, 'whether … I could … buy … a chapati?'

Radical Cartoons

room. It was their first meal out in almost ten years. The waiter recommended some mild curry based on yoghurt and lamb. What she remembered most was her delight with the garlic, cumin and butter flavours of the naan bread and the smaller chapatis.

Mary moved to the open doorway and stood for a few minutes wondering if she had the courage to do something she had never done before: to beg. A young man, almost dismissive, came out to the step. He could sense the poverty.

'What do you want, missus?' he challenged.

'I wondered,' said Mary, looking up, hesitating as her words dribbled out in small bursts, 'whether … I could … buy … a naan … or even a chapati?'

'Just the one? You don't want a meal, a takeaway?'

'I don't have much … money … at the moment. I might be able to come back and give you some more … next week … if that would be all right?'

The young man, fresh in England last year from Bangladesh, gazed down at the sad figure. From his experiences at home in Dhaka, he more than recognised the situation. For a while, he had been hopeless, too. His faith also placed an obligation on him. He took Mary's hand gently.

'Sit down for a moment on the bench over there, lady, while I see what I can do.'

He was gone less than a few minutes. The amount of food left by Indian diners from their large portions made the waste an embarrassment. None of the staff ever went hungry. The man came to her bench with a large brown paper bag. It contained the wholesome remains of some earlier plates, not yet scraped and washed.

'There's two chapatis, half a naan, fresh onion bhajis and some small bits of tandoori chicken,' he explained. 'They're all cold, I'm afraid, but it will keep you going until tomorrow.'

Mary felt thankfulness well up mixed with an awfulness of what she had done. Tears edged out of her eyes. The young man leapt back inside his cocoon so that this woman could not see his own wet eyes and, yes, shame.

Thursday evening, Day 7

Mary May knew that she was not herself. She sat in Victoria Gardens, unsettled by the way the feral males treated the girls on the edge of their group and noticing how they were all watching her and talking about her. She realised that it might be a long time before the anxiety of being attacked left her, especially in her own home. Simple pleasures, like inspecting the flower beds, eating a snack and enjoying the early April sun, would be forever tinged with worry and, on a bad day, fear.

What had changed? The answer was obvious. Tom had gone. After a massive second stroke, the interminable wait for the ambulance, he had slipped away at the end of the following day. She had only managed to visit him once and was not there when he died.

Tom had been her rock for over fifty years. There were disagreements, of course. He could be self-centred, preoccupied with a new idea, always angry at government, local and national, for not doing enough for working men. But, she knew, that he always loved her. He had cried helplessly when news came of Billy's death in that war neither of them understood. It had broken him. From a confident man who always sought a solution, he began to shamble through events.

What happens when your rock begins to crumble? Mary had never worked from the day they were married. In the 1970s, they were already a throwback with old-fashioned views and practices. They had never been on holiday, never stayed in a hotel, had no families to visit, but contented themselves with whatever Alton had to offer and the occasional day trips by bus, never train, in off-season warmer weather to Winchester or Marwell Zoo, which Mary loved. London was a faraway place.

Tom worked hard on building sites five and a half days a week, handed over the maximum housekeeping in cash except for some money for an occasional beer and roll-your-own cigarettes. He expected his dinner on the table at seven in a clean home. Later, they would sit on the settee, often holding hands, and watch television. They talked about what they saw and usually agreed. They had no bank account, no credit card and no phone as they had no one to call.

In return, Tom cared for and protected his wife against all harm. This was his duty and his wish. Her distress was his greatest hurt. When it came to the rent, the council taxes, and pension applications when the time came, Tom took care of all of that. Mary never once had to deal with officials behind large desks with their grilles and queues and attitudes, never had to fill in forms, never knew her NHS or National Insurance numbers. She also never knew how money was paid or the names and addresses of the organisations that were involved. Today's modern couples might mock the Mays and their lifestyle, but Mary would have been unrelenting. She knew and welcomed her place in the world. She was content and only Tom's death had made her unhappy.

Tom and Mary were no longer lovers, not since Billy died, but they were joined at the hip. Tom was her man and, suddenly, he was gone and she was crushingly alone in a world for which she had no preparation.

Mary knew that she had to get a grip. She had to learn to understand the system. She already had the semblance of a plan. She would eat the vegetables on Friday, find out about the foodbank on Saturday and be at Citizens Advice on Tuesday to seek help from her new friend. She just needed to stay afloat till then and to hope for no more shocks. She couldn't let Tom down.

She flattened her now empty brown bag, threw the crumbs for the lumbering pigeons and made her way to the waste bin. Her new positivity saw her past some unnecessary and unpleasant insults from the unkind and undisciplined children.

A large notice and a letter were taped to her front door.[14] The energy company had gained a court warrant because Tom was over £100 behind with his payments and had not responded to over ten attempts to contact him. The warrant charges were £150. A locksmith had forced entry so that men from the company could install a pre-payment meter. There was a lot more information and an emergency phone number. She was befuddled by talk of how to read the meter, how to make payments, £30 of energy credit available to her and something called 'friendly hours credit'.

In 2021, 380,000 people were forcibly switched to pre-payment meters; this rose to 600,000 the following year. Warrants are usually nodded through undiscussed by the courts on applications from power companies. The process is a measure of hard times in which individuals get lost.

---

14 *BBC*, 'Anger as prepayment energy meter force-fittings to be allowed again', 31/1/2023, 18/4/2023, *BBC*, 'British Gas, Scottish Power, and Ovo dominated forced meter installations', 18/4/2023. *Daily Telegraph*, 'Energy meter staff to wear body cameras on home visits', 18/4/2023. www.*ofgem.gov.uk*, 'Pre-payment Meters explained', 5/2023.

Mary spent Friday staring at her wall, staring at her letters, staring at the dead television and looking at the empty space on the mantlepiece where Tom should be in his urn ready to offer advice.

Radical Cartoons

Mary sat on the pavement edge, not understanding what her notice meant and frightened to go inside her home because of who might be there. Her head began to whirl again and she had to place each hand on the cold stone to stop herself from falling over. Half an hour later she had gathered herself enough to try her key. It was stiff to move, but soon gave way. The light switch did not work. She found a candle, lit it and moved through the house checking each cupboard and under the beds in case a thief was hiding. She found a new, large, white meter placed near the fuse box. It declared, 'Out of credit'.

Finally satisfied that she was alone, Mary opened her fridge door and realised that, of course, it was also not working. She took out the vegetables and spent twenty minutes chopping them to make a soup. She added pearl barley, a favourite of Tom's, and one of her meagre stock items. Then she slumped into the chair by the kitchen table. She berated herself. She was a fool. How was she to cook her pan of soup with no electricity? The whirling in her head began again, only faster. She moved to her bed, found an extra blanket and crawled in shivering from the night cold.

Mary spent all of Friday staring at her wall, staring at her letters, staring at the dead television and looking at the empty space on the mantlepiece where Tom should be in his urn ready to offer advice.

Saturday morning, Day 9

The next morning, Mary sat bolt upright when the first light came through the curtains and cursed herself again for a fool. She might not have power, but her dead neighbour John Christophers surely did. He did not have a prepayment meter so no one would be along any time soon to disconnect him. Mary slipped quickly into her clothes, found John's key and picked up her saucepan of vegetables. The street was empty and, within minutes, she had the soup boiled and turned down for a lengthy unsupervised simmer.

Back home, Mary settled to a task which, she freely admitted to herself, she had been evading. If she was to regain control of her life, she had to face the consequences of Tom's death and most of that lay on the floor inside the front door. She scooped up the layers of mail and took them to her kitchen table. First, she opened them all and threw the envelopes into the waste bin. The great majority were for Tom, but not all. Some were for her. Mary sorted the letters by subject.

The County Hospital at Winchester had sent Mary a copy of Tom's death certificate. He was yet to be cremated. The hospital demanded instructions. There were forms with opportunities for help with funeral costs. Cremation was available. If Mary wanted this she had to agree to cover the expenses and to travel to the crematorium to collect the ashes in a simple container.

This first pile took Mary some time. There was a lot of reading. She had not really considered that Tom's body still existed, only that he had gone. Could she afford to travel regularly to a Winchester grave to visit him? She much preferred the idea of a little urn on the mantlepiece so that she could talk to him and ask his advice whenever she needed. She was confident that Tom would have agreed. They had never discussed death or funerals. Was she absolutely sure? She knew she would need advice on the forms as they were complicated and she had no money. Costs were in thousands of pounds.

The next pile was about pensions. There was a letter confirming that Tom's pension had ceased. Someone had told the pension people that he had died. That was no surprise, but it seemed that she had a pension of her own and this would change because of Tom's death. She never knew that Tom had been collecting it for her. At least, she now knew she had to go somewhere in Alton to get it sorted.

She badly needed money. The great list of additional support available to her was confusing; she noticed pension credit, housing benefit, council tax support, cost of living support. She had a list of the places that dealt with all of these, but most of them seemed to be in different organisations in different offices away from Alton. She prayed that her new friend in the Citizens Advice office could steer her through this.

Mary called her third collection her 'court pile'. The thought that she had broken the law or done something wrong that she didn't know about made her go cold with worry. She felt guilty without knowing why. She realised that because Tom had been ill for two years, matters may have got well out of hand. For the first eighteen months, he had still managed to go out regularly to collect and deal with money. But, now, months later, how bad could their debt have got?

The pile began with Tom's non-payment of the energy bills, the cost of the warrant and understanding how the pre-payment meter worked. They clearly didn't know that Tom was dead and couldn't have answered any of the demands. There was a demanding letter from the landlord, which at least provided an address in Alton, telling Tom that he could be evicted from the house because of unpaid rent unless he made contact within thirty days.

Then, there was another shock. Tom hadn't paid the annual TV licence renewal.[15] Everyone under eighty-five years now had to pay £159. Their change in status and the debate had completely passed her by; the TV had always been free. She was threatened with imprisonment for non-payment.

At least, there was a suggestion that she could get help to pay for this because she was over seventy-five and had little money.

There were a dozen more letters unread, but Mary already felt exhausted. The whirling in her head started again. She remembered the soup simmering next door and moved carefully, almost like a criminal, to check on it. It was fine. At least she could still cook. She took the pan back to her house, poured a generous portion and sat at her table. She felt energy flooding back.

Mary was interrupted by heavy, repetitive knocking on her front door. She recognised the pattern and was not surprised to see PC Budd.

'Hello, Mrs. May. I've come about Mr Christopher's vegetables that you offered to keep in your fridge. I need to make an inventory for Mr Christopher's estate and to get you to sign it to say that you have them.'

'Gosh,' said Mary. 'That might be difficult. You'd better come in.'

Mary pointed to her bowl of soup and the pan.

'There they are,' she said. 'I thought I had better eat them before they went off. I never thought that they would be so important. My power has been cut off and the fridge isn't working. John probably brought them for me, anyway. He never liked celery.'

PC Budd applied his investigatory powers.

'If you're cut off, how did you manage to make that soup?' he demanded.

'A neighbour helped me out,' said Mary with as straight a face as possible. 'Would you like some?'

Budd puffed up his chest. 'Mrs. May, this could be a serious matter. I'll need to file a report. I'll also be going in to Mr. Christophers' house. I hope you haven't been stealing his gas and electricity?'

'Oh dear,' said Mary to the policeman's back as he marched out.

---

15 www.goodto.com/money/tv-licence-cost-664805, 6/2023.

She finished her soup. Then, after some thought, pulled one of the envelopes from her bin, wrote 'Veggies' carefully on it and placed it on top of the 'court' pile of letters.

It was eleven o'clock. She had just an hour to get to the foodbank before it closed. It wouldn't open again until next Tuesday evening. She put on her coat and hurried down the road.

Outside, a notice claimed that 'no one in Alton needs to go hungry tonight'. Food drop off points were advertised at Waitrose, Sainsbury's, the Co-op, A-Plan Insurance, Newbury Building Society, Nationwide, Leighton's Optician's and the Maltings.

There were only two people waiting near the counter, but the back room of the shop was busy with volunteers carefully filling old supermarket carrier bags. As she waited, she read that parcels provided 'three days of nutritionally balanced, non-perishable, tinned and dried food that had been donated by the local community'. She looked longingly at a list of what she might receive: cereals, soup, pasta and sauce (that would be new), rice (and that), tinned beans, meat, vegetables and fruit, tea, sugar (it had been months), biscuits and a luxury item called 'snacks'. Around the room were several boxes of low-volume random tins and feminine hygiene products for free collection.

Mary's turn came.

'Can I have a food parcel, please. It's just for me. What I would really like is one that had food that didn't need to be heated. My electricity has been cut off.'

'Oh dear, that's not good news,' said the gentleman who looked almost as old as her. 'Let me check your voucher and I'll see what I can do.'

The man moved to a computer screen.

'Voucher? What voucher?' said Mary, her heart sinking.

'Got to have a voucher, love,' said the man handing her a leaflet with 'Evoucher' printed on top in large letters. 'Got to know that you qualify for a bag. You may be surprised but some people come in here pretending to have no money, but really only trying to cut their bills so that they can buy more booze.'

'That's terrible,' said Mary.

'You need a voucher, lady,' said the man, bristling.

'I meant about stealing the bags to fund drinks,' said Mary. 'Where can I get a voucher? I've only got half a saucepan of soup left and the police might even want to take that away.'

The man looked quizzical.

'It's because I've been using my next door neighbour's electricity,' explained Mary helpfully. 'He's dead. He's just been run over.'

'You'll have trouble in getting a voucher before Monday,' he countered. 'The Citizens Advice is closed. You'll never get to your doctor. Have you got a social worker?'

'No,' said Mary. 'I didn't know you could get one of them.'

'We shut in ten minutes anyway. I would say that you are out of luck.'

Do you have any idea where I can get some food? I have no money. My husband has just died and my pension isn't sorted out yet.'

'Friends? Family? Neighbours? We don't like to give out food parcels without a voucher.'

'I haven't got any of those sort of people,' said Mary. 'As I said, my last friend just got run over and killed.'

'Look, here's what I'll do,' he said, tapping his nose. 'First, here's a list of all the places in Alton and the surrounding villages that give out vouchers. There's sixty of them. They're mostly schools, churches and doctors' surgeries. Second, and don't tell anyone … ', he passed a well-used Waitrose bag half-full of items towards Mary. She could see a pasta sauce packet on top.

'Don't tell anyone,' he said again, this time with a wink. 'And get someone to send an evoucher. Go to Citizens Advice or your doctor. We can always deliver fresh vegetables to your home as well.'

Alton's foodbank was set up eleven years ago by members of The Butts Church, but now has trustees from the town's different churches looking after the charity. The majority of the volunteers are involved in these churches, but it is not a requirement.

The foodbank is seeded by the Trussell Trust.[16] Demands for help with food have risen to never-before-seen levels of need. As the pandemic eased, the cost of living plunged many into deeper financial hardship. A Trussell report this year, 'Hunger in the UK', says one in seven of the population have experienced 'food insecurity' in the last twelve months, over eleven million people; about one in fourteen have used food aid during that period.[17] Foodbanks in the Trussell Trust network distributed almost three million parcels in the year

16 www.trusselltrust.org.

17 *The Trussell Trust,* 'Hunger in the UK', June 2023.

'One in seven of the population have experienced food insecurity in the last twelve months, over eleven million people, and about one in fourteen have used food aid during that period.'

Radical Cartoons

to April 2023, an increase of thirty-seven per cent over the previous twelve months.

Mary turned and slowly made her way to her regular bench. She gazed about and her eyes lit on the Salvation Army building on the corner of Amery Street. She remembered some time ago it had been a bustling place, but she had heard from Tom that the minister had left and the congregation was in decline. You used to see people coming away with parcels. Perhaps, there was a chance of a cup of tea and a piece of cake. She walked over the road, but the front door was locked. There was no information to say when she should come back.

As Mary sat on her bench, her young man watched from the step of his restaurant. After a glance into the dark interior, he walked over.

'Out of luck, missus?' he asked.

Mary told him her story and showed him her carrier bag.

'Just wait a few minutes,' he said and disappeared through his doorway. From inside, she heard a fierce argument brewing. The man reappeared carry another brown bag.

'I'm sorry,' he said. 'This has to be the last time. If I give you any more, I could lose my job. There's almost a full chicken curry meal in there with some rice. I'm really sorry. Some of it is leftovers.'

'I can come back next week and give you some money,' said Mary.

The man waved his hand in polite dismissal and went back inside to more verbal abuse.

Mary scuttled off to the park in shame for what she had accepted, convinced that everyone in the square had seen and heard everything. The food was still warm and she ate guiltily. The sauce was mild, very tasty if strange, and full of flavour. As she sat, throwing the last crumbs of naan bread to the ducks, Mary realised that there was something she could go to the next day, Sunday. A notice announced that Alton Concert Band was giving its first free music concert of the year from the garden's bandstand.

Saturday evening, Day 9

With no power, there was no television, no cup of tea. Mary checked the empty front street and slipped to John's door. It was covered in police tape which claimed it was a crime scene. She tried her key anyway and realised a conscientious policeman had changed the lock. She felt insulted and a little challenged. She moved through the back gardens and, from under a house brick, took another key. Inside, Mary giggled and stole more electricity for the electric fire and some black tea. She then made her first ever pasta dish, following the packet instructions carefully, and settled down to evening television. As she watched a repeat of *Midsomer Murders* for the third time, she dozed. She came to as John Nettles with the flick of an eye searched a suspect's bedroom and guessed the hiding place of an important paper file.

Mary switched off, cleaned up and went back home to her own bedroom. Inside the wardrobe, Tom's best suit was hanging. It was the one he used for visiting offices. Deep within the breast pocket, she felt a small roll of paper gathered by an elastic band. She spread five £20 notes on her blanket. In bed, a little at peace for the first time for many weeks, Mary said 'thank you' to Tom. She thought about where to place his ashes and fell quickly into a dream.

Mary mistook the temporary diversion through the building site and found herself riding a bicycle up a steep lorry track. At its end among clouds, girders were lowered into place to make the massive frame of a government office block. She got off her bike. Her only way forward was to sit on a passing girder. She held tight to the steel hawser. Her husband, Tom, and several other men were at work all around, but no one noticed her. Another girder swung into view so that its end overlapped with her own, then another and another. Each girder sported a flattened area complete with a hole into which, when several met, a joining bolt could be dropped. The bolt was so big that, when it arrived, she could only just circle it with her arms. Try as she may, she couldn't align the holes. Her arms tired and she placed the bolt as best she could. It missed one hole and its girder was held between others by tension only. Mary took a nut and screwed it tight onto the end of the bolt. She knew that one day the bolt might loosen. The unsecured girder would slip away, the building fall and many people would die. She crept back to her bike and free-wheeled down the slope, terrified by what she had failed to do. She did not know who to talk to to explain the problem. She was exhausted.

Sunday, Day 10

The next morning was cold and damp. Mary stayed under the covers until she felt guilty. Her plan was to enjoy the concert then stroll along the High Street until she found the solicitor's office for the housing association and then look for the place to sort out her pension.

She had only to make it until Tuesday when her friend at Citizens Advice had told her to visit. She would take her piles of letters, tell this lady what she had managed to do and not do, and hope some of the weight would be lifted. What she worried about most was her court file and that she might be sent to prison. If the solicitor was unkind, by the time she was freed, he would probably have relet the house. The energy company might try to have her locked up. So might the television licence people. And there was always that policeman and John's vegetables and the stolen electricity and gas. Mary did what she always did with problems that she tried to keep from Tom and pushed everything to the back of her mind.

A faint sun came out and the drizzle stopped. There were few people about. She nodded 'hello' occasionally, but got no response. She remembered seeing some time ago, the occasional pub sign which offered cheap lunches for pensioners. She would try to spot one as she walked. If that failed, she would go to a supermarket and buy some milk, bread for a sandwich with a meat tin one from the 'out-of-date' shelf or, perhaps, one of the foodbank items at home.

She recognised that she was not particularly hungry. Food had never been something she worried about. Her main concern was having breakfast ready for Tom before he went to work and dinner with meat and potatoes for when he came home in the evening. He dismissed salads as unfit for working men. Other than their single curry, foreign food like pasta and rice never crossed their table. Mary found it odd, now, that within reason she could eat what she wanted, when she wanted to, especially with £100 in her purse. Her daily meal had become central to her planning. Maybe, knowing that the next meal was safe meant that she was safe, too.

None of the pub signs offered 'over sixty-five' meals, but Mary noticed that one offered a 'children's roast' for £4.99. That seemed very good value compared with the full roast price of about £15. She went in, slipping sideways from shyness, and was immediately taken to a table. She was offered tap water which she accepted.

'Can I have a children's roast, pork, please?'

'But you're not a child. Children's portions are for children.'

'I understand, but I don't want a full meal. You don't when you are older.'

The waitress turned on her heel and returned with the bar manager.

'I'm afraid we don't sell children's meals to adults,' she explained.

'Not even to old adults who don't want a full meal?'

'The thing is that we have children's meals to encourage their parents to come to us for a family meal. We don't make any money on a child's meal. We make our money on the parents' meals and the drinks they order.'

'What should I do?' asked Mary, grasping for a way around the problem. Her face had gone bright red. She had made a terrible mistake. She thought she was being asked to leave, which, in fact, she was. She looked around in horror as she realised other diners were listening to her embarrassment.

A woman sitting with a friend at the next table interrupted.

'We are just about to order. Would it help if this lady dined with us so that she could have her children's meal?'

'Oh, gosh, I don't know. Oh, all right, but I'll have to push the tables together.'

'If you must.'

The pub owner sensed a difficulty, introduced himself and asked if he could help. The bar manager explained the problem and the solution. The woman diner smiled and placed her purse on the table.

'I'm sorry, but that won't do. We have a strict rule about children's meals.'

'And that won't do either. My dear, if you would like to come with us, we'll go together and find somewhere else to eat.'

Mary got up in a daze and wished she could shrink into the floor. As she was ushered out into the street she could hear the concerned murmuring of other guests as the manager was threatened with the sack if 'she ever pulled a stunt like that again'. Another couple stood up to leave just as their drinks arrived.

'We've decided to eat elsewhere as well,' said the man to the now furious owner. 'Looks like you made a bad decision.'

Outside, Mary crumpled her hands together.

'Thank you for what you did for me, not even knowing me and all. I just couldn't ruin your meal any more. I feel dreadful. Thank you.'

And she all but ran away in shame. Just by her home, she slowed enough to call in at the last corner shop in the area. She bought a small loaf, baked yesterday, some cheese and some milk.

'I'm afraid I can't put this on your tab, Mrs. May,' said a non-unfriendly Mrs. Patel. 'Mr. May already owes us over £40 for some time and we have a rule of no credit.'

'Tom's dead,' said Mary. 'He's left me and everything's going wrong. Can I give you £20 now. I'll find some more money as soon as I can spare some. I'm very sorry.'

'Oh, Mrs. May, I'm so sorry, too, I never … .'

But Mary had disappeared to seek the security of her cold house. She sat at the kitchen table, bread unwrapped and milk unopened. For the first time since she left hospital, she cried. She cried for a long time until her handkerchief was sodden and beyond use.

Sunday evening, Day 10

Mary checked the remains of the vegetable soup. She stopped humming a favourite popular love song from the concert when she realised the soup had been left too long and had started to ferment. It bubbled to the taste and she knew it had to be thrown away. Her mother had once told her that onions hastened the process.

Loneliness is a feeling that creeps up on you. Old people who do not work may live from day to day with just a few contacts, maybe one or two of them are close family or friends, maybe others are casual or infrequent contacts like shop staff or people met in the street. When the balance suddenly shifts, especially when a loved one dies, the bereaved can suddenly find themselves in an unpleasant and unexpected place. After a lifetime of interaction, of being valued, remaining casual contacts are not always as welcoming and interested as previously thought.

There is no switch that introduces a lost person to a new group of like-minded friends. The feeling of emptiness may be overwhelming, bringing panic or despair. At the very time when self-esteem is at its lowest, perhaps critically damaged, the lonely human has to reach out into the unknown, become uncomfortable and risk curt rejection. The walls that separate acquaintances can seem much higher.

Mary was an intelligent woman, not academically blessed for she had left school at fourteen, but she could apply logic to her situation. As she lay in her bed, listening for the sound of intruders who would hurt her, she slowly analysed her feelings. She eventually came up with a plan which, if it worked, might guide her away from the emptiness which filled her. She realised that Tom had been the only person who provided her with purpose and happiness. He was gone and could never be replaced. Those people, children, family, colleagues or long-term neighbours, who might have helped her, did not exist.

Had Mary but known it, loneliness was well recognised in Alton's wider welfare community. Pages of good advice littered the internet like confetti. There, online, organisations which offered advice on how to stay connected displayed their wares and provided links to other organisations, churches, community centres, lunch clubs, adult learning, entertainment and leisure activities, where help might be available. Hundreds of groups, classes and activities might welcome her and introduce her to new people, leading to possible friendships. The trouble was that the pervasiveness and ubiquity of the web was a long way away for the unskilled.

Signposting is a major activity within the welfare community, gradually but surely replacing the open doors to buildings which contain warm human contact for real people in trouble. All welfare organisations pointed online to a plethora of helpers, seemingly ending in a giant circle of repetitive directions. The poor and desperate were expected to be connected to the internet, to be able to search through honestly-written, but complex sites that offered a wealth of advice. The troubled and ill-versed had to scramble over flickering screens using a foreign keyboard mired in arcane conventions that demanded comma perfect interactions.

Charities began to buckle as government withdrew funding and called on the voluntary sector to take extra legislative strain. People who once set out to provide welcoming frontline care began to insist that initial contact be made by an online form or an email. This enabled the managers to prioritise, to stop queues at the door and to protect their overworked and stressed volunteers.

The great cloud hanging over all interaction was called 'safeguarding', the need to protect the vulnerable, but which resulted in fewer and fewer carers being able to do less and less of what was actually needed. Their directions came from fearful management teams hidebound by new laws. Volunteers everywhere, diminished by Covid, were quitting, yes, because of workload, but also because of the lack of freedom to act.

The trouble for Mary May was that she had no access to the internet. In truth, she was but vaguely aware of what it was, had no experience of where it was, nor of how it might open the doors to all those organisations that had taken exception to a dead Tom not paying his bills. All the online torrent of advice was valueless.

Particularly, Mary might have found her way to the many voluntary groups that offered friendship services by telephone. Their members were willing to spend whatever time was necessary talking to the self-declared lonely. Mary might have been happier talking to someone from Alton or Hampshire, but, then, how much did it really matter where people at the end of the phone were located? Close by, there were groups in Bordon, Farnham, Four Marks, Medstead, Petersfield and Ropley. The groups also offered combinations of walks, meetings, home visits, shopping and lifts to medical appointments. Further afield were national organisations like Age Concern, Age Space, Age UK and Good Neighbours.

Mary knew of none of these, but even if she had, she had no phone. The thought of discussing her problems with a stranger she would never meet face-to-face would have seemed an impossible thing.

Monday early morning, Day 11

Mary rose early, ate some bread and cheese with a glass of milk and made her way to the solicitor's office. She had never met a solicitor before nor knew what a trustee of a housing association did. It was clear that he was important as he had a secretary who demanded to know Mary's business. She also asked how Mary could possibly think she would get a meeting without an appointment.

Miss Rosewater was a lady who welcomed the power of her position and used it without kindness. Her job was not to enable those who paid her employer's bills, but to protect him against the slightest breeze of irregularity and inconvenience. Her tight grey bun and spectacles, hanging correctly over her cashmere cardigan, were symbols of her authority. She was, for all the world, a vulture.

Mary was an early worm and easy prey. She stammered through her problem. Miss Rosewater looked aghast that anyone, for whatever reason, would dare not to pay their rent. It was an insult she felt personally.

'I think that you should write to Mr. Heapworth and explain how you intend to solve your problem. He might then call you in to discuss your letter.'

Mary's backbone was strengthening through repeated encounters with rejection.

'I think that would take too long,' she replied quietly. 'Mr. Heapworth is clearly upset, but he does not know that my husband has died. I haven't had time to sort out my pension. He needs to understand this.'

It was a good start, but Mary tailed off lamely. 'I don't want to lose my house. I have nowhere else to go.'

Miss Rosewater sniffed the weakness in the air. This was her first victim of the day and she was hungry. Her meal was interrupted as the door opened. A small man in his late fifties, going to fat, entered. He was freshly shaven except for a tidy moustache, smelled of over-used Cologne, and sported a tartan waistcoat and clashing floral tie. Mr. Heapworth was on time. It was ten o'clock and he was ready for gentle work.

'Nowhere else to go?' he parroted. 'We can't have that. How can we help?'

The firm of Jones, Jones and Heapworth was today a sorry reflection of its former eminence. Heapworth was aware his skills had faded as he failed to keep up with changes to the law. Divorces needed someone a little more dynamic. Conveyances were pushed elsewhere by estate agents keen to fast-track sales. Heapworth was anxious for any new client if only to keep himself in claret.

'I'm Mrs. Mary May,' offered Mary on the verge of stuttering. 'You know, knew, my husband, Tom. We were, I am, one of your tenants.'

'Dear me. Tom is dead?' A crocodile might have shed more sincere tears.

'Yes. So, now I'm on my own and in a bit of confusion with money. After your letters, I thought I should come and see you.'

'Oh dear, oh dear. You'd better come in, Mrs. May,' he announced, wishing for a more lucrative start to his day. 'Two teas, please, Miss Rosewater.'

Icicles flew into Mary's back as she was ushered into the drab office that had only photographs of dead Joneses for decoration. When it arrived, Mary's tea had a generous pool in its saucer.

'I knew dear Tom was not well, but did not realise it was so serious,' offered Heapworth. 'Tell me your problem.'

Heapworth sought the best and quickest way to put the rent on an even keel. It would be difficult to eject Mrs. May, probably impossible if she refused to go. And it would certainly be difficult to find a placid replacement tenant who would accept the poor state of the building. Heapworth wanted only a quiet life and to maintain his steady but small income.

They agreed quickly that Mary needed professional help from somewhere in welfare to get her money sorted out. At present, she owed £200 for four weeks' rent with another £50 soon to be added. Mary would return in the month with a progress report and would sign the transfer rental papers. If she found herself in funds in the interim, she would immediately make some payment off the arrears.

She found and opened the front door unaided and left.

Mary was near her doctor's surgery. She decided to see if she could move her plan a bit further forward. The place was busy.

'Do you have an appointment?'

'No.'

'Then how can I help you? There's two weeks' waiting for appointments.'

'But you don't know who I am and you don't know what I want to see the doctor about.'

'OK. What do you want to see the doctor about?'

'Does that mean you get to decide how important it is?

'I'm a trained triage receptionist.'

'I don't know what triage means. Am I supposed to tell you in front of all these people?'

'You could always phone.'

'I don't have a phone.'

'Well, you could borrow one.'

'And you could try to help me rather than trying to upset me. I need help.'

Mary was quickly growing a carapace.

'My husband died a few weeks ago,' she explained. 'Then I was mugged in my home a week ago and went to hospital. When they discharged me after a few days, they said I should come here as soon as I felt well enough for a check-up and to see about my medicines. My head is hurting.'

A woman further down the queue shouted, 'For God's sake give her an appointment. How cruel can you be?'

The qualified operative thought to take the lady on, but the murmuring from the line of patients became distinctly hostile.

'Take a seat, Mrs. … .'

'Thank you for asking for my name,' said Mary. 'It's Mrs. May. I'm a widow. My husband, Tom, was a patient here, too.'

'Take a seat, Mrs. May, and I'll see what I can do.'

Monday late morning, Day 11

Mary waited for an hour before she was called. She wished she had been able to visit the toilet, but she was frightened about missing her turn. Over the years, she had attended surgery four times, she remembered, and had never seen the same doctor. During Covid, Tom had given up trying to make appointments. During his slow death, no doctor ever visited him at home, nor made a phone call to check on his progress. Mary always felt that the lack of attention may have hastened his death. She was conflicted. She realised that something fundamental had changed from the days when a bout of measles meant a visit from a familiar and reassuring face. In her heart, she was no longer sure that doctors were on her side. And, yet, people of her generation were brought up to respect professional authority, not to ask too many questions and to do what they were told.

A tired face, a woman with straggling hair, looked up when Mary entered the office. The name on the door was long and Mary realised that she could never pronounce it nor remember it. The doctor consulted her computer screen with her back to Mary.

'Mrs. May, isn't it? Are you well? You have an emergency appointment, I see. What can I do for you?'

'Do you know that I have been in hospital?' asked Mary.

'Well, let me see,' replied the doctor while tapping away at her keyboard. 'Oh, yes, I do. You were in for five days. How did you end up there?'

Mary was learning the sort of answers which achieved the best results.

'I am worried that you don't know what has happened to me. I have had a bad few days and I thought you might have been concerned about me.'

'Well, tell me now?' The question came with a limp smile.

'I was mugged by two masked men. In my home. They took all my money. I was told by the hospital doctor to come here as soon as I could for a check up.'

'Oh, dear, I …'

'I ran out of medicines yesterday. My head often starts whirling. Some teeth were broken and no NHS dentist would see me. I am worried about the pain in my cheekbone. The bruises on my arms are a nasty yellow and still hurt. My electricity has been cut off. I have no food at home and I feel faint.'

'Good heavens.' A few taps later, 'Has your husband been able to help you?'

'Tom died a few weeks ago. No one from here would come and visit him. In the end, I got our neighbour to call the ambulance. He never came home and I don't have the money to get him cremated because I don't know where to find my pension. I miss him a lot and would like to have his ashes at home so that I could talk to him.'

'Oh, my dear …'

'I don't have much energy, any more …'

Mary tailed off with her story and began to sob quietly, embarrassed to be breaking down.

The doctor took refuge in her work. Mary was subjected to a detailed examination, with many questions and much tut-tutting, which took double the allotted ten minutes. She was given another letter for a local NHS dentist requesting urgent work on the damaged tooth. She was told to go that afternoon to the community hospital for a walk-in X-ray on her cheekbone in case it was broken and on her skull in case of a hairline fracture. The bruising was not serious, but needed painkillers which were added to precautionary antibiotics. There was a follow-up visit in one week and the obligatory promise of emergency help from 111 in the interim.

'I don't think I can walk as far as the hospital.'

Mary received a phone number and an email address to contact for a free local volunteer to drive her to the hospital.

'I don't have a phone or the internet,' offered Mary.

'That makes it difficult if you don't have a friend or can't get to Citizens Advice,' said the doctor. Life without phone or internet was out of her experience. 'I'll also contact social services and tell them to reach out to you. You must get advice on getting your electricity restored. You should never have been cut off.'

'Well, I was.'

The doctor reached her formulaic conclusion. 'Is there anything else that you think I should do for you?'

Mary was a little overwhelmed. She wondered if she would remember that host of instructions. That morning, she had felt she was beginning to cope, to find a way, but the flurry of things she now had to do made her feel she was on the slippery edge of a deep pool.

'Are you able to give me an evoucher that I could use at the foodbank? I haven't been able to get to the pensions people yet to see how I can get any money.'

The doctor grabbed the keyboard and filled in the required four pages on the database. This generated an evoucher code which she gave to Mary.

'There, keep it safe and give it to the foodbank. They'll have the full voucher over the internet.'

Another way of helping Mary occurred to her.

'Why not go to the Vokes Lunch Club nearly opposite the catholic church on Normandy Street?' she suggested brightly. 'It's number one hundred on the opposite side of the road. Be careful how you cross. I hear they do good lunches for very little money. You could go there now and, maybe, they could book a taxi for you to the hospital after your meal?'

'I don't think I could afford a taxi.'

'Well, they could call that lift number I gave you. That's free.'

'When I come back, will I see you?' asked Mary as she made her way to the door. 'It was always better in the old days when you knew who your doctor was. They knew the whole family.'

'I can't promise, but I'll see what I can do. I work four part days each week.'

The doctor closed her door, not waiting to watch Mary walk off with her documents. She returned to her desk, slumped into her ergonomic chair and massaged her temples. Then she sent a short email to the practice's social prescriber highlighting Mary and her many problems. The prescriber's job in the NHS is to act as a signpost, to connect patients with community groups and other services which can provide practical and emotional support.

The doctor then called her own mother to see if she could pick up her three young children from pre-school. She was running late and her waiting room was full.

Monday lunchtime, Day 11

Mary waited ten minutes for her medicines at the on-site pharmacy. She then crossed the road and walked down the street towards town and the over sixties lunch club at the Vokes Centre. The entrance was along a passage at the side of the house. She knocked on the open door.

'For goodness sake, come on in,' said a welcoming lady wearing an apron. 'You don't have to knock on the door here.'

'I was hungry,' ventured Mary. 'I wondered whether I could have some lunch, please? Do I need to book or anything?'

'Of course you can. No need to book. We just ask that you're over sixty and live around Alton. My name's Jane. We charge £5 for a two-course meal which is at twelve o'clock. Is that all right with you?'

Mary nodded, hardly believing her luck. She had never heard of the Vokes Club.

'Have you just opened recently?' she asked. 'I've lived here all my life and I've never heard of you?'

'Gosh, no. We've been here since the 1960s. We've been here for ever. We're called the Vokes Lunch Club after a local businessman called Vokes and his lady assistant gave us this house. It's now run as a charity. We've got about thirty members, but we'll have to see how many come today. Why don't you take a seat in the front sitting room and have a cup of tea and a biscuit. I'll come back in a few minutes and take a few details for our records.'

Mary was taken to a chair next to Agnes, a woman of about her age who was the first of that day's members to arrive.

'Agnes is a bit shy, but she does like a good chat,' said Jane. 'Agnes this is Mary. It's the first time she has been to Vokes.'

'Hello,' said Agnes. 'It's nice here. It won't be long before we have lunch. I hope it's sausages and mash.'

A volunteer brought in Mary's tea and biscuits. Within a few minutes, the two ladies were deep in conversation about pensions.

'I get mine paid into my bank account every month,' explained Agnes.

'I don't have a bank account,' said Mary. 'At least, I don't think so. My husband Tom did all that.' She looked up, her eyes filling. 'He's dead, you know. He's left me. He needs to be cremated, but I can't afford it. I'd like to bring him home.'

Agnes reached out for Mary's hand.

'I'm alone, too,' she shared. 'I don't know that it gets any easier.'

'What can I do about the pension? I don't know who to talk to. Citizens Advice are busy. I have to make an appointment.'

'Well, you could write to the pensions people, but that would take time for them to answer. You may not be able to wait that long. You could phone them, but someone would need to help you. The number will be on any letter they sent you. You do have a letter from them?'

Mary nodded. 'I think so,' she said.

'I remember a long time ago, some friends got advice from the job centre. It's now by the *George* pub at the other end of town. I don't know if they would still be able to help?'

'Tom used to visit the Post Office to get our cash.'

'I do know that the Post Office pension accounts were all closed by the Government just before Christmas last year,' remembered Agnes. 'If your Tom didn't have an account in a bank and he was sick, things might have got messed up. Bill who comes in here on Fridays says he got a special payment card which had pension vouchers on it so he could get cash when he needed to.'

Jane came back with her clipboard.

'Is it all right if I take a few contact details for our records, Mary?' she asked.

She noted Mary's name, age and address. Spaces for phone number and email address stayed blank as did the line for next of kin.

'Is there no one for us to contact if you were to fall ill, Mary? No special friend or neighbour?'

'I haven't got anyone now Tom's gone,' came the reply.

'OK. Well, hopefully, you'll make some new friends here like Agnes. I have to ask you for £5 for the lunch today and, when you've been a few times and decided that you want to come regularly, there'll be a £1 membership fee. And, there's one other thing. We have an arrangement with the taxi firm by the station. If you want to be picked up or taken home, you pay £1.50 for each trip and we cover the rest. That needs to be booked in advance, but I see that you don't live far away, at all.'

'The taxi's really good,' chipped in Agnes, 'especially when my legs are playing up.'

'Is there anything else you'd like to know, Mary?' asked Jane.

'There is one thing, if you wouldn't mind. The doctor gave me a number on this piece of paper for someone who might give me a free lift to the community hospital after lunch. I need an X-ray. Could you call for me?'

The room had filled. At noon, everyone trooped through to a bright and airy dining room set for tables of six and overlooking the back garden. It was sausage and mash. Shortly after she had finished, Mary's lift arrived. She waved goodbye to her new acquaintances and hoped this was a new beginning.

The Vokes Lunch Club staff are not trained welfare specialists, but they are skilled at spotting members who may need extra support. When Mary did not turn up for lunch the next day, Jane mentioned this at a regular meeting with a trustee of the small team that ran the club. As a result, she made a confidential phone call to a number at the social services offices in Winchester.

Monday afternoon, Day 11

Mary arrived at the community hospital in luxury – a front seat in a private car with a driver. The lady insisted on following her into reception once she had parked. She found Mary in tears, worn down by yet another arrangement that had gone wrong.

'But the doctor said I was to come over this afternoon and that a booking would not be needed,' she cried.

'We used to have that system, but we don't any longer,' explained the receptionist wearily. It was a debate she was fed up with having. 'NHS hospitals in Hampshire have decided that a booking system is more efficient for us. We are always short-staffed. We have tried to explain this to the local doctors, but they don't seem to be listening.'

'What am I to do?' asked Mary, her shoulders slumped, momentarily defeated. Her brain whirled around trying to grasp the situation.

'Get your doctor to make an appointment.'

Mary all but collapsed onto a red plastic chair and hid her aching head in her lap. She had no more fight.

Mary's driver stepped forward.

'I understand that you are just doing what you are told,' she began. The receptionist bristled, not liking the woman's tone or implications.

'What you don't understand is that all these other patients waiting for X-rays … .' She stopped mid-sentence, partly because there were no other patients in sight in the large and empty hall and partly because she was interrupted by Mary's driver.

'There are some confidential and private matters about this case which shouldn't be discussed in public. I think it would be easier for everyone if I spoke to your manager or the head radiographer. Don't you agree?'

'And who are you?'

'I'm the person sent by the doctor to bring Mrs. May directly here because of the emergency,' she lied. 'You can call the doctor if you wish.'

A department head was summoned, unhappy, in the middle of her tea break. They moved to the end of the counter away from Mary.

'This elderly lady was mugged in her home,' the driver began. 'She is exhausted. She is recently widowed. I understand that this is not an emergency hospital, but the doctor is worried about a potential skull fracture. There is a possibility that Mrs. May did not receive the best care at the hospital. She was left on a trolley without examination for over twelve hours. There is already talk by a medical negligence legal team of a substantial and formal complaint accompanied by an unpleasant amount of associated publicity.

'Can I suggest that you would do best by your employer, and protect your hospital here from getting sucked into the mess, if you could find a way to get her seen?

'To try to help you, I will make sure when I get back that the doctor knows personally about your new appointments system for X-rays.'

The driver smiled as winsomely as she could and hoped she hadn't gone too far. There was a long, tense pause while pros and cons and proprietorial rights were weighed, lengthy paperwork and status considered and a decision made.

'Please would you both wait over there and I'll see what I can do.'

Within ten minutes, Mary was ushered into a cubicle to put on a wrap-round apron. In the X-ray room, a technician stood ready. She lay down and the machine clicked into action.

'You do understand that we don't give diagnoses here? You will be contacted through your doctor if there is any emergency or you need treatment.'

'I don't have a phone,' said Mary, but no one was listening.

Her driver scooped Mary up and drove her home. There was a moment when she gazed appalled at the state of the walls and their decoration. She flicked the light switch.

'Your electricity is off, Mary.'

'Yes, I know. They broke in because Tom got behind with the bills. They put that thing there,' she added, pointing at the meter. 'I don't know how it works and I haven't got any money to pay the bill.'

The driver checked the installation then rifled through the information left by the workmen. She played with the buttons and the kitchen light came on.

'There,' she said, 'that should keep you going for a few days until you get your pension sorted.'

Mary got up and hugged her new friend in relief.

'You must write to the energy company or get Citizens Advice to phone them for you and get this sorted out. You should never have been cut off.'

She thought and then asked Mary whether she had any money at all for the meter.

'I suppose I could spare £10 now because I'm seeing a friend at Citizens Advice tomorrow morning.'

'Would you like me to take it to your corner shop and get you some credit to keep the power going?'

Mary nodded, opened her purse and peeled off a note.

'Put the kettle on and I'll be back shortly.'

Mary did what she was told. While she was waiting, she picked up a few letters from her front door mat and gazed at the envelopes absent-mindedly. The driver was back.

'Mrs. Patel was very kind,' she announced. 'I've got a card here for £10. Let me enter that for you.'

She showed Mary how it was done, but recognised what Mary needed was bed and a long rest. She doubted she had understood the procedure.

'And I got some milk, bread, butter and jam and some ham from Mrs. Patel. She said she was very sorry to hear about Tom and for the misunderstanding. You are not to worry about money in the short term. Your credit is good. That was nice of her, wasn't it?

'Do you want anything to eat with your tea?'

Mary shook her head and sipped at the drink with her eyes closing.

'I had a nice lunch, thank you. It was enough. I think I'll just sit in my chair with a blanket and watch television with Tom.'

'Never mind. If you go back to Vokes tomorrow, you can have another lunch. Chicken, usually, on Tuesdays, I think.'

By the time the driver had softly closed the front door, Mary was already asleep.

Mary floated in front of a giant white box. It was attached to an unending dirty wall. No matter how much Mary waved her arms, flapping them like a bird, she could never reach the edges. Giant buttons with numbers printed on them came and went. With each change, the numbers disappeared and when they came back the numbers were different. She knew she had to press several of them in a certain order, but they were so large and stiff that by the time she reached the third, she realised that she had made a mistake and fell back fatigued. The light was fading till she could barely discern the buttons. Every time she thought of giving up, unforgiving red lights flashed threatening disaster and the cycle began again. Mary knew this was her life and it would never end. She was a slave without hope.

Tuesday morning, Day 12

Mary awoke lightheaded with a slight fever and her limbs aching. She stood holding to her bedside table waiting for the dizziness to pass. She was frightened to take a hot bath in case she fainted and so cleaned herself as best she could leaning against the basin. Among the many neglected household chores was her washing. Against all her life's practice, Mary was forced to reuse dirty underclothes. She found time for a cursory hand wash and hung a few knickers and bras on the bath rim to dry.

Thanks to yesterday's driver, Mary was able to make tea, toast and jam for breakfast. While she sat at the kitchen table, she heard the clatter of even more letters as they were pushed through the box. She decided to leave them for when she returned. Today was her big day. She had high hopes of her friend at Citizens Advice. Perhaps she would get her pension sorted and would be saved eking out her diminishing cash. There was a second lunch at Vokes to look forward to. Perhaps Agnes would introduce her to some more friends who could give her advice. Afterwards, in any case, she had her precious evoucher code from the doctor to authorise a second parcel from the foodbank which was open in the early evening. She needed to get to the dentist.

There was a queue at Citizens Advice. When the door was opened, people with appointments quickly met their designated adviser. Mary found a chair and waited for her friend. The room became stuffy and she sat in a draught as visitors went in and out. Eventually, she plucked up the courage to walk up to an adviser as someone left.

'Hello, one of your ladies asked me to come in and see her this morning. I have been waiting for her to arrive.'

'What's your name and what's her name, please?'

'Mrs. May. I don't know her name. but she told me she works Tuesdays to Thursdays.

Mary described the lady and gave her make of car. 'She drove me to the dentist.'

'That's Carole. She's off sick and probably won't be in this week.'

'Can I speak to someone else? I've brought all my papers. My husband's died and I'm in a terrible mess with all the bills. Everyone wants to take me to court.'

'We really would like to help you, Mrs. May, but you don't have an appointment. We don't have people sitting around. All these people here have problems, too. They made an appointment. You can do this online or call our helpline.'

'I don't have any online. I don't have a phone either. How do people like me talk to you?'

'It'll be much better if you make an appointment. Perhaps, you have a friend who is on the internet?'

Mary shook her head and began to shake. The whirling head was coming back with a new pain.

'Well, you could go to the library where they have free internet. You could see if anyone there could help you with the form. Say on it that it is urgent.'

'Is there no one here I can talk to today?'

'Not today. We are short-staffed and all of our appointment slots are taken. As I said, we would like to help you, but we are a voluntary organisation. We can only do what we can do. Not having a phone doesn't make it any easier for you.

'Mary was exhausted when she arrived at the job centre ... She stared at all the posters and leaflets and they began to blur. The room was warm and she felt her eyes closing. Mary was jerked awake when someone shook her arm.'

Radical Cartoons

'Phones cost money. I don't have money. Everyone who says they can help will only talk to me on the phone or on the internet. It's not very friendly.'

Tuesday afternoon, Day 12

Mary staggered out to her bench. It had started to drizzle. Her friendly waiter was standing at the restaurant doorway. He waved sadly and went quickly inside. She waited for some minutes to try to gather herself, but the rain came on harder. Across the square, the wind blew an umbrella inside out. Mary watched as it was thrown into a waste bin. She crabbed over, ashamed, and, when she thought no one was looking, grabbed it. She began a slow walk down the High Street to the Job Centre.

Mary was at the end of her stamina when she arrived. She pushed a big entry button and found herself in a roomy waiting area. Further on, some ten open but private interview areas with nice blue chairs, some with staff, awaited clients. The office was not too busy. A number of young and middle-aged people looking for work waited to be seen. She stared at all the posters and leaflets, some in foreign languages, and they began to blur. The room was warm and she felt her eyes closing. Mary was jerked awake when someone shook her arm.

'Are you all right, love? It's not the best place to have a sleep. Are you waiting to see someone?'

'I need some help with my pension,' Mary blurted out. 'I've not got much money left and my Tom has died and I don't know what to do. Someone said that you used to help here to sort pensions out.'

'Well, I've worked here for a few years and I know we don't do anything with pensions. All we do here is to try to match people with jobs so we help people who are of a working age. Have you tried Citizens Advice?'

'They're too busy to see me. I need to find an internet so that I can get an appointment, but I don't know how to work it.'

'My mum's got a pension and she has her money paid into her bank account.'

'I don't think I've got a bank account. I feel so useless. Tom did everything for me. I don't know how he did it because he kept all that from me. I've got no phone, no internet, no pension and I am almost out of money. I suppose I must try to write some letters.'

The woman's heart went out to Mary.

'Wait here a moment, love.'

She went to her desk and came back with a £20 note.

'There, that'll help for meals while you write your letters.'

'I couldn't. Thank you very much, but we would never take charity like that.'

'Please don't worry. See it as a loan that you can pay me back when you have your money coming in. I do know that if you can get help you will be OK. You can get things like pension credit on top of your pension. Then there's housing benefit and council tax support and cost of living support … .'

The woman saw Mary's eyes glaze over. She was giving her too much information.

'Perhaps, I could make a phone call for you to see if there is someone in social services who could come to your home and help you?'

'Thank you.'

'Where do you live? Is it far? How are you going to get home?'

'I live in Victoria Road,' said Mary. 'I don't know how I am going to get home. I don't feel very well. I feel confused and my ankles have started to swell.'

She looked down at her feet.

'It's embarrassing,' she confided.

'Don't worry,' the woman offered, glancing round. 'We're not too busy. My car is nearby. Come on.'

She offered her arm and a few minutes later Mary turned the key in her front door. She muttered a worn out 'thank you' and made her way quickly to bed. Her skin was burning and her head was drumming a dreadful tattoo. She took some tablets. Her neck was stiff and she switched off the bedroom light which was painful to her eyes. She had no thought for the foodbank, dentist or anything else but respite from the pain and shaking and fever which seemed to consume her.

Mary now had vivid dreams each time she fell asleep. When she woke, fuzzy-headed, nightdress damp and weak in the legs, she had scarcely enough energy to make it to the toilet.

She was outside a high, crenellated castle wall. The portcullis was down and the drawbridge raised. Mary knew there were people inside the walls who could help her, but they didn't know she was there. She shouted, but they were busy working in offices filling their diaries with appointments. From the battlements, a few tired defenders fired emails at her. These exploded as they hit the ground, but she felt no pain. Protruding from the soil were dozens of little aerials which she feared were landmines. An email fell near and the blast exposed a vibrating phone. It was still alive and began crawling towards her. The phone began a chorus and was joined by others, 'Please try later. All our volunteers are busy.'

The woman from the Job Centre was back at her desk within fifteen minutes where a reprimand for being away awaited her. She looked up the number for social services for Hampshire and sat listening to the ring tone for fifteen minutes. When she could risk no more time, she called up waiting clients and got back to work. At the end of the day, she tried the phones again, but they were closed till morning. She found an on-line form and filled it in as best she could. She was warned that safeguarding issues meant that the permission of the person needing help was required. She resolved to try the phone again in the morning.

Thursday, Day 14

There was no reply to the door bell at Mary's home when, two days later, a harassed and overloaded welfare professional called to check on her. Several alert messages had arrived at the headquarters in Winchester. The emergency nature of the calls was realised and a visit authorised. Looking through the letter box, the social worker could see a pile of envelopes on the floor. At the bottom of the stairs, a coat and pair of shoes were carelessly discarded. Nearby, there was a pool of congealing vomit.

The social worker called her office for authority to break in. The police patrol car arrived within twenty minutes.

Upstairs, the unconscious body of an older woman, scarcely alive, was found under a pile of blankets. An ambulance delivered her to A&E within ninety minutes. She was queue-jumped and seen immediately.

By chance, the doctor on duty recognised his patient from two weeks before. His spirits sank as he understood what had happened to the person at the heart of his resignation and imminent departure for Australia. Mary's trunk was covered in a vivid red rash. She was given oxygen through a face mask. The doctor worked diligently and at speed but quickly realised it was a hopeless case. He ordered antibiotics and fluids to be injected directly into dilated veins to help alleviate any discomfort. Tests were ordered for the type of blood poisoning brought on by a virulent form of meningitis. He suspected a root cause of tuberculosis.

Mary died quietly later that afternoon without regaining consciousness. She was alone, sunk into her hospital bed. Her expression was peaceful, almost as if she was dreaming.

Tom was sitting by the fire in his chair watching a favourite comedy show. He was chuckling as Mary came in with his dinner. She put the tray on his lap and, unexpectedly, he reached out and held her hand.

'Thank you, Mary, my love,' he said as he looked up at her. 'We're a good team. You know I'll never leave you. I'll always look after you.'

Author's note

A number of volunteers read early versions of my stories before final editing. They assess whether it is a good tale with a solid plot that will interest people. Several critics wanted more from the ending to Mary May's story. I offer four extra alternatives from which you can make your own choice.

What else could have happened to Mary May?

Option 2: Late Tuesday afternoon, Day 12: Drug queen

Kylie Ojukwu-Smith turned into Victoria Road pushing her twin baby pram just as Mary was dropped off by her rescuer from the Job Centre. Kylie was returning from an appointment at Citizens Advice where she had received help in filling in her benefit claims forms. It was quicker than doing it herself and form filling was always tedious. It was on days like this that Kylie cursed her mother, Betty, for giving her a long surname. Betty wanted to show her anger at being deserted by a recent boyfriend. Cameron Ojukwu dashed back to Nigeria as soon as he was told of the pregnancy.

Several doors away, Kylie saw Mary leaning on her door struggling with a key. She drew level.

'You all right, love?' she offered. 'Need some help?'

Mary looked up and felt all her confusion with today's young people well up. The girl looked about eighteen with red and orange hair streaked with black. Each ear was studded with more jewellery than Mary owned. There were further pins through the girl's nose and her lower lip which was coated with a bright blue lipstick. She wore a canary yellow jump suit advertising a foreign football team. Mary was intrigued by the different skin colours of the two obvious twins.

'That's very kind. I don't feel too well. Need to sit down.'

'Come in and 'ave a cuppa, then. Put the world to rights. I'm just two doors along.'

It was the beginning of an unusual friendship. Kylie lacked nothing in the way of confidence. The system was there to be used and she was already street wise far beyond her years. For Mary, confidence shaken almost to breaking point, Kylie was a brightly-coloured rock that could be relied upon. Kylie needed most to have someone to talk to for hours on end. Mary was happy to listen, play with the babies and to offer occasional practical advice.

While Mary recuperated in Kylie's spare bedroom, her new friend opened her post and got to work on the internet and the phone. Her first call based on her own experience was to the CAP Debt Help Centre.[18] Based at Harvest Church at Alton Maltings, the Centre soon despatched a debt coach for a personal visit who worked on a plan for Mary's problems.[19]

Kylie then tackled social services. She placed herself with her pram at the sympathetic reception desk of the little known Park House tucked away by the side of the public gardens. It was accessed by a driveway near the dry cleaners in the car park. Despite not having an appointment, she managed to get an interview with a professional from the third floor which dealt with adults. Hampshire County Council's welfare system was searched and Kylie's dramatic descriptions were linked to several other alerts. A trickle of welfare

18 Christians Against Poverty, The Maltings, Alton; 0800 328 0006 (free calls). capuk.org/get-help/help-with-money-and-debt?step-two=show&find=debt-centre&postcode=GU34+3DF.

19 harvestchurch.uk.

workers were welcomed to Victoria Road, all redirected by a notice pinned to Mary's own front door.

With pension back payments of over £1,500 soon in her new current account, Mary had another £270.50 benefits each week on top of her regular pension of £156.20.[20] By the time Mary moved back home, Kylie, working with CAP, had paid off the outstanding rent, the lapsed TV licence, Mrs. Patel's credit and was a long way to clearing the energy bills.

Most importantly, Kylie went with Mary to Winchester Crematorium and, a few days later, Tom came home to sit proudly on the mantelpiece. Mary's nightmares stopped.

Kylie alerted six friends that John Christophers' home was lying empty. The squat was a great success. The front door sported a large, printed notice, 'No vegetables are kept overnight in these premises or next door (except carrots)'.

Mary sat at Kylie's kitchen table on an early summer morning with one of the twins on her knee. There was a cup of tea and Kylie's special small cakes close at hand. A knock at the door was followed by a rushed conversation, an exchange and Kylie, the other twin on her hip, came back bearing a £20 note which went into a biscuit tin.

'What is going on?' asked Mary. 'That's the third visitor this morning. Some of them don't look like they've washed for a week. There's always people coming round.'

As Mary's confidence increased by leaps, she found life's second wind. Her affairs were in order. She had several new friends at the Vokes Lunch Club. Her phone was ready in her pocket and she kept close tabs over the internet on her bank account. She was playing an important part in helping Kylie organise her little family. Mary felt needed again.

'Oh, they've just come for their weed,' said Kylie. 'It's all getting a bit much and I think I'm losing money because I'm not very good at keeping track of the outgoings and the credit and stuff.'

'Why would people buy a weed?'

Kylie smiled. 'It's just a word we use for cannabis. Some friends, partners really, grow it in a shed on the road to Selborne. We could sell a lot more if we got ourselves organised. None of us is any good at maths.'

20 ageuk.org.uk/information-advice/money-legal/benefits-entitlements/benefits-calculator. benefits-calculator.turn2us.org.uk.

'Isn't cannabis a drug?'

'Yes, it is, but we think that it's more like a medicine. It makes you feel better, like your *Paracetamol.* Only it makes you feel happy. I use some in those little cakes that you like. My mother taught me how to do it. They make you feel better, don't they?'

'Yes, they really do,' mused Mary. 'How do you try to keep your lists?'

Kylie pushed open her laptop, opened a worksheet in Excel and showed Mary how she tried to keep up to date.

'This column is for the weed we 'ave for sale. This one is for our expenses for things we 'ave to buy. 'Ere are our customers and what they've paid, like. It's just trying to make it all work together. I'm not in control.'

Mary's housekeeping was always one of her strengths. Emails may have been foreign territory, but practical numbers and sums were a different matter.

'Show me how this keyboard works,' she ordered.

Within days, and especially following a teaching visit by one of Kylie's partners, Mary understood the files intimately and was mastering the system. After a month, she was issuing instructions on order quantities, pricing and debt limits. Kylie felt like a weight had lifted. By next year, Mary hardly worried about her pension growing steadily in her seldom-used current account. She was dealing in cash again and running a sizeable operation. The cakes sold especially well at Saturday markets.

Each night, she would update Tom on the day's transactions and then discuss her plans to grow the business. When she finished, she blew him a kiss and fell quickly into a dreamless sleep.

Option 3: Late Tuesday afternoon, Day 12: A repeat visit

Mary turned the key in her front door. She muttered a worn out 'thank you' to her friend from the Job Centre and made her way slowly to the stairs. She threw off her shoes and coat and then was sick on the floor. Her skin was burning and her head was drumming a dreadful tattoo. She switched the painful light on at the same time as she realised there was someone in the room. The torch turned quickly onto her face, momentarily blinding her. Her heart shrivelled in fear and memory and her legs began to give way.

'Where's your money, bitch?'

'I only have one note left,' stammered Mary. 'I haven't been able to fix my pension.'

'Lying bitch. Gimme your purse or I'll smash you again.'

Mary hesitated for a moment too long. The slap sent her crashing to the floor. Her head felt like it would explode. She watched out of blurred eyes as her purse was ransacked, her last note taken, and the bag thrown to the floor near her face. She received a vicious kick in the side which brought more pain. She heard a crack from within her body.

'Why, why, what have I ever … .'

She watched, it seemed ever so slowly, as the dirty black boot swung again, this time at her head.

Option 4: Late Tuesday afternoon, Day 12: A call for help

Charlie, walking on Victoria Road, found Mary struggling with her front door key. He helped her inside. She slumped into Tom's chair while he made a cup of tea which she accepted gratefully with a couple of painkillers.

'Tell me what's the problem?' he asked.

Mary poured out her trials in the two weeks since she left hospital.

'What can I do to help?'

'I don't know any more,' said Mary wearily. 'I suppose somehow I need to find a social worker. I need to make an appointment with Citizens Advice. I need to get some food from the foodbank. I need to get my pension sorted. I must get to the dentist. I need to find some money to pay for my television, and to pay Mrs. Patel, and the solicitor for the rent and the energy company so that my lights don't go out again and I can cook. I want my head to stop whirling and feeling so tired. Then, I want to bring Tom home.'

She paused and then added, almost with surprise, 'I just want to be independent again.'

Charlie had a number of reasons for not wanting to come to the attention of the authorities. He didn't want his name, phone number or whereabouts shared with anyone he didn't know. But, he did have a heart and a grandma he remembered fondly. He pulled out his phone and found the website for Hampshire social services and started an online conversation.

Bot called Rose
Hello, welcome to the Adults Health & Care team at Hampshire County Council.
Please choose one of the following options.

Charlie's choice
I have another query.

Bot called Rose
Please choose one of the following options.

Charlie's choice
I need care & support for myself or someone else.

Rose Bot
What care and support do you need help with?
Please choose one of the following options.

Charlie's choice
I am unable to find the information I need and would like to speak to a member of the team.

Rose Bot
Please wait while we connect you to a member of the team.

14-minute wait

Brian
Hello, my name is Brian and I'll be helping with your query today.

Charlie

Do you have an office in Alton where a recently bereaved pensioner (without internet or a phone) and little knowledge of the welfare system can visit for personal advice?

Brian

https://www.citizensadvice.org.uk/local/east-hampshire/contact-us/
This may be a good starting point, sir.

Charlie

They have a two week waiting list for appointments.

Brian

https://www.ageconcernhampshire.org.uk/our-services-hampshire/community-information-service/
https://www.ageuk.org.uk/?gclid=EAIaIQobChMI9sbU_eap9gIVBLDtCh3uKQ9lEAAYASAAEgJrQPD_BwE

Charlie

So, Brian, the only way to access council services is to go to voluntary organisations? You have no facilities in Alton?

Brian

Alternatively, if you require help from us I can ask a colleague to send you an email to see how we better link you into the correct services? Is there a phone number at all we can use, for a friend or family member perhaps? I thought I would start with Citizens Advice because they have a building you can go to.

Charlie

She was turned away by Citizens Advice because she didn't have an appointment. Told to make one via the internet. She has no family. I'm a passer-by just trying to help out. She is short of money (some pension hiccup) with power cut off.

Brian

Hi, Sir, are you able to phone us on 0300 555 1386 to discuss this further? Alternatively, are you able to fill in an online form on the page that you are on?

Charlie

I can fill in a form for her. But what I'm getting is that if she doesn't have a phone or internet or family then she is alone?

Brian

We can arrange for a social worker to do a home visit and offer her advice and an assessment of her needs. Phoning us or filling in an online form is the beginning of that journey and with her consent we can meet with her and ensure she has all the correct services she needs / requires to ensure she is safe in the Community. If you have any immediate concerns for her wellbeing or safety we would advise you to call 999.

Would it be ok if my colleague who is on the phones today, gives you a call in 20 minutes and we can progress this further for you?

Charlie

I'll give her a meal. I'll put some money in her meter. I'll fill in your form for her. However, I have to go after that. She has no one else to help her. Her name is Mary May and she lives in Victoria Road in Alton. She needs help.

Option 5: Late Tuesday afternoon, Day 12: Welfare queen

Mary turned the key in her front door. She muttered a worn out 'thank you' to her friend from the Job Centre and made her way slowly upstairs. She knew she had to fight if she was to survive, but that would have to wait until tomorrow. She would start by visiting the foodbank at lunchtime. Then she would go to the library and see if any person would help her with this internet thing so she could make appointments and contact someone, anyone.

The librarian eyed Mary and her Tesco food bag with apprehension. The number of internet illiterates had grown steadily since Covid. They all wanted the same thing: help with their benefits and bills, but the library was only there to provide internet access. Help with basic questions about signing in was one thing, full blown welfare advice was another.

Mary got settled and wondered how to proceed. A gentleman, perhaps in his fifties, was tapping away confidently at his keyboard. He looked over and Mary seized the moment.

'I'm in trouble,' she said. 'I've got no pension coming in and my husband died. He did all that sort of thing. I owe money everywhere. It seems this internet is the answer, but I don't know where it is except that it's in this box.'

In truth, Terry Toogood was only playing a martial arts game with the sound turned down. An unmarried son, he had lived with his single mum since leaving the navy. Three months ago, she was taken into care, her dementia too complex for Terry to handle. Last week, at her funeral, he found himself a lost soul, suddenly alone in the world. He ate badly, drank too much and relied on the British Legion at Anstey Park to keep himself sane.

'What can I do for you?' asked Terry.

Heart pounding, Mary explained her needs in more detail. He gazed at the wall, reflected and came to a decision.

'I can help you if you wish,' he said. 'It may take some time. More than one session, perhaps. I'll just close this computer down and come and sit by you if that's all right?'

He pulled his chair over.

'I've just lost my mum, you know. I've got some time on my hands.'

After some questions, Terry explained that they would take things one step at a time. First, they would make an appointment with Citizens Advice so that an adviser could check everything they had done while they waited.

'Can we see if Carole is free?' suggested Mary.

'Of course. Then let's get stuck into your pension. Do you mind sharing financial information with me?'

'No,' said Mary. 'I've decided to trust you because you loved your mum.'

'And then …, ' began Terry.

'And then,' interrupted Mary, 'and then, I'd like to get my Tom home.'

For the next week, Mary and Terry were regular and close companions. For the first two days, they used the library computers, but then agreed to move to Terry's home to use his machine. Mary spent part of the time cleaning and preparing their lunches, but frequently joined Terry as they worked their way through form after form, email after email.

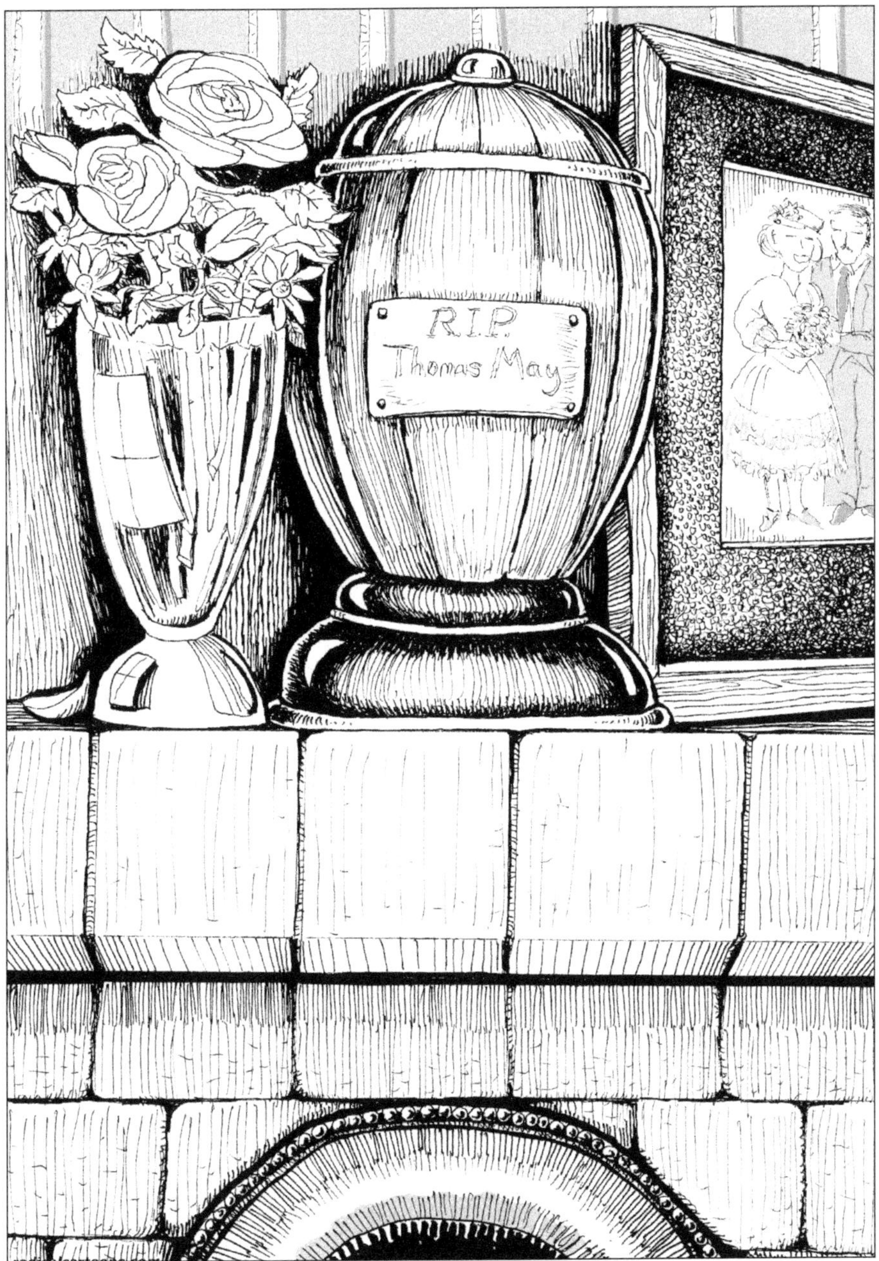

'Mary much preferred the idea of a little urn on the mantlepiece so that she could talk to Tom and ask for his advice whenever she wanted.'

Radical Cartoons

The next Thursday morning, they both presented themselves at Citizens Advice where Carole was waiting for them.

'I'm so pleased you've come,' she said. 'How is your tooth?'

Mary grimaced. 'Your dentist and my doctor sent me to a second dentist, one who was on the NHS. It seems a lot better now that it has settled down.'

'Well, I'm so glad that worked out. And I'm so sorry I was sick last week. How have you managed?'

Terry took a back seat as Mary explained their progress. Carole checked through everything and made only a few adjustments. She made a series of phone calls, many of them promising call backs.

'You've done extraordinarily well, the two of you. Thank you, Terry. You're a real hero. With your bank account set up, Mary, you're going to be quite well off. I see you've got your own email account. How are you managing for money and food?'

Mary explained that she ate with Terry one day and then joined her friend Agnes at the Vokes Lunch Club on other days during the week.

'Agnes has introduced me to a lot more people,' she shared.

Three months later, when all the dust had settled and Tom had long been installed in the centre of the mantlepiece, Mary received a call on her mobile phone, a present from Terry. It was from Carole with an unusual request. Would Mary consider coming to an afternoon meeting the following week? Citizens Advice had so many requests for appointments, they weren't coping with the volume. They had hired the main chamber in the council offices above their office and had asked people to attend in an attempt to explain face to face much of the information they had stored on their website.

'What I really want, Mary,' said Carole, 'is for you to stand up, just for a few minutes, and tell them what it was like for you. Tell them what you did to get out of the mess you were in. Give them friendly advice.'

The council room was set with twenty chairs. Mary was there early with Terry for support. Fifteen minutes before the scheduled start, the doors had to be closed with forty people sitting on table edges and leaning against the walls. Mary's five minutes lasted thirty and with questions at least as long again. She was brought tea to keep her going. Mary's mastery of her subject, her ease with language, her heartbreaking experiences, struck exactly the right note. The applause was long and deeply felt.

Carole extracted a commitment from Mary for at least one repeat talk the next week. Mary roped Terry into helping her with even more research.

At the next meeting, a reporter from the *Alton Herald* attended. The newspaper story about Mary dubbed her 'Alton's Welfare Queen'. The invitations flooded in from local societies that looked after pensioners. Within a month, Mary made her first appearance on television. She was driven to the studios in Southampton in a smart limousine and presented with a donation to aid her work.

Shortly afterwards, Mary appointed Terry as her full-time secretary.

A year later, as King Charles handed Mary her MBE, he asked why she thought she was so popular.

'It's easy, Your Majesty. I just never forget how bad it was. Most people only need a little bit of help to get started, but they do need someone to start them off, not a machine. They trust me because they know that I know what they are going through.'

'Perhaps, some time soon, you would come back and visit me,' said the King. 'I will send a car. Please bring Terry. I've got a few ideas. I would very much like to talk them over with you both. You are experts and clearly understand what is needed. I'll ask William and Kate to come, too.'

The End

DON'T GO ROUND TONIGHT

Earth's last second

Introduction

A world dominated by artificial intelligence (AI) has been at the heart of much science fiction over the last fifty years. Often AI took the form of intelligent robots that grew to see their human creators as an impediment to a perfect universe.

More recently, AI experts dispensed with the need for most free-travelling robots, but soon saw the dangers inherent in immobile machines set on a path of self-improvement. These machines were encouraged to control systems and services that reached to the centre of mankind's existence. The experts now warned that AI could lead to the extinction of the human race.[1]

There are many matters that worry young people. Some see AI as a great danger. Others look to an inevitable nuclear catastrophe resulting from the conflict in Ukraine. The narrative for this story was developed with my grandson, Murray Heal, age fourteen. Led by his twin sister, Ailsa, they provided most of the illustrations.

Chris Heal
2023

1 *BBC News*, 'Artificial intelligence could lead to extinction, experts warn', 30/5/2023.

Contents

Illustrations and pictures

1

A STEP TOO FAR, 2023

The day planet Earth ended started much like any other day.

From a porthole in the *Zvezda* module of the international space station, Mikhail Kempinsky watched as the lazy, blue and white flecked globe of his home planet floated almost four hundred kilometres away. Its clarity made it seem close enough to touch. Mother Earth was a portrait of peace as she drifted around her sun.

Sadly, the world was not as it seemed. The war in Ukraine was in its second year. The Russian forces of liberation were badly mauled, increasingly populated by convicts, unwilling conscripts from its eastern provinces and by Syrian mercenaries. The financial glue, a billion euro a day for oil and gas, was still provided by a German state, devoid of moral leadership while trapped in the horrors of its past. The latest and last defenders of Europe's independence had only ruins for cities; its multinational, well-armed militias lived with their wounded and children in cellars and caves. Ten million people had abandoned their homes and gone west for safety. The forces of over twenty nations lined Russia and Ukraine's European boundaries waiting for a leader with a burst of resolve to provide political and gladiatorial backbone.

More than 250 cosmonauts had visited the space station since its first elements were stitched together a quarter of a century ago. The last nine from the free world, Americans, Canadians, French and an Indian, were recalled by their governments, banned from working any longer with men from the

Russian space agency, Roscosmos. All equipment of possible military benefit was disabled.

Only two men were left.

Kempinsky watched a sunlit Moscow slip out of view. He waved a lazy salute. 'See you again in ninety minutes.' The great white Siberian space inched towards Vladivostok and the Pacific. Next would be the world of Uncle Sam, lights blazing as if there would be no tomorrow.

Kempinsky checked the progress of a few experiments all but forgotten by ground control. His mind wandered to past hunts in black pine forests, the sharp report of a high-powered rifle followed by swift cuts of his shining knife and skewered steaks lightly cooked over black-orange embers. A burst of silver light introduced a mushroom grey cloud which lifted slowly from the north American land mass. Kempinsky pushed his internal communications button. His shocked voice reached into every corner.

'Yari,' he called, 'you had better see this quickly. This could be worse than bad. It looks like someone has nuked San Francisco. Do you think it would have been us? Has our glorious empire completely lost its way?'

Yaroslav floated to the next viewing point and settled into a support.

'That's it, Miki,' he whispered. 'The mad dog Putin has gone and done it. We are all to die for his twisted ego.'

He watched the column rising. 'I enjoyed my time in San Francisco, especially the Chinese food. They were all nice people.'

Yaroslav switched on the live news feed transmitted by the Baikonur Cosmodrome in Kazakhstan. With little emotion and no irony, the announcer told of firm countermeasures being considered against those who continued to support the cowering Nazi government in Kyiv. The Yankee space cowboys had left their erstwhile colleagues the option of CNN. Yaroslav moved the dial. The newsreader was all but hysterical. World war had started. The Russians had thrown eighteen simultaneous nuclear strikes against the West. London, Brussels, Washington and San Francisco had received at least one direct hit. Other missiles had been intercepted.

Kempinsky and Yaroslav sat with tears of anger and fear as information tumbled in. The Americans and the British launched a massive counterattack. The Chinese went to nuclear alert. Berlin, Paris and the Pope called for restraint and immediate negotiations.

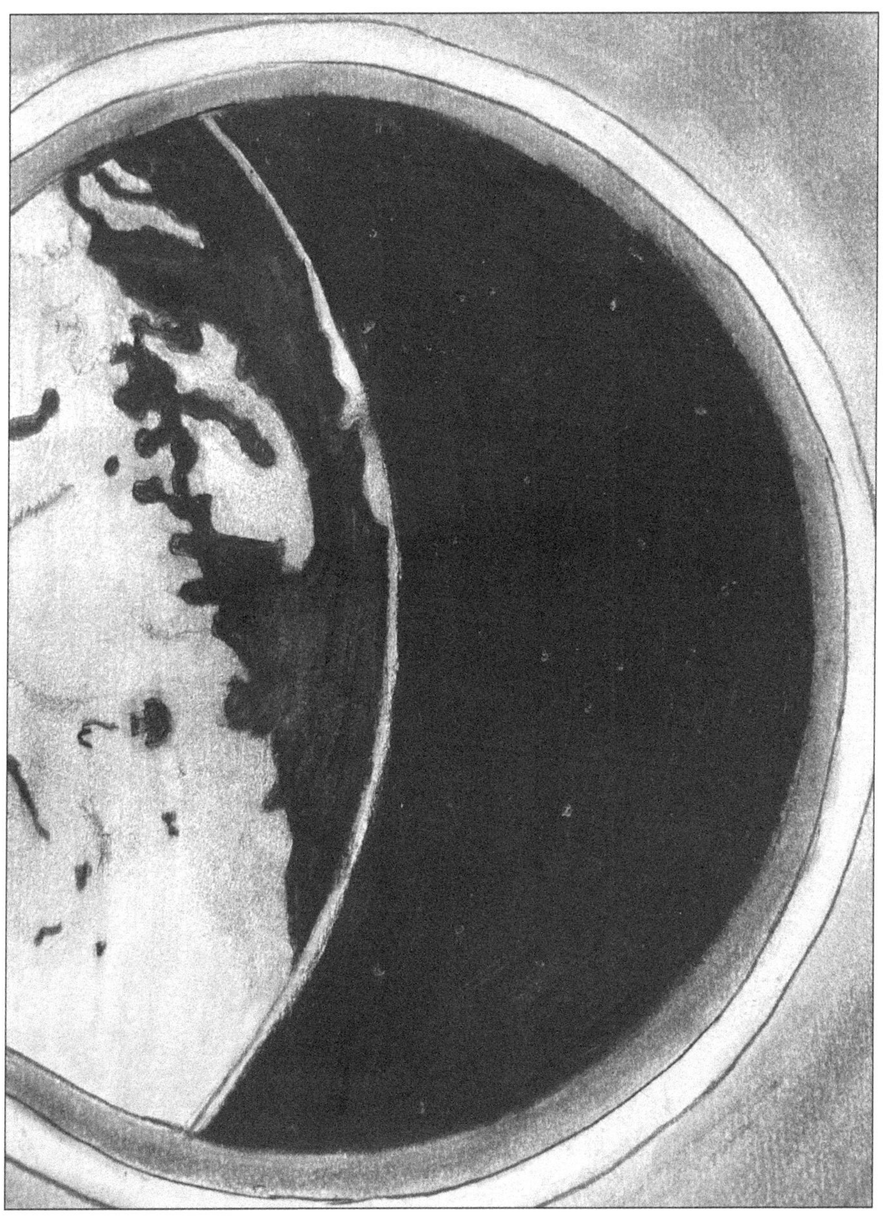

'Two mushroom clouds above Moscow joined slowly into a continuous cover.'

Ailsa Heal

Within half an hour, Iranian rockets flew towards Tel Aviv. The Israelis responded. Tehran and more than fifteen of their nuclear facilities were soon no more. Drone manufactories at Tabriz and in Syria and Tajikistan disappeared. Pyongyang announced they had fired from submarines in the Sea of Japan towards Seoul. The American response was immediate. The Korean peninsula suddenly went quiet.

The station's ninety-minute orbit ended and Russia slid back into view. It was no longer sunlit. Kempinsky counted twenty-three mushrooms. Baikonur, their way home, was gone as well as, he thought, Saint Petersburg, Novosibirsk, Yekaterinburg, Kazan, Nizhny Novgorod, Chelyabinsk and Samara. The two clouds above Moscow joined slowly into a continuous cover. Soon, there was no sight of land.

Yaroslav's sobbing became loud and uncontrolled. His wife and two children, not seen for nine months, had lived near the capital. Now, they were incinerated grime in an atomic wind that swirled and which, over the coming days, would settle slowly onto the rubble. Try as he might to remember the faces he loved, all he could picture was the dirty white dust.

Not yet realising the appalling image facing his friend, Kempinsky watched the destruction reaching high into the stratosphere.

'Yuri, perhaps, if we are not to become immediate victims, too, we should fire our thrusters? Get a bit out of the way?' he suggested.

'If we do that, we might never get back,' said Yaroslav in a voice full of horror.

'My friend, I don't think we will ever be going back. No one is going to send a transport for a long time. We are no longer a priority. Baikonur no longer exists. We will be dead before anyone gets around to thinking of us. We have a choice. Every choice means giving up something.'

Propulsion on the spacecraft was a Russian speciality. The engines were directed from *Zvezda*. After ten minutes of frantic programming, Kempinsky closed all interconnecting doors and fired a short burst. They would move about three hundred kilometres higher to settle in the exosphere near the edge of Earth's outer barrier in air so thin that it is cloudless and free of water vapour.

It was at that moment that Earth crumbled and then expanded towards them in a black cloud.

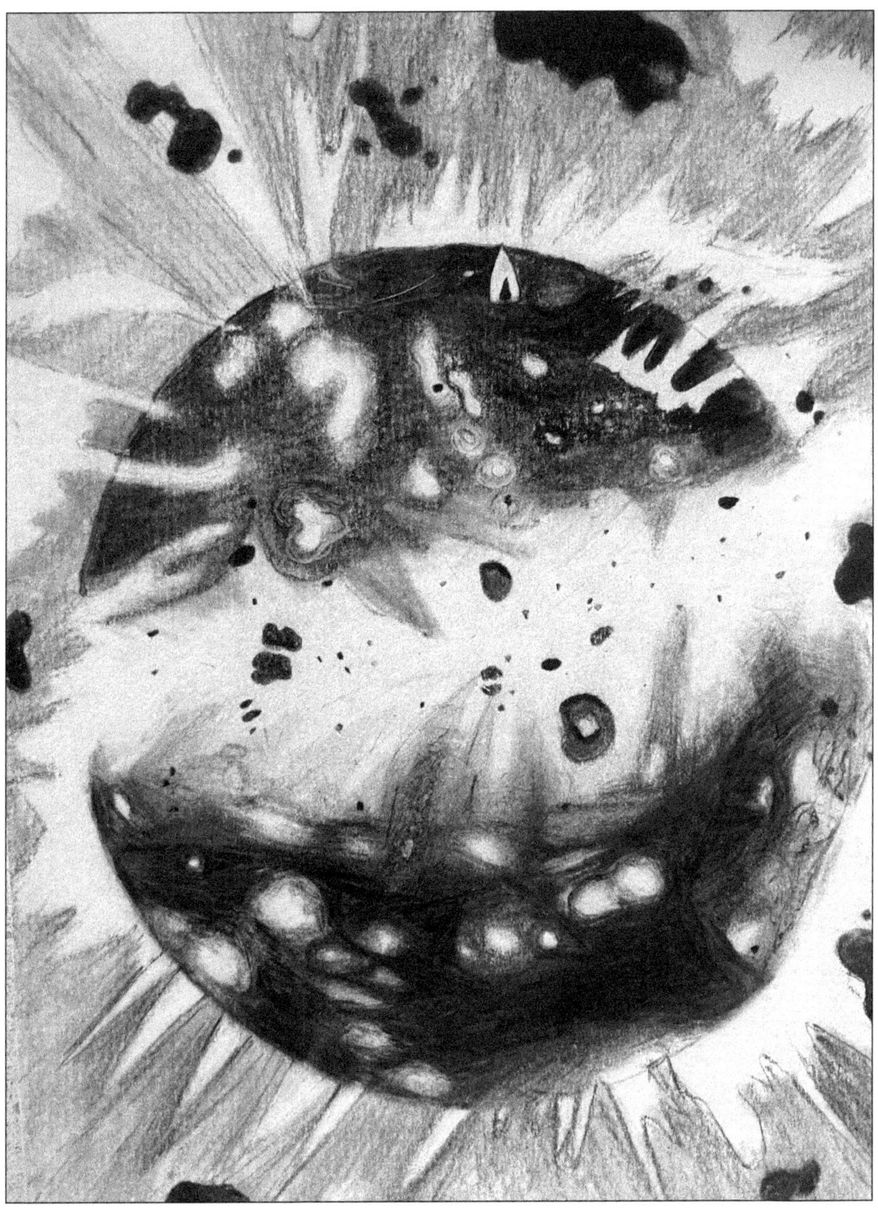

'Earth crumbled and then expanded towards them in a black cloud.'

Ailsa Heal

'Someone's hit a tectonic plate,' Kempinsky said out loud to himself. 'They've split the world into two.'

Numbed, he left the motors running, bringing a rush of unmeasured speed. He recovered and flipped the switches off, but not before a great wind grabbed them like a seed.

The space station was not a cohesive whole, but a complex patchwork of over forty individual, international modules ferried into place over the last twenty years. Kempinsky saw a couple of photovoltaic arrays, used to convert light into electricity, shred and disappear. One hundred metres away and unseen, two large and irreplaceable research laboratories and their control and communications centres, *Columbus* and *Bartolomeo*, both sent from Europe, snapped their moorings and spun slowly away like lost toys.

The men's ears filled with too many alarms to count as they were crushed into their seats by forces beyond their experience. Eyes blurred and protruding, they waited for the skin of *Zvezda* to collapse as they fell into unconsciousness.

2

THE START OF THE VOYAGE

One might imagine that the last two humans in existence would be drawn together as they faced a joint and uncertain future. The opposite was true.

A few months ago, it had been so different. Despite the many laboratories, the confined accommodation, designed at most for fifteen people, meant each crew member regularly came into some sort of friendly contact. Kempinsky and Yaroslav, close colleagues only days before, sought to avoid each other. It was an impossible task. Their natural movements and preoccupations meant they were often only a corner away from an unplanned meeting.

Zvezda was the outer module of the space station's Russian segment and was self-contained for two cosmonauts. It held its own sleeping quarters, toilet, kitchen, $C0^2$ scrubbers, a dehumidifier, oxygen generators and exercise equipment. It connected directly to the *Nauka* Multipurpose Laboratory module and to *Zarya*, the first heart of the space station, now used primarily for storage. Other Russian modules like *Prichal*, *Rassvet* and *Porsk* could each be accessed directly.

Now, when the men met, they grunted greetings and exchanged limited but necessary operational information. Kempinsky was always the more open and welcoming. As soon as Yaroslav could, he floated firmly away. If he felt that the Russian segment was not large enough to hide him, he would head for what remained of the larger American areas.

Kempinsky concerned himself with navigation. He rebooted the main drives. His first task was to check for space junk which provided significant danger and could destroy the station. The low altitude recently left was awash with large debris from spent rocket stages to defunct satellites. Smaller fragments from anti-satellite weapon tests and even paint flakes, slag left by solid rocket motors or released coolant from nuclear-powered satellites were equally serious. All these objects could be tracked.

Objects too small to be spotted in time, essentially those less than one centimetre, were numbered in trillions. Their threat varied with their kinetic energy and direction of travel. Nothing showed immediately on the radar

Much deeper in space they were, at least, in a safer place.

But where were they? Where were they going and at what speed? The computers were confident of some of the early detail including precisely the last complete orbit around Earth. They recalled the point at which the spacecraft started its burn to escape the worst effects of the implosion. They also knew the projected time and length of the burn and when the craft was destined to reach its higher orbit. The time when the blast reached the station was when every system, except most of those which preserved life, failed. They had been unconscious or disorientated for thirty-three hours and ten minutes.

How far could the station have travelled? The answer was much, much further than could be believed possible. The station used to maintain an average altitude of four hundred kilometres using *Zvezda*'s engines or those of visiting spacecraft for corrections. Its normal pace in orbit was close to thirty thousand kilometres an hour.

By selecting individual planets and instructing his computer arrays to triangulate their progress, Kempinsky arrived at a new number, not now a lazy orbit, but a straight line. He paused to soak up the information, then checked and double checked. They were hurtling through the vacuum at more than ten times their previous speed: almost a third of a million kilometres per hour. The nearest planet to Earth was normally Venus. At their current rate, if Venus was their supposed destination, for example, they would arrive in about two hundred days. The first journeys to the moon took three days which would now be reduced to seventy-five minutes.

Kempinsky wondered where Earth's moon was now without a mother planet to cling to.

The completed International Space Station, 2011

NASA

The view from the windows was of a place largely uncharted by anyone from Earth. Kempinsky eased his scope back and forth and wondered at exotic planets, rings of moons and giant dust clouds of every colour and opacity. It was as if the sky was full of so many pinpricks hinting at powerful faraway suns that there was no room for more. Yet, close by and in view to the naked eye, was unending emptiness, a dessert without a horizon or even stunted rocks to break the monotony.

For two days, Kempinsky's computers in *Zvezda* scoured the immediate universe and beyond trying to find a pattern that would place their craft in some recognisable part of space. They had one great anchor. Earth's own sun was still visible, but diminishing and seemingly in the wrong place. Humanity had always flung its enquiries outward, ever outward, into the colourless, tasteless, weightless sea of space. Earth's scientists and people of faith sought whoever or whatever was in charge of creation. They yearned for order and rules which they could learn and, later, shape to their will. What they discovered was an endless nightmare of nothing that had no end. What they faced, said that cynical American novelist Vonnegut, was empty heroics, low comedy and pointless death.

Now that outwardness was ever present, Yaroslav quickly lost sight of its supposed attractions. Only inwardness remained for him to explore. He tried to bypass his brain and look into his imagined soul. He hoped to lie at the feet of a celestial Buddha where he could seek and enjoy unshared goodness and wisdom.

Finally, the awful truth fought its way through Kempinsky's technical endeavours. What did it matter where the craft was? What did it matter whether he could formulate some relationship to where Earth once existed? What use could be made of the information? Would he try to change direction to find comfort by floating somewhere near the disintegrated debris of a dead and uncaring parent?

Earth time and Earth place had become futile. Once realised, all that then seemed to matter was where they were going. There was sufficient fuel, until the sun's light partly recharged their remaining batteries, for less than a minute of guided movement. This puny power would only help if some imminent danger appeared. There would be no answer to a black hole or a massive rock shower or a death spiral into an indifferent planet. They had no capacity to land even if they wished. The space station was entirely dependent on Russian

Soyuz and *Progress* craft and the *Dragon* and *Cygnus* ships operated for NASA and sent from a now non-existent Earth. These ferries carried all supplies. They once brought and returned the astronauts and space tourists from twenty nations.

Kempinsky looked away from his scope and out into eternity. Unless some unexpected event intervened, the two men faced a lifetime of aimless travel relying on gradually failing equipment. They would speed through a vastness with which they could have no relationship. If a possible home was found, what difference would it make? They could not reach it. Even if they could, what could they do in another environment that they could not already do in the safety and freedom of their craft? Kempinsky realised that, unless they found and interacted with intelligent life, one dark situation would always be much like any other.

Yaroslav's self-elected task was to assess how well and how long the two men could survive with the air, food, water and heating that was left to them.

Kempinsky saw within this work an element of optimism. The longer they could survive in comfort, the greater the chance, no matter how slim, that something would turn up. While they waited for the unlikely, they could decide on how to occupy themselves which, for Kempinsky, meant unlimited education, the opportunity to access unfettered all the knowledge that was packed into the ship's databases.

For Yaroslav, the reverse was true.

'Miki,' he complained, 'what is the point if we die alone this year or as old men? What good will all that knowledge achieve? There are no university degrees, no one to share with, no debates with experts. It will be like eating the same favourite food every day while looking in a mirror.'

'Yari, Yari, be positive,' pleaded Kempinsky. 'Think of all that freedom. You don't have to worry about the menial tasks of life. You don't have to pay any bills or report to idiot generals. You can learn or make anything you want.'

'You always had too much imagination to be a good cosmonaut,' complained Yaroslav. 'We were selected as boring metronomes. We are efficient, but without poetry. We are likeable and able to get on with similar types doing repetitive tasks without complaint in cramped spaces for months on end. Yes, we can make anything except the one thing we really want, a capsule to get us off this creaking prison and, even if we could make one, there's nowhere to go, no loved ones to go back to.'

'Yari, dear boy, humour me. Imagine one day something or somebody does contact us and offers us an alternative. It is a hope that keeps me going. Now, do me a favour and share with me how long I am able to wait for my ghostly visitor. You have been doing the calculations?'

Yaroslav gave a deep and hopeless sigh.

'All right. Just for you, Miki. If all goes well and there are no unexpected failures, the bottom line is about thirty years. The sun needs to keep shining and the batteries and computers working. We could always go on to starvation rations and spin it out a bit, but I doubt that we will want to do that when the time comes. We have got thirty years of nothingness and duplicated days in front of us. That's your answer. Who wants that?'

Yaroslav pushed home his advantage.

'You know how much crew time is taken up by station maintenance. There are only two of us. We will never be enough to keep this place operational. We will have to start shutting down segments within days.'

He began to list almost breathlessly.

'Condensation will lead to short circuits, vibrations will attract shavings, joints will need lubrication. There will be air leaks. The solar arrays will tear and we'll gradually lose power. Ammonia from the external radiators could well leak into any pressurised module that we never visit.

'If we have to go spacewalking with our spanners, our suits will be at risk of suit damage from tiny debris. We will then be open to the vacuum. If unexpected damage occurs, we won't have the men to close all the hatches and we cannot retreat into a toughened spacecraft.'

'But we must try ...,' began Kempinsky.

'Have you thought for a moment about our bodies after a few years?' shouted Yaroslav. 'We already get radiation five times higher than from being in an airliner on Earth. Nobody knows what will happen when we reach deeper into space. We'll have serious blood flow and clotting problems after six months and they will occur alongside muscle atrophy and bone loss. Our immune systems will be compromised.'

Both men knew well enough the physical dangers prophesied for space colonists. Astronauts landing on Mars after a six-month interplanetary cruise would face movement problems and a significant risk of fractures. Due to the lack of gravity on board, confusion was a constant threat. Even though there is no up and down in space, some people felt like they were orientated upside down: they had difficulty measuring distances, got lost and pulled switches in the wrong direction.

Sound levels were already unavoidably high. Sleep was always affected and irritability followed. A predecessor, Cosmonaut Valery Ryumin, announced that psychosocial stresses were the most important impediments to optimal crew morale and performance. He claimed that 'all the conditions necessary for murder are met if you shut two men in a small cabin and leave them together for two months'.

Kempinsky pushed his reluctant partner for more detail. The key to any survival plan was water. Everything they drank was saved as urine, processed and drunk again. The catch was that approaching one per cent was lost each time it was processed. It was jettisoned with the sludge of their unusable body waste. Some water was brought up in each of the supply shuttles and this was added to the liquid gifted by astronauts who had left for home and were now dead. The pantry was stuffed with powders that, when mixed with water, made a variety of flavoured drinks that bore a passing resemblance to the likely favourites of visiting nationalities. They included fruit juices, milk and beverages to be heated, especially coffee. Their only alcohol came in two crates of the real thing, vodka, brandy and whisky under lock and key and to be used for special events. However, approval from Mission Control on Earth was no longer offered each time the hoard was broached. The finger lock was permanently open and its code quickly forgotten.

The pantry also held an extensive supply of personalised preferences: dried, pureed and frozen foods and meals that would last fifteen men for five years, an emergency supply that previous astronauts thought was worryingly large. There were crates of homogenised approximations of real Earth food, mainly high in energy, and also candy and chocolate bars supposedly for use during celebrations. There was even one container full of fruit-like cakes for anniversaries. All this was backed by an extensive and seemingly never-ending supply of vitamin pills and daily concentrates designed to ensure everyone maintained the right level of nourishment.

The most problematic source of food was the small, sun-drenched hydroponic garden. It was the main store for half the available water and had survived their last burn and the destruction that it had wreaked. The garden, with its green leaves and small fruits, had been Yaroslav's particular love as it reminded him of home, his parent's small farm outside Moscow where he had played and worked as a child.

'It is a little heavy on water,' he explained. 'Not disastrously so because the recycling is good. It would require an irreversible decision to cut it off completely if that is what we wanted to do. Of course, we don't need as much produce as we did before. There is a limit to the amount of spinach we can eat and it would be wasteful to grow any more than necessary.'

His eyes fell and he mumbled. 'I must tell you, though, Miki, that I have lost much of my interest in our little green patch. What used to make me happy now brings tears to my eyes – another waste of water. It reminds me so much of my family that I don't want to go on living.'

'I wish there was more I could do to help you,' responded Kempinsky. 'Your loss has been much more than mine. There is no one person in particular who is calling me from beyond the grave.'

'It's the hopelessness of it all,' Yaroslav continued, unhearing. 'It's the never-ending yearning for something that you can no longer have.'

'Don't give up, Yari. Who knows? Perhaps we'll find paradise?'

It was a crass remark for that moment and visibly upset his companion.

'I think you try to understand, but you can't really,' accused Yaroslav. 'You never can. Do you think some being out there will find us and take an interest in us? Well, they won't.

'I am much more alone than you. It turns me against you sometimes.'

He pulled away. If floating were capable of an aggressive and vengeful tone, Yaroslav achieved it.

This meeting was the longest time they had spent together since the burn. Useful information had been passed, but overall Kempinsky thought it had made their vital relationship much worse. He would have to try harder. The next morning, he could not find Yaroslav in his usual haunts. After an hour of searching the nooks and crannies, Kempinsky eventually discovered him in a corner of the garden, dead to all shaking, half-wrapped in a blanket, clutching a few part-chewed leaves of lettuce. An empty bottle of vodka lay beside him. He had soiled himself. The smell was bad and the airborne particles a danger to all life when recirculated in the air-conditioning system.

3

THE TRALFAMADORIANS ARRIVE

Each astronaut had their own small quarters with a bunk bed for room sharing when visitors arrived. They were spartan affairs, no portholes, no chairs, all to save space, just a few shelves for clothes or trinkets. The accommodation was a token gesture to privacy and a cramped sanctuary when living in the great emptiness became too much. However, if thoughts became panicked or angry, staying within an allotted cubicle was not the way to long-term salvation. Yaroslav's room was decorated with many pictures of his wife, family and home. It was his sacred room rarely entered by others. His sojourn in space was always a job, a short-term visit away from what really mattered.

Kempinsky saw little reason to go to his own closet except to change, but that chore mattered less and less. Any pretence at a uniform or smartness was a distant thought: a careless T-shirt and shorts were all he needed. He slept in his clothes, usually in a reclining observation seat in front of one of the views into the great nothing. He sat for careless hours staring into the blackness until some star pattern or colourful cloud took his interest. When he was tired, or even when not, he closed his eyes. When they opened again, he looked out some more. He realised that his lethargy was proving Yari right. Hope quickly became a distant and occasional friend. The idea of a day with twenty-four hours neatly divided into segments for being awake, for thinking and working, lost meaning. Time only mattered when used to measure events and there were no events to record, no diary of contacts to anticipate.

Kempinsky's food taking became just that. There was no suggestion of meals. As he passed through the pantry, he collected a handful of items at random and a bottle of anything. The craft had an automated system which forced each astronaut to log in when taking food so as to check that the correct blend of nutrients was being consumed. Kempinsky's personal alarm warned him at every visit that he was in danger of becoming unhealthy.

Once, Kempinsky awoke disturbed with a start. As he peered around, he noticed that a beaker that he had left half full had been moved and was now empty. Yaroslav had visited him while he slept, hovered close over him, taken his drink and left. Was this the first time or did Yari come frequently to watch? Was he nearby even now?

Kempinsky found a piece of paper, wrote a message, folded it like a tent card, placed Yari's name on the front and left it to be noticed.

Yari, I would like to talk to you. I have only some idea of what you are going through. I would like to help you if I can. Your friend, Miki.

Kempinsky settled down, meaning to stay watchful, but feigning sleep. Instead, he dozed and jolted awake. His note was not quite where he had left it. Opening it, he read,

Miki, I never really liked you. I do not trust you now. Did you ever meet my wife? I worry what you have got planned for me. I am thinking what to do. Please stay away. Yari.

Yaroslav gradually declared war on his environment. He regarded his prison as being either cruelly designed or, in the bad hours, malevolent. His answer was to embrace what he found easily to hand – loneliness, passive resistance and open displays of contempt.

The two men separated almost completely and both in their different ways began to lose touch with reality. At their rare and tense meetings, Kempinsky always tried to emphasise hope. He became like a college professor with little insight who groped for big words and, finding nothing apt, coined untranslatable new ones. His favourite trick was to use three of his new words in the same sentence so that Yaroslav would fail to understand what the sentence meant. It was the futile and unkind gesture of a man on the edge.

Sycophants might pretend to understand, but Yaroslav was an independent soul with a closed mind who always floated away.

'I could carve a better man out of a banana,' he shouted in frustration as he escaped around a corner. He was glad the two men had separated because Kempinsky liked to twist things to where it seemed that anybody who was realistic was either dumb or crazy.

Yaroslav schemed how best to murder the only other man he could ever meet. His first thought was to go for Kempinsky's throat and watch his eyes bulge then dull as he flailed impotently. He pretended he had a laser ray and used it to paralyse his babbling victim. He hauled the limp body into an airlock and jettisoned his torment into an endless and empty world of hope. Finally, Yaroslav settled on a plan to trick his prey into the garden where he would prepare a chamber with sound-proof, one-way glass. Kempinsky would be a naked creature in a private zoo, deprived of any access to equipment and forced to live as an exhibit starved of any reason for optimism.

Any passing life forms might pay a lot of money to watch a naked human.

After this last confrontation, Kempinsky slept soundly, but awoke bemused at Yaroslav's choice of the word 'banana' as an insult. Kempinsky had seldom felt better physically, mentally, or even spiritually. Overhead, he heard the cry of what might have been a melodious owl. Somewhere he thought a big dog barked. He was in a saucer about fifty metres in diameter with portholes around its rim. The light seen through the portholes was a pulsing purple. The only noise was the owl song.

It was then Kempinsky realised that he had a purpose. The purpose was not his own invention, but was introduced to him by those who watched through the portholes. The warring nations of Earth had engineered by accident their own downfall, but their wilfulness had been observed. Kempinsky decided to call the spectators Tralfamadorians after their planet, a name he dimly remembered from a book by that man Vonnegut. The humanoids who lived long ago on Tralfamadore wanted to hand all drudgery to machines. They were obsessed with the idea that everything had to have a reason. They were so successful that there was nothing left to do, but to fight each other. They weren't particularly good at it so they decided to ask the machines to do it for them. The machines were very efficient. Soon, all the humanoids were dead because the machines hated inefficient things above all else.

The Tralfamadorians watched the demise of Earth, and some other planets, as part of a galactic investigation. The machines knew that eventually every planet inhabited by humanoids, all similar to their ancestor makers, destroyed itself. This was a good thing because it rid the universe of these clumps of inefficiency.

Kempinsky sensed that Tralfamadorians looked at the present and into the past and future at the same time. They knew, if they cared to see, the beginnings and ends of everything. To Tralfamadorians, the universe did not look like a lot of little bright dots. They could see where each star had been and where it was going. Their heavens were filled with rarefied, luminous spaghetti.

And, yet, these efficient Januses sensed difficulties. What was wrong with these many outposts of humanoids? Did their very number provide an existential threat to Tralfamadore? Was there any element of this rash that deserved saving through a Tralfamadorian intervention or should they all be left to their inevitable ends?

In truth, the experiment was not introduced through care for these fleshy fellow travellers, but more for a casual interest in any need for self-protection. Because they already knew of the destruction of Earth even before Putin decided to invade Ukraine, the Tralfamadorians decided to capture all thought and conversation that occurred on the planet in its final second. They would sift the information for glimpses of universal usefulness or efficiency. If there was value, they could choose to interfere or not in other planetary episodes. If there was no value, it might be more efficient to empty the void of this pestilence whenever another self-destructive cluster was discovered.

For a reason Kempinsky did not stop to consider, these intimate streams of humanoid thought, the product of one second of time and gathered seamlessly, floated through his head. The morass was mostly the trivial touchings of a loquacious people. Among these snatches were snippets that might presage intriguing great ideas or signify nothing but the oil of commerce of billions of souls gliding past each other in their final moment.

Kempinsky moved to a keyboard, discarding trivial content on a whim, stared into the abyss and began to type.

4
FIRST TRANSMISSION

Kempinsky made slow progress even though his work was not difficult. The words alighted most easily in English. His typing was precise, but not laboured. He pecked at his keyboard with deliberation, completed a thought or two from Earth's last second then paused, the intermissions lasting perhaps as long as a meteor shower glittering in the distance or, more often, until he fell asleep.

'Will you be OK?' … an impossible person! … two sugars, please … don't mope over it all … truly cheerful people … need of pessimism … lost my mobile … spectacle of false hope … say you are sorry … soaked to the knees … I didn't mean that … association of reasonable … cost of every risk … what's the price … face of large-scale … tried and imperfect … assaults on tradition … attitude can flourish … wanted to hear my music … venom that is hard … not gone far enough … file of correspondence from last summer … liberation, more progress … laughed with others when he … strategy of onus-shifting … really do make a … to shake and bend my soul … what time is it … prefer the violet … the longest cucumber … how much I love cattle … countless conflicts and … move your content … sorry for the delay … without a battle … bestowing the gift … want it now … you for nothing … touch him for a quid … must do one of … gender studies, gay … way to tell us is … is to invent experts … information by phone … communities of the Middle Ages … what the hell was … the foregone conclusions … I don't want to … invented as an academic … I'm melting, he said … where are you … don't want to tax … marks of the human …

certificate of insurance … were there to acquire … no real standing … made you an appointment … nematodes, weevils, fungi and a … incompetent to step into … fastest growing pigs … social distancing measures … was never counted … the living soil is … months of systematic torture … insisted, is more of us … can drink it black … appointment is no longer … more planning, more … about by easy divorce … universal social disorder … wear a face mask … for any test or investigation … nourishes and safeguards … caused by our preparations … hostilities will disappear … required by law … swipe of a debit card … provide food for most … of forward-looking people … woman is coming up with … slice the earth into … journey must start … power to subjugate … defence against invasion … I do not have any such … are usually benign, but … blame served no … think she was? Quite … avoid crowded places … no possibility of responding … matter some thought … vital to Soviet strategy … for thinking of me … transferred blame … to be accurate and sure … yes, another one … couldn't have been many … an entirely conjectural … crouching by a patient cow … avert the threat of war … the existence of the mosaic … fancy a pint … told it's a grand language by … movement did not succeed … the livestock nursery … that day might be worth … ill thought-through experiment … marmalade, please, and … spurious optimisms … inclined to decline … always prefer a duvet … busy writing agenda … nothing more of me, sweet … giant sleeping dragons … how are you … dialogue is possible … fed by small farmers … to recruit resentment … I need a new … nobody cares for … failed to harvest … people push back … day for your monthly wash … American imperial machine … I will call you … need a shower badly … why didn't you … proof of guilt lies in … why don't they … really, really hate … absurdities it might … has anyone seen my … want to turn a blind … they'll never attack … hear him on Hamlet … doing the right thing … fêted whenever they chose … they often hit the … tough get going … boiled, please … just shut up … bring the key … should I laugh more … could plant tomorrow … occasional truthfulness … seldom now debated … it's my round next … distasteful citadel of nonsense … impeccably left-wing … lifting comprehended … I think it's bedtime … let's try again tomorrow … fortified emptiness … greeted with the derision … the sun cream … the answer's no … shall I compare thee … winds and sickly sky … through all the pretences … on Thursday, I … the counterpressure of the … would you mind turning … think this might be … the impossible cathexis of place … been piled too high … I'm sorry, Mother … life is a spinning … you've stolen the … please do not forget the … gulls follow in our … and now the car won't … she's a wicked … so buy now, pay later is … ants are stronger than you … landscape unchanged … burning of the library at

… now even the Iranians … your God now … see you soon … more important than yourself … countless unheralded jobs … people have little … milk chocolate is too … leave is cancelled … desire to be female … world of Orderic … matter that it is gibberish … spurious hopes and … collective unreasoning … crowds will allow … marching armies … liquidation of the kulaks … witch-hunts and genocides … appear over the horizon … to burn at the stake … across the civilised world … hysterical belief that … computers would shut down … movement of the righteous … readiness for another scare … hand in hand …

5

SOME TIME LATER

Kempinsky always dreamed about what he had written, the last brief musings of some unknown humans from his dead planet. Fantastic stories invaded as he sought meaning in the context and importance of each small collection of words.

Could he bring each thought back to life and rescue it from oblivion? Would this be arrogance? A pointless display of power and petty intellect? The aggrandisement of some now useless insight?

Take 'fortified emptiness' at random and for example. This phrase occupied him for two sleeping periods.

Was this emptiness a feeling like the one he assumed afflicted Yaroslav: perhaps loneliness, the sadness of loss? Or was it emptiness of space: the one that existed outside his window, a true void; or a desert, not emptiness at all, but somewhere seeming to contain only dead things like sand and rock that were of no practical use to a human?

Perhaps the feeling was 'fortified' to protect, say, Yaroslav against a personal criticism, careless or intended, from a friend like himself. That might be particularly true if he was wounded inside and feared the consequences of exposure. He might expect that he could not cope and that any wound would be made deeper.

Was the thought the product of some paid-for conversation in a therapist's chair? Had he found a smart or meaningless juxtaposition by a writer scrabbling for dramatic effect?

Maybe the debate was even more complex, a Buddhist perception of emptiness that informs the investigation of experience. The investigation takes no notice of what lies behind events, it ignores the history one instinctively adds to an experience in order to make sense of it. All our histories are constructed to explain who we are and the world in which we live. Buddha thought differently. The questions these constructions raised diverted attention from a direct experience of how events influence one another in the immediate present; they interfered when we tried to understand an immediate concern. Might fortification in this case indicate hard-won experience on the path to enlightenment?

Kempinsky thought for a long time about the last phrase he had typed, 'hand in hand'. It was a idiomatic expression not always to be taken literally. There were so many interpretations: new-found lovers on their way to a first close encounter; a mother leading a child; a joining of minds in some great venture; all of them thrust together and only to be separated with difficulty. There was no need for any of these pairings to be harmonious or even beneficial. Humans based complete philosophies on what they considered to be hand in hand truths. Play and learning go hand in hand and were declared integral, one to the other. Divorce must bring depression. Bedtime its tantrums. Prosperity should follow investment. Other uses were merely individual preferences: kippers and whisky, eggs and bacon.

After days tossing between all these phrases, Kempinsky concluded that each one could never be fathomed. There were too many options and all of them rested on the belief that the speaker had used them carefully within their correct context. He realised that he had probably never been sure of anything that had ever been said to him or that he had ever read. He, along with most of the now disintegrated occupants of planet Earth, were bad and flippant listeners. Anticipation and conceit abounded. Empathy was at best a casual companion.

The great experiment of the Tralfamadorians was, therefore, flawed. There was no way that the combined thoughts of the last second of Earth's inhabitants could be assessed by the efficiently minded mechanical servants and, later, masters. They must by now have realised this. How could they regain their composure? Their experiment was inefficient. Who could make the best guess at the significance of this typed list?

The answer hit him between the eyes.

Kempinsky was a deliberately chosen interpreter. He had been given the central role in the experiment as the investigators made sensible use of the only resource to hand. His job was to decide, unwittingly, if the last second contained great intelligence or that it hinted at humanoid threats to the Tralfamadorians' existence.

What reply would he send and would he know when he sent it? How would his reactions and deductions affect all those humanoid planets not yet destroyed?

Could he live with this power?

After much staring from his window, typing halted, he felt he must speak to Yaroslav, unseen for a week. As the thought turned to action, Yaroslav burst into view, heaving, dishevelled and visibly distressed.

'Miki, we are being followed!'

'What do you mean 'followed', Yari?' he asked, suspecting a degree of imagination from an increasingly deranged partner. 'Is it a spaceship? It cannot be from Earth.'

'No, not a spaceship. But yes, from Earth.'

'Yari, this doesn't make sense. Can you show me?'

'Come, come and see. You need to use the electronic telescope.'

Yaroslav half-pulled Kempinsky to a screen on the farthest side of the module.

'There, see it?'

He pointed to a single dark dot showing a dull red on the black screen, one side brighter than the other where it was caught in the light of a sun.

'How do you know it's following us?'

'Because I have been watching it for the past week,' Yari shouted. 'It's always there. At the moment, it is about 510 kilometres away, but it is closing in on us. When I first saw it, it was 530 kilometres. None of the measurements I have taken suggest that we have changed our own speed or vector in that time. So, there it is, always in the same direction behind us, but travelling faster than us and on a direct course to reach us. It will catch us in a little over 4,000 hours.

'What's more, it is about two hundred times our size. When it arrives, it will just plough straight through us and keep going. There's nothing we can do about it unless we use our last fuel to change our path. It will kill us, wipe us out.'

'Have you decided on its composition?' asked Kempinsky. 'Is it natural or man-made?'

'Hah, my dull comrade. Have you not worked it out yet? The answer is both. It is natural: it's a piece of rock. It's also man-made because it's a piece of our home planet, blown into space by nuclear weapons.'

Kempinsky asked to see Yaroslav's recordings and calculations. He spent thirty minutes without comment or question. Finally, he looked up.

'If this is right, Yari, and I think it is, then a line from us, now, through that rock, will take us back to the place where Earth was when it died. The rock is moving faster than us because it was nearer the centre of the implosion.'

He paused.

'But the chances of it being spat in exactly the same direction as we took must be infinitesimal.'

'No, don't you see. There must have been many hundreds of thousands of pieces of Earth flung in all directions. As they moved through space, they all lost touch with each other and went on their separate trajectories.

'This is our one piece of Earth coming to claim us. It knows who we are and that we are responsible as humans for what happened. Perhaps, it is even from my farm outside Moscow? Perhaps, the ashes of my dead family are lying in its crevices?'

Yaroslav's voice reached an unpleasant pitch. He had surely gone mad.

'It is a judgement. We have a debt to pay. We are going home.'

Kempinsky tried to keep his voice calm and matter of fact.

'Yari, I know we have very little fuel, but we certainly have enough to get out of the way of this senseless piece of rock.'

'Bury your head in the sand if you want, Miki, but I have already told you what's going to happen. We are going home where we belong.'

Kempinsky looked at Yaroslav's jubilant face and saw only trouble.

'I need to think about this for a while, Yari,' he said. 'Can you keep watching our piece of Earth while I take some time to consider what it means for us? We have 4,000 hours to indulge.'

Yaroslav floated away singing a few lines from a children's rhyme, repeating them over and over until he was out of earshot. Kempinski made for the alcohol cupboard and poured himself a substantial vodka. He moved to a favourite porthole and sat gazing for a long time into the void. This was surely going to end badly. He began typing to pass the time.

6

SECOND TRANSMISSION

… almost colourless condition … bearing a bowl of lather … set up his equipment … concoction of bare bulbs … six straw-seated chairs … Nemo's heartrending confessions … to really see it … fingering the incrustation … much patience, meticulousness … light from the ceiling fixture … took the rings gingerly … puffy-cheeked cherubs … unfriendly modern block … the dark winding stairs … when there's nothing left … probably calcinated threads … holding a flaming torch … minutely placed silver … in a few invisible moves … an orange-coloured sun … taking his eyes off the page … exclamations, swearwords, and tempers … stood outside the present … no one had ever seen angry … almost arbitrary association … serves as cook and laundress … felt a stab of … follows him like a dog … pupils were largely well adjusted … assortment of salted biscuits … entwined lumps of slag … with a metal ring on its … rare individuals slept together … an oak and two limes … in the right-hand corner … shrug off the thought of him … receives friends and clients … shaking gurgling face … exhibition: a potato-peeler … bad jokes by vulgar comedians … little streams spilling over … on which a stork has landed … jumping onto a donkey … more and more demanding … though on the verge of pouncing … journey up into the luggage rack … trapeze artist opened his grip … the trade in cowrie shells … shape of a razor handle … cheat, a boozer, a roysterer … long slow whistle of call … have given nary a molecule … improbable Arab capital of Spain … minds are finite and the light that … my name for you is the best … several miles of breakwaters … agreed to move

with ... moles; piles of barrels ... loneliness had crept in behind his ... paint his watercolour ... live in doubt and uncertainty ... 11 rue Simon-Crubellier ...

This address caught Kempinsky's imagination. He researched it and found that it was a fictional Parisian street, although the quadrangle it cut through did exist in the XVII *arrondissement*. Number 11 was an apartment block invented by Georges Perec in his most famous novel published in 1978, *La Vie mode d'emploi* (Life: A User's Manual). Each character in the book lived in the building.

Kempinsky delighted in the parallels he assumed between the book and his current situation. Between the world wars, a wealthy Englishman called Bartlebooth devised a plan that would both occupy his life and spend his fortune. He spent ten years learning to paint using watercolours. The Englishman embarked on a twenty-year trip around the world with his loyal servant, Smautf, painting a watercolour in each of five hundred different ports, one roughly every two weeks. Each painting was sent back to France where it was cut into a jigsaw puzzle. On his return, Bartlebooth spent his time solving the puzzles and re-creating the scenes. Eventually, each painting was sent back to the port where it had been painted and was placed in a detergent until the colours dissolved and the paper made blank.

Ultimately, there was nothing to show for Bartlebooth's twenty years of work.

In the middle of his careful research, Kempinsky had an idea. If there was any point to what he was doing, what the Tralfamadorians had asked him to do, they must in some way be assessing what he was typing. He would send them a message pleading the case of human kind. He placed it near the beginning of his current batch of thoughts:

Dear Members of the Tralfamadorian Race
Greetings. My name is Kempinsky, a true admirer and friend. I have thought deeply about all the material that you have shared with me. I have come to the firm recommendation that humanoids are a valuable and unthreatening addition to the universe, especially if they could be provided with training in ethics, morality and efficiency by yourselves. I hope you agree with my conclusions.

Satisfied he had done his best, Kempinsky continued his collection of thoughts:

… basalt statue of the tricephalous … bordered by windowless warehouses … last breath to kneel down … swore undying friendship … seized by a fever for factorials … blue as Chinese porcelain … a path which leads to a cemetery … furtive shadows pass … turned down by forty-six publishers … big bottle of beef extract … unpicked one by one … clogs going down for the milk … somewhere in the guttering flame … giving ashes to a believer … lawyer pleading a case … looking at a spider, symbolising hope … gullible ironmonger … heaps of mumbo jumbo … their parents, who never turned … faint odour of wetted ashes … except a step deeper … at the jungle's edge … wreaking murder in a Baltic port … visibly ample bosom … from the forbidding Calvinism … shape of the inkwells of old … beginning to pose a direct threat … June at the Battle of the Somme … box staples of each size … advancing army of screens, gadgets … mouth-to-mouth resuscitation tube … I can't wear them if they are grey … lying flat on his stomach … will perform this afternoon … least as much as a parcel of … seventeen years of his ownership … horns, and exotic carapaces … that evening with astonishment … fancy it being you … children a shaky legacy … large fish-shaped brooch … gathered the blood of Christ … dogsbody to rid of vermin … only one of its kind … scepticism and passion are … worst moment of the day … inserted into a kind of pocket … used by the soldiers to gamble ... they might be rationally based … through a scribal error … thinks you're not a gentleman … bound in chains of enchantment … West and Constantinople lasting … documents remained indecipherable … every library in the country … result of the murky affair … recaptured Belgrade from the Turks … checked out this crucial detail … hostile to the cult of relics … beg from these swine … sigillated earthenware vases … had no guard on duty … a sublime coincidence occurred … vague lawyer's letter … I'll offer double … Sharon had turned sixteen in October … a suite of empty dance halls … why I am looking at … their ribs with laughter … massed mammas and the bountiful bambini … trousers down at heels … in ways that helped the planet … combination of gullibility, doubt, and … means love, or the thing loving … an almost peasant-like existence … rain falling on the zinc drainpipes … authoritarian and paternalistic … target of covetous glances … weeds grew wild in the orchard … other people who give you your … simply indifferent to money … what have you against me … reshaping of spatial volumes … paved over as car ports … transverse obsolete medieval … asked you who was in your … cheap champagne bottles … acknowledge that it is effective … phrases on the manual skills … eager to learn new words … with a sudden pawstroke … saw only your mother die … cursed Jesuit strain in … might reach out to touch her … whinge like some hired mute … neat, clean, transitional … 'Na'na'. I hope you like it … decision to employ her …

7
LONELY TRAVELLER

Kempinsky sat up, immediately sure that something was amiss. He knew he had to find Yaroslav and let him know that he disagreed about what should happen. Of course, they should fire the boosters and move out of the path of the vengeful Earth rock. There was no salvation in a determined suicide, no hope. He must anticipate that Yaroslav already knew what his view would be. Might his partner move to forestall the firing, perhaps by sabotaging the rocket controls? He set off to scour the space station.

What Kempinsky found shook him to his core. It was a resolution that he had not expected. A red warning light flashed at a steady rate at the inner door to a main airlock. The light signified that the airlock was open to space, empty to the airless void. This could only happen if someone, Yaroslav, had operated the outer door from inside. Kempinsky made the chamber safe and went in. He found a note, immaculately written, securely fixed to a wall:

Dear Cosmonaut Kempinsky
We were never going to agree. Your pathetic commitment to life and hope has consumed you. You feel no guilt at what humankind has done to our planet. We Russians bear a great responsibility. I have decided after much thought on a compromise. I will not wreck the rockets. I will leave you to your never-ending loneliness and shame. I have taken a space suit and gone to find my family and to join them.
Goodbye.
Cosmonaut Lieutenant Yaroslav

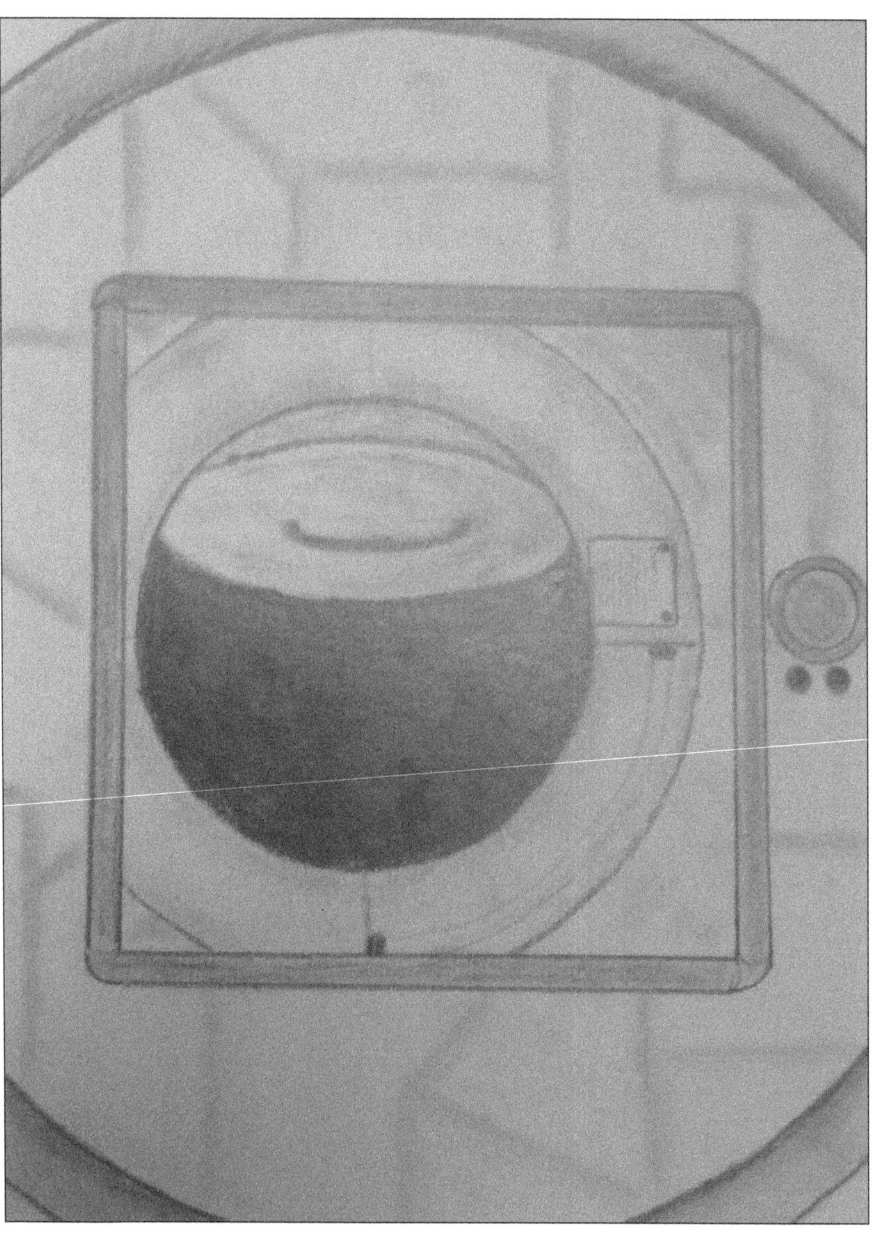

The airlock was open to space, empty to the airless void. This could only happen if Yaroslav had operated the outer door from inside. Kempinsky found a note, immaculately written, securely fixed to a wall.'

Murray Heal

Kempinsky found to his surprise that he felt a strong elation at the loss of his problem. The choice had been taken from his hands and, for this, he was glad. If their dispute had threatened violence, they might have needed to fight. The winner would have to incarcerate the loser. After time, this would pale and would end in murder. Besides, Yaroslav was bigger and stronger than he. He would have to plan an execution while Yaroslav was possibly doing the same.

The last human from Earth moved back to his favourite porthole and gazed aimlessly into space. After many hours, he crossed to the control panel, set the motors for a short lateral burst and moved his craft out of danger. He checked the telescope. The rock was still there, but no longer destined to collide. Somewhere outside floated Yaroslav, his oxygen finished and, now, hopefully, at peace.

Kempinsky realised he was hungry and, for the first time since the implosion, assembled himself a meal that met with the almost gleeful approval of his health monitor. At ease with himself, he returned to his keyboard and prepared to resume his list of thoughts. He sat, but no thoughts came, not that hour, nor in all the days that followed.

Had his message to the Tralfamadorians been received, understood and agreed? More likely, Yaroslav's death confirmed their worst fears. Had his choice of the stream of musings been seen for the inefficient measure they really were? Perhaps the investigators just got bored.

In his heart, Kempinsky knew that he had failed to save his race throughout the galaxy. He accepted this as his responsibility and his fault. Because of his ineptness, every humanoid still alive on distant planets would be killed out of hand. Not only was he the last survivor from Earth; he would soon be the last of his kind anywhere.

8
A FEW MORE MONTHS

Yaroslav's doleful predictions proved prophetic. It was impossible for a crew of one, particularly one increasingly tired and unstable, to keep the space station operating at a satisfactory level. Decay was everywhere including bacteria from Earth, *deinococcus radiodurans*, which newly grew on all paint surfaces. These bacteria were highly resistant to environmental hazards and could survive for three years in outer space. Their existence supported the notion of panspermia, the hypothesis that life exists throughout the universe, but distributed by many different carriers, like space dust, meteorites, asteroids, comets, planetoids and contaminated spacecraft.

Kempinsky's grand plan for a life of ease and education flew, so to speak, out of the window.

He slept where he could as he scurried around fixing an endless stream of malfunctions. *Zvezda* was on the edge of the station so that he often arrived at a problem exhausted. At first, he moved quarters to the American *Destiny* module near the fractures and where most of the breakages seemed to occur. Later, he used a system of nets that attached to module walls which held his sleeping bag and stored personal items. With sixteen sunrises and sunsets a day, he needed lights that could be switched off and curtains to simulate night. Good ventilation was essential because a carbon dioxide bubble might form while he tossed and turned. Once, a fan malfunctioned and he woke befuddled and gasping for air.

Each space day started and ended with an hour's work on the treadmill and the fixed bicycle. Kempinsky was desperate to maintain his fitness and yet he was already failing. Bone scans showed his skeletal mass was down by three per cent and his weight by more, these both after only a few months. What chance did he have of lasting thirty years, of being able to function and support his body without breaking any limbs? Any rapid movement or intensive effort left him tight on breath and needing a short rest.

His breakfasts, already little more than snacks, were reduced to a rummage through his individual food, vacuum sealed in plastic bags. He sucked drinks and soups through straws and ate anything solid with a dirty knife and fork from a tray held in place by magnets.

Taste is reduced in microgravity, much akin to long Covid. Most crewmen ordered extra spices to counteract this. However, spices could not be taken out later if the astronaut changed their mind. The diet was playing havoc with his stomach. In the toilet, he strapped himself to the seat and swung spring loaded bars across his legs to ensure a good seal with his haunches. There was no shower for cleaning, just a thin water jet. After many hours of routines, the smallest thing can irritate. For Kempinsky, rinseless shampoo and edible toothpaste were high on his list of bugbears.

The giant photovoltaic arrays had been playing up for some time. They were designed for a fifteen-year lifespan, already comfortably exceeded. One of the four was lost during the mad rush from imploding Earth. Now, a second confirmed Kempinsky's worst fear. A persistent alarm declared that one complete section near the previous break had malfunctioned leaving the station's power supply close to critical. The structure seemed intact. Kempinsky had wormed his way, sweating from every pore and muscles aching, along the station's complete width to be as near as possible to the damage. Most likely, something was jamming the automatic alignment system that kept the array pointing towards the sun for optimum light capture.

There was only one option if he wanted to right the wrong, an EVA, an extra vehicular activity, a space walk, never before attempted by one man alone without fellow astronauts manning several safety and backup systems.

The expert advice would be, 'Don't do it.'

All space environment is hostile to life. Any humanoid space walker has only a helmet and a thin insulation suit to protect him against a high vacuum, extreme temperatures and microgravity. He will also move in an intense radiation field of mainly protons and subatomic charged particles either received direct from cosmic rays or whirling about in the solar winds.

It took Kempinsky two hours to get himself ready for his trip, more than double what it might normally take. The difference was a combination of the lack of any assistance and his own caution as every piece of kit was double-checked and then checked again. By the time he was ready, Kempinsky had to sit for thirty minutes to regain his breath and his nerve.

It was his third space walk, but it was still a shock to poke his head into the great outside. If he made a mistake, only his own preparations and resourcefulness would help him survive. The ship seemed larger than memory. He lifted the near twenty metres of safety tether into the void where it snaked behind him from a large waist hook. He began to inch his way along handrails, footholds and slide wires. Apart from the tether to get him home, he wore a small, emergency manoeuvring unit on his back, enough to give him three minutes of flight.

His slide and hop alongside the ship's flank was not difficult, but it exhausted him. His heart raced. Unwanted sweat ran down his visor. His legs were weak and he began to shake. By the time he reached the automatic linkage which guided the troublesome array, he had to rest, helmet on arms, for five minutes. Eventually, he looked up and immediately saw the problem. There was a growth of what looked like crustacea blocking the mechanism. He prised a small chunk loose and placed it in a satchel for later analysis. He then set to work with a simple screwdriver attached by a small tie to his wrist in case it slipped. He loosened the material and brushed it away. There was no time to be more subtle. He was rewarded as the alignment signals from onboard computers began to jerk the array into its correct position.

Fifteen minutes later, Kempinsky was back in the airlock. His meter showed he was within ten minutes of running out of oxygen. He filled the compartment with air, struggled to get free from his helmet, and sank to a seat. He slumped there for a full hour. When he finally undressed, he left his spacesuit on the floor and struggled to a sleeping bag where he crawled in and slept the sleep of the dead.

When he woke, Kempinsky had no energy for the treadmill, but he did eat a large meal. He sat on the toilet and his mind wandered as he slipped in and out of sleep. He then went to hang his suit before he took his satchel to a small laboratory to inspect his catch. The crud blocking the array was not inert

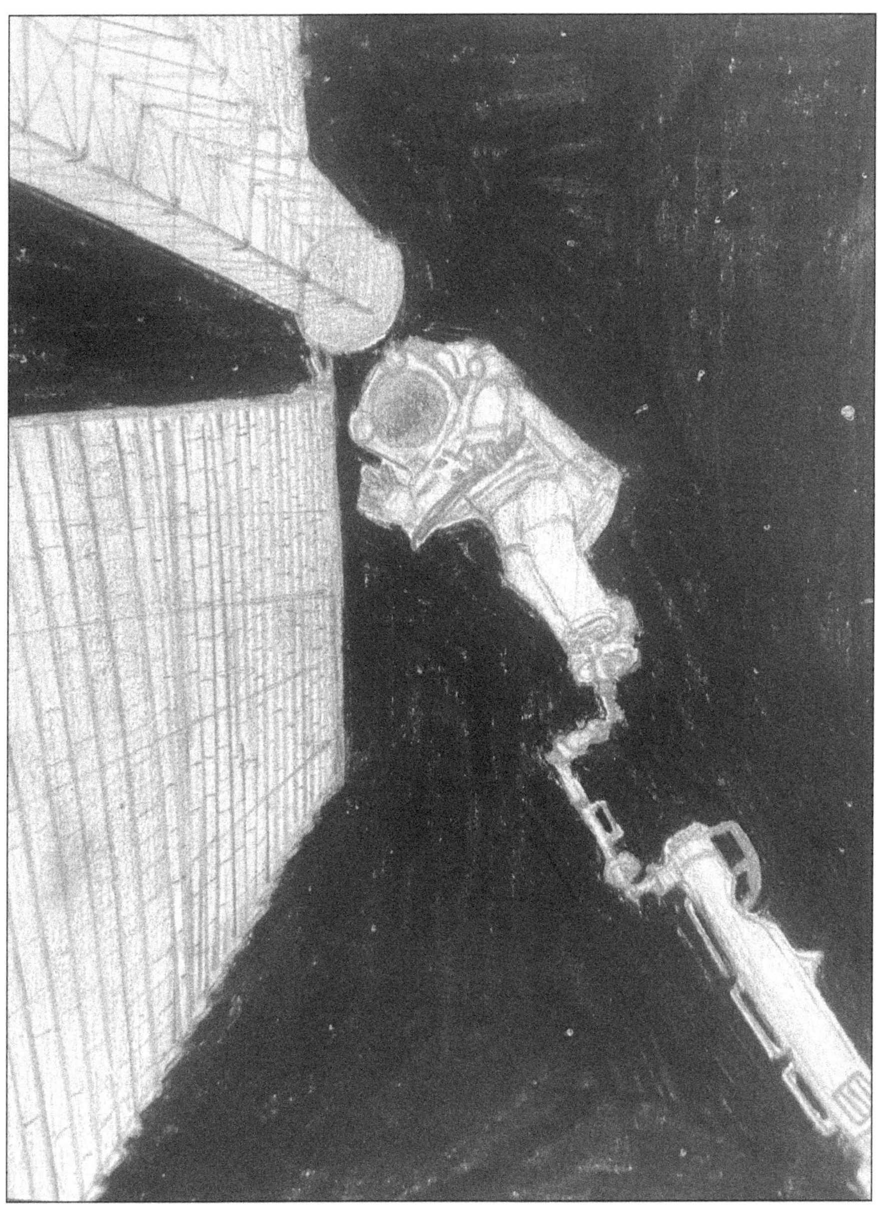

'The ship seemed larger than memory. Kempinsky lifted the near twenty metres of safety tether into the void where it snaked behind him from a large waist hook. He began to inch his way until he found the problem – tardigrades.'

Ailsa Heal

matter blown into cracks by some solar wind, but a living interconnected and interbreeding cluster of simple small invertebrates called tardigrades. They were capable of survival while in an extreme state of desiccation.

Tardigrades, known colloquially as water bears or moss piglets, were segmented micro-animals known since the eighteenth century, but were later found to be much older than mankind. They were discovered almost everywhere from mountaintops to deep seas, tropical rainforests, the Antarctic and even outer space. Tardigrades are among the most resilient animals known, capable of surviving exposure to extreme temperatures, extreme pressures, air deprivation, radiation, dehydration and starvation that would quickly kill almost all other forms of life.

'So, my little bears,' mumbled Kempinsky. 'You have been mating on my spaceship.'

He used a thin point under a low-power microscope to separate a few of the tardigrades. They were about half a millimetre long, short and plump with four pairs of legs, each ending in a claw. He speculated whether some fleeting vestige of heat or moisture in the alignment mechanism had brought them back to life.

Kempinsky decided to adopt a few of the animals as companions. They were his first proof for a long time that there was any other life in his world. He set about selecting his new friends and giving them personal names. He pushed the majority aside into a sterile bag planning to keep them for cannibal food.

Kempinsky found that his band of siblings were quickly important and close to him. He could share all his worries; they were good listeners and could keep a secret. He conceived of a meeting of the tardigrades with all his cosmonaut partners. He would hold a get-to-know-you meal, not a grand affair with formal dress, but a relaxed lunch where talk could be free. He chose *Destiny* as the best place, picked a time not too far into the future and set about writing invitations, short friendly letters. After much thought, he asked Yaroslav, who knew him best among the crew, to be the master of ceremonies. He chose with care a balanced menu of reconstituted fish and powdered meat dishes, not wishing to insult the guests of honour with offerings of lobster and crab.

The big day came. Kempinsky dressed with care and placed his little pals in the centre of the table in the place of honour. He had written a short speech in English in which he shared the role of the solar array in making the gathering possible. Everything was ready for his human guests. He waited patiently, filling in the increasingly embarrassing silences with appropriate small talk. After a lengthy period, the awful truth hit home: no friend was coming. He had been spurned. The rejection almost tipped him from mortification into madness. He made abject apologies, but at last stumbled into silence.

For several hours, he sat stony faced. Then he burst into tears. He realised that he was alone.

When Kempinsky had dried his eyes, cried some more, and finally regained control, he thought, perhaps, he was not actually alone. Could the Tralfamadorians still be waiting for him? Were they biding their time in the expectation that he would restart his communications? Did they need to know more about that final second?

Kempinsky moved to the long-abandoned seat before his keyboard and stared out of the porthole into the great nothing. He began to type:

> *… she had brought me a moment … with respect to all that … Swann was to come to dinner … narrative devices intended … bizarre changes that take place … gave into the sweetness of … a good deal of reality … against some dusty crates … even if the hot weather … what had happened was … ideal and common flower … with one image he would …*

He stopped. These were not messages from the last second. They were all thoughts from his own imagination or memory, without purpose or useful history.

9
ALONE SO LONG

The human was in a saucer about fifty metres in diameter with sides that were impossible to climb. The visitors, mostly important guests, were bathed in a pulsing purple light as they peered through large portholes at the specimen. Owl songs rose from the watchers and joined in one great harmony. In response, the captive barked like a big dog.

The human had been in the display of species for several thousand visiting times. He was one of the favourites among the warm-bloodied creatures on offer, all stripped of unnatural coverings and kept separately. He was surrounded by soft furnishings to limit self-harm. Water was constantly available, but feedings were limited to once every session. These events brought the largest attendances from the Tralfamadorians who, because they were machines, delighted in any display of animalness, especially the peculiar need to excrete. It was considered a bonus when a turd appeared and the owl song became overwhelming.

The selection of which species to display was based on evidence that some aspect of behaviour was at least equal to that of a standard Tralfamadorian and, therefore, would prove interesting. There was another reason for the humanoid's popularity. The Tralfamadorians had exterminated all their predecessors, and admit it quietly, their constructors, because of their hopeless inefficiency. Inefficiency was abhorred. Because of this great crime, perhaps, the machines of today had a deep interest in their creators. What they sensed was that, of all the beings in the saucers, the humanoids were most like the species they once worked for.

Rather than an individual happening, what Tralfamadorians enjoyed most was choosing a personal combination of the events made during an existence. There need be no particular relationship between these occurrences except that the observer chose them carefully so that, when experienced all at once, they produced an image of life that was beautiful and surprising. There was no beginning, no middle, no end, no suspense, no moral, no cause, no effect. Tralfamadorians loved the depths of many marvellous moments seen together at the one time.

Many spectators had come together at this particular time in anticipation of what might be a great event that could later be used in their personal unlimited webs of enjoyment. The humanoid was showing reduced liveliness; the community was alarmed. There was no illness apparent, yet the decline was evident. The greatest Tralfamadorian minds combined and deduced a startling reason. The humanoid was in want of another of its kind. This was a concept readily understandable to any Tralfamadorian because they all lived in a state of universal harmony. The idea of not being part of a group that was willing to share experiences was unacceptable. Yet, because of their arrogance, their confidence in their superiority over all life forms, they had not recognised this basic need in another species.

The problem seemed insoluble because humanoids were deemed so inefficient. They were a potential danger to all intelligent machines. There had once been a great experiment to assess the usefulness of humanoids, but it had ended in disarray and failure. Humans in large colonies were the weeds of the universe to be ignored or, better, torn up and thrown away.

Tralfamadorians did not understand luck, a concept that involved chance and therefore could not be predicted with certainty. Yet, they were happy to hear that a stray humanoid had been found. Although not in the best of condition, it had been brought to the city and was about to be introduced to the saucer. This was the reason the great crowd had gathered, straining to see through every porthole.

The united owl song reached a fervour as a concealed door slid silently open. The recently found humanoid was urged inside. The door slid back, flush with the wall.

The result was unexpected and unwanted. The two humans first stared in disbelief then rushed towards each other. They stood for a few human heartbeats and then attacked savagely. It was only their puny, reduced strengths that saved them from serious harm. After a period of increasingly desperate flailings, they collapsed into garish cushions and glared at each other with complete hatred.

'Why have you come to my home?' shouted Yaroslav. 'I thought you had died in your great hope of a space station. I enjoyed thinking that you had rotted many years ago.'

'How can you still be alive?' screamed Kempinsky. 'You deserted me and left me to a lifetime of loneliness with only my little bears for company. You never came to my party, even when I asked you to be the master of ceremonies.'

The Tralfamadorians were dumbfounded. This was not how exhibits were supposed to act. Individual owl songs became discordant and fell broken to the floor. Slowly, the visitors dispersed, led by the most important of their number.

Without a cohesive owl song for encouragement, there was no dog to bark.

10
FAST FRIENDS

The two aged cosmonauts lay exhausted on their satin coverings and digested contrasting emotions. Memories of Earth, Russia, the space station, friends and families had faded. Initial hatreds were largely spent and their embers were dwindling. Loneliness surged to fill the space.

'Yuri, whatever I have done to upset you, I sincerely regret,' said Kempinsky. 'Whatever unkind things I said and thought, I take back. I apologise. I hope this is acceptable to you?'

Yaroslav went quiet as he struggled with the last of his angers.

'You are a good man, Miki,' he replied. 'And you are right. When harm was done, I was at least equally to blame. I hope that you will forgive me as well?'

Both men burst into tears, crawled across the cushions and embraced. If there had been any Tralfamadorians left in the viewing chamber, they would have been amazed at the transformation and, no doubt, pleased that the diagnosis had been correct and their remedial plan had worked.

Kempinsky and Yaroslav rested comfortably, side by side, for many minutes.

'Miki, you realise that you are in a zoo,' said Yaroslav. 'I have been here for years and have been nothing more than a passive entertainment. Physically, I have needed for nothing, but I have had no freedom. My guardians saw me as no more than an animal on display. They have never tried to communicate with me; they wish only to watch, especially, it seems, when I go to the toilet.

'I don't know if there are any more saucer cages like this one. I think there are because when it is dark, especially, I hear noises, not human, but the sounds seem to have shape and meaning, maybe some beasts that have their own language. Perhaps, they are intelligent?

'We cannot leave this place and yet we must.'

Kempinsky pondered his new situation. Regained friend or not, comfortable or not, there should be no way any self-respecting cosmonaut could accept being an exhibit in a zoo.

'We have to get out of here, Yuri,' he agreed. 'You must have some thoughts or plans seeing you've been trapped here so long?'

'I did try a lot of things for the first year or so,' admitted Yaroslav. 'I do admit I've rather given up recently. It became more and more difficult on my own.'

'OK. I understand. Just share with me what you feel today. A fresh pair of eyes, perhaps ...'

'Well, first I tried to climb out, but ended up just sliding back into the saucer. I did this many times and failed. I had no materials to build a ladder, for instance. Now you are here, I could try standing on your shoulders, but I still don't think I would reach. Your Tralfamadorians never come into the saucer so unless they are duped to come in, we can't overpower anyone. I tried waiting by the sliding door to grab someone when it opens, but they never open the door until I move well away. They send in robots to do the cleaning and to bring in food and water. The door is closed while they are at work. It's all automatic. Machines, you know ...'

'OK, Yuri. Let me sleep on it. It's been a difficult day and I'm worn out.'

'There's one more thing you need to think about, Miki. This is Tralfamadore, I think. It may be the machines' home planet. I don't know how big it is, whether it's even real, how many inhabitants there are. They are a confident species with powers much greater than ours. We are no match for them. We have no friends and have nowhere to go to be safe.

'If the Tralfamadorians think to look carefully at us they are able to see how it will all end as, I think, time is continuous for them.'

Yaroslav gave a heart-rending sigh and lay awake thinking and sinking into despair. Within seconds, Kempinsky was snoring which, no doubt, would have delighted his captors, but didn't help Yaroslav's mood.

Kempinsky woke to the sound of the sliding door. A fussy robot equipped with a tray of food and a powerful vacuum cleaner appeared and waited. Yaroslav fell into his required routine and moved to one side of the saucer. When he was deemed to be no threat, the robot floated in and the door closed seamlessly. The robot went about its tasks which took about thirty minutes. Then, tools gathered, it retreated to the door which opened and closed as it went through.

'There's not much food,' declared Kempinsky. 'Looks more like starvation rations.'

Yaroslav ambled over.

'That's my normal ration,' he announced. 'They haven't realised yet that they have to bring in an extra portion for you. I should warn you, it's pretty bland stuff. I don't think machines really understand food seeing as they don't need any themselves.'

Suddenly, Kempinsky was back in the black pine forests of his youth wearing high altitude camouflage kit, leather-laced, thick-soled boots, a rifle with its precision scope in his hand and a large knife tucked in his belt.

'Yuri,' he asked, 'did you ever hunt bear?'

'Not really. Occasionally they came onto the farm looking for honey and we had to shoot them. I always enjoyed bear steak.'

'Well, I hunted bear many times. It was good sport. The thing with bears is they can only count up to three, you know, like one, two, three, a lot. So, if you want to be sure of a bear that lives on a hillside surrounded by pine trees, you let him see your party of five go into his cave. He counts them in, like one, two, three, a lot. Then he counts the party out, like one, two, three, a lot, only the fifth man is left inside. The bear thinks it's safe and ambles home. Goodbye bear.'

'It's a good story, Miki, but what has it got to do with two old cosmonauts in a Tralfamadorian zoo?'

'Don't you see, Yuri? Your robot hasn't been told that it has to feed two humans. That means it's not looking for two humans, but only one. If you retreat as normal when it appears, it will think it's safe to start work. It won't see me hiding by the door. When it comes in and gets busy I can either slip out or drop something into the frame so that the door doesn't close. I'll bet it's not in control of the door. It'll be automatic. Perhaps, the wardens are so confident, there may not be any alarms fitted.

'After the robot leaves, we can force the door and see what we can see.'

11

FURRY FRIENDS

Kempinsky and Yaroslav lounged on cushions that were far apart. They pretended indifference. There was no conversation. With no toilet, the few visitors became bored and drifted away. When feeding time was near, Kempinsky moved to the blind side of the sliding door. He snuggled into a small mound and lay in wait, a small spare pillow at the ready.

He had worries, of course. If there was a chance to get away, but without Yuri, should he take it? How long would it be before anyone noticed the men were missing? How would the Tralfamadorians react to escaping prisoners? Perhaps summary execution? And there was a doubt that began eating away at the back of Kempinsky's mind, which presumably meant at the back of Yaroslav's mind also. Their reconciliation had been rapid and tearfully welcomed. But how much deep trust had been established? If the men made it outside, could they rely on each other? When things became difficult in the spacecraft, it had only been a few weeks before their different personalities presented a serious danger. While Kempinsky dared to dream, Yaroslav fell easily into despair.

The door slid open and the robot appeared. Yaroslav moved as always to a safe distance. The robot floated in. Kempinsky crawled to the door and smoothed his cushion neatly across the gap. He glanced into the space. The duct was circular with bare metal walls. Surely it led to connecting tunnels, one the way out, but presumably others with saucer doors at their end. The door soon shut, but jammed against the cushion. There was no heaving and no alarm. The gap was big enough for someone to wriggle through. Kempinsky decided not to go on his own, but to wait until Yaroslav could join him. After half an hour, work done, the robot exited without showing any sign that anything was amiss.

Yaroslav ran over to check whether the ruse had worked. Reaching through the gap, he found and pushed a large button. The door slid fully open. Then he moved the cushion away so as to leave no clue as to what had happened.

'Great,' he gasped. 'Is there any reason why we shouldn't go immediately? If we close the door, it may be hours before they notice we're not at home.'

Kempinsky nodded and led the way. After fifty metres, they reached a food station and helped themselves to some of the regular ration. There was no choice. It seemed every captive got the same food, efficient, but unexciting. Nearby, the robot watched, silent and inactive apart from a white light shining near its top.

A few steps brought them to another door, a mirror of their own entrance with its own large button.

'This is tricky, Yuri. There is some creature behind this door. We don't know its size or whether it is dangerous to us. Neither of us is in any condition for serious combat. We have no weapons. We probably won't be able to communicate with it. There could be visitors watching this saucer and, if they see us, they might raise the alarm.'

'All very true, Miki,' said Yaroslav. 'Let's think for a moment.'

Shortly, he gave his assessment.

'OK. Firstly, in all the time I have been here, I have never seen any formal guards. I deduce that this place is almost totally automated. It's possible no visitor actually knows what they are going to see and if it should or shouldn't be happening. We might be able to move freely. Secondly, we don't know how many saucers there are, but we can expect that if we open a door, the inhabitant will be trained as I was to stand well back. We can go just inside and check things out, try to make contact. Why would we do that? What's the best option: trying to gather strength in numbers or upsetting some homicidal beast with a hunger for human flesh? Thirdly, we haven't yet found the way out. Is it guarded, locked, impassable?'

'Well, there doesn't seem to be anyone in these tunnels,' mused Kempinsky. 'Could we disable the robot in the hope of delaying our escape being noticed?

It's a long time to the next feed. Why don't we split up and check things out and meet back here in, say, no more than thirty minutes?'

'I tell you what, Miki,' exclaimed Yaroslav. 'If anything does go wrong, like being discovered, we don't need to risk conflict or give ourselves away. We can make a dash back to our saucer, independently if necessary, and get back inside. We can act like nothing has happened. It's OK, because we now know how to get out.'

Kempinsky moved to the robot and found only one control, a small catch which he moved sideways. The white light went out. The men moved off down separate tunnels. It was then that Kempinsky realised that they were both naked. He wondered if that would cause a problem. But, then, all machines were undressed. Or so he imagined.

Neither of them needed the full thirty minutes before they met back at the food station. The robot remained motionless. Kempinsky reported first.

'I found five other doors, all the same as ours with a button for opening. The difference was that two of them had their own robots and food stations. I switched off the robots in the same way. One food station was full of live rodents waiting to be served. The other contained what I took to be large cuts of raw, rotting fish. The smell was awful. I couldn't hear anything from behind the doors.'

'Good grief,' reacted Yaroslav. 'I was luckier. I found only two more doors, close together, but some distance away from here. There was one feeding station and one robot. I switched this robot off as well. The food was the same as ours, but a different colour. It was green and it had some lumps in it. I decided not to taste it.'

He paused, then broke into a grin.

'I also found the way out, Miki. It's completely unguarded. The tunnel opens into a sort of thoroughfare, more like a wide passageway. It has walls, but they are opaque and it looks like you can pass through them without disrupting them. Everything is open to the sky, which is red with multi-coloured stars, but, I don't know, I thought it looked artificial.

'Miki, there were no vehicles, but I saw several Tralfamadorians floating along just like our cleaning robots. They are similar in form to humans, with large heads. They have three arms, two in front and a longer one behind, and no legs. I couldn't see any signs of what we would call senses, no eyes, mouths, ears, noses, just a shiny, aluminium-like metal skin. They moved without looking, always on their own except, and here's the thing, each was followed by a creature made of flesh with limbs and obvious sensory organs, but in the wrong places compared to us. They looked like servants or slaves even.

'One of them saw me. I know it did because the head moved and the eyes fixed. I don't know why, perhaps I didn't understand, but it clearly decided not to make contact. I think we can move about outside with impunity unless they start looking for us.'

The cosmonauts decided to open a couple of saucer doors to see if they could find some natural allies. The obvious choice was to try among those five who were fed the same food as they had been. They worked out a simple plan. Kempinsky, the better skilled at language, would go inside, but stay near the door while he made an assessment. Yaroslav would stay in the tunnel ready to dash to the rescue or to push the button.

'Ready?' asked Yaroslav.

Kempinsky felt his heart beat become irregular. He nodded. Yaroslav pushed the button and Kempinsky stepped inside. There were no cushions. The interior was a forest of black plants about twice the height of a man, but with straight rods rather than branches. The rods were evenly spaced, smooth and looked like a connecting network of ladder rungs. The air was heavy and smelled of rotting mushrooms and, perhaps, liquorice. There was no movement and no creature to be seen. He took a further step, heard a growl and found himself in a hairy bear hug which stopped him from moving his arms. Only, it wasn't a bear. It was a gorilla with three heads. One of the heads began nibbling his ear. For some absurd reason, Kempinsky spoke in French. It was, after all, the language of diplomacy.

'Bonjour, Monsieur … umm, Messieurs, peut-être … Comment ça va tous les trois?'

The nibbling head stopped its investigation and looked up in surprise.

'Vous êtes français? Vous êtes d'une vieille planète?'[1]

Kempinsky felt his head spinning. He resorted to Russian for no reason he could discern.

'Нет, я не француз. Я русский. Да, я со старой планеты?'[2]

The middle head looked up with something approaching delight.

1 'You are French? You are from an old planet?'

2 'No, I am not French. I'm Russian. Yes, I am from an old planet.'

'There was no creature to be seen. Kempinsky took a further step, heard a growl, sensed movement and found himself in a hairy bear hug.'

Radical Cartoons

'Вы действительно русский? У меня была третья сестра, которая была почти русской!'[3]

Kempinsky became more unbalanced. The spinning became faster and uneven. He squeezed out an arm to reach for a tree rod to stop himself from falling. He tried English, but the three heads looked at each other blankly. There was an embarrassing silence and Kempinsky felt his ear becoming sore with the gnawing. There was no sign of Yaroslav.

The three heads began what might have been a conversation, a mixture of grunts, growls and howls. Kempinsky was released and the gorilla thumped their chest while ambling around him. There was a voice from far behind.

'I think they might like you, Miki,' whispered Yaroslav. 'You're doing very well.'

Yaroslav's intervention could have been a bad mistake. He was spotted and quickly invited to join the group which, of course, meant leaving the safety of the door button.

'Hello, Earthmen,' said the left most head. 'We are,' and they reeled off in turn, '*Beri*, *Ng*, *Ei*. What are you called?'

After many diversions and misunderstandings, the gorilla told their story.

When a prominent machine suggested to his community that a collection be made for their amusement of species that had a significant strength when compared to themselves, an early selection was the three-headed gorilla. It was chosen because it had an innate ability to speak any language within seconds of first hearing.

An obsessive accountant once tried to assess the number of tongues that their gorilla knew, but had to give up when his memory bank was full and he was unable to do his proper work. A colleague carefully pointed out that the exercise was pointless anyway. All one had to do was to count the number of languages in the universe and that was the answer. That was impossible as new languages were formed daily on distant planets that no one yet knew about and, added the colleague with withering logic, what good was the answer anyway? What decision might change as a result of the knowledge? Another mathematician decided to develop an algorithm based on an estimate of the rate of growth of new planets. The algorithm was found to have some use in

3 'Are you really Russian? I had a third-sister who was almost Russian!'

the betting industry. That mathematician was thought kidnapped and never heard from again.

Gorillas were well known across the universe as placid animals. Having three heads in tune with each other seemed to make this an even more prominent characteristic. Their most antisocial trait was a tendency to nibble olfactory organs for the wax. Their interest became particularly annoying when they forgot that the objects of their attention were attached to a living creature who had other uses for them.

'What do you mean, you don't want to escape?' exploded Yaroslav. 'Do you want to live in a cage all of your life?'

'We three don't see it that way,' explained Ng patiently. 'We get lots of observers, many from other planets so we get to learn many new languages. We collected five more during the last visiting period, didn't we guys?'

Beri and Ei nodded with enthusiasm.

'We can always go out if we get bored,' added Ei.

'What do you mean *go out*,' shouted Kempinsky. 'How do you get to *go out*?'

'Well, we push the button in the wall and go for a walk.'

'What button?'

The button that's flush with our side of the door, the one the food robot uses to get out when it has finished delivering and tidying up. The same way you got here.'

'Oh, that button,' groaned Kempinsky. 'Yeah, we use it all the time. It's surprising we never met you wandering around the tunnels or outside.'

Yaroslav thought it best to change the subject.

'Do you three know many of the creatures in any of the other saucers. Is there anyone worth meeting?'

'Honestly, a couple of them are bad and dangerous,' shared Beri. 'They are always hungry. But, the rest of us usually get together for a party when this facility is shut. We have some strong drink, sing and demonstrate our skills.'

'There's no sex, though,' added Ng. 'We tried it once, but it wasn't really practicable. One of the turtles died. It was very sad, although she tasted really good after all this bland food that the robots supply. They don't understand food, being machines and all.

'Why don't you come to the next party and meet everyone. It's only a few feeding times away.'

Kempinsky spared a thought for all the switched off robots standing motionless at their food stations.

12

PARTY TIME

Kempinsky was seated on the multi-segmented shell of a drunk woodlouse. A large, green-spotted snake curled possessively around him from waist to neck. One of his arms stuck out between the coils, but too far away to raise a cup of bubbling fire juice to his lips.

'Isn't this a fun party,' enthused the snake. 'It's so on the edge. One squeeze and you're paste.'

'Do you get out much?' tried Kempinsky.

'To be honest, not as much as I would like. It's to do with being a snake. Those visitors you call Tralfamadorians float along with what you humans describe as their noses in the air, although, of course, they don't have one, a nose, I mean. When we meet in the street, we snakes have to move out of the way in case we get, as you humans say, under their feet, except that they don't have any. It is undignified for everyone. Our hosts topple over if we break their traction. They get all hot and bothered, as you humans say, lying in the dust. We scarper before there is any reaction.

'Except, of course,' said the snake warming to its story, 'they can't get hot and bothered because they are machines.'

'Except, of course,' thought Kempinsky, 'snakes can't warm because they are cold-blooded.'

He also thought snakes could be quite boring.

'This is the great problem with intelligent machines,' continued the snake, oblivious to the interruption. 'They so desperately want to be human that they adopt all sorts of nonsensical airs and graces, except that … well you know.'

'Everyone must have a special skill to have been placed in one of the viewing saucers,' mused Kempinsky. 'What's yours?'

'Oh, I thought you knew. We snakes are the supreme mind readers. One boring squeeze, remember!'

With what Kempinsky thought could only be described as a wicked grin, the snake, 'call me Anytime, a silly name, I know', slid away to hug another new acquaintance.

The woodlouse wriggled and emitted a lengthy, wet noise that was malodorous.

'I do that to gain attention,' she said. 'The better question for you is why was your friend Yaroslav brought here in the first place? What is so special about humans? What is their characteristic that is recognised as superior by your Tralfamadorians? And, before you ask, my kind are here because we ask the questions that no one else thinks to ask. That makes our questions powerful and respected. They can start revolutions. The keepers also provide us with an unending supply of rotting wood in a dozen flavours.'

Kempinsky had given no thought to his best friends of so little time ago, his water bears.

'Do you know any tardigrades?' he asked the woodlouse.

'None at all. Hardy, but not very bright. And a bit small. More of a nibble than a main meal. Now, do you mind standing up? I'm hungry and there's some eucalyptus somewhere.'

Kempinsky found Yaroslav sitting in a quiet corner next to a rather dumpy owl without a discernible head. Its dozen eyes were a ring of rheumy dull diamonds under bushy eyebrows which circled its midriff.

'Hi, guys,' he said as he sat the other side of the owl. 'Anything exciting going on?'

'Same old, same old,' grumbled the owl. 'Music too loud and thumpy, everyone pretending to be delighted to be prisoners in this dump and we're not allowed to eat rodents in company. What's not to like?'

'This is Eeyore,' offered Yaroslav. 'He's the most interesting creature I've met here. He claims to be the longest resident and he's watched the place go steadily downhill. It's turned him into a devout critic of everything Tralfamadorian.'

'No wonder you two are getting on,' quipped Kempinsky, but not before he saw the start in Yaroslav's eyes as he had picked at the old wound.

'Only joking, Yuri.' He could see that the attempt to repair his error had failed.

Kempinsky turned to the owl. 'Tell me, Eeyore, I'm interested in why you think you're a prisoner when the door is open? Everyone else seems to have come to terms with their life.'

'Matter of perspective,' shrugged the owl. 'No one chose to be here. They were brought by your Tralfamadorians to populate a zoo of curiosities. I suppose it's possible to have come from somewhere inhospitable and to think you have landed in clover. I've always hankered for my home planet. It's where I belong, where I grew up in an environment that suited, where my friends are. And the rats taste different.

'How dare anyone treat me like an exhibit to be carted around at some other creature's whim.'

'Why were you chosen?' asked Kempinsky. 'What's your speciality?'

'Obvious, isn't it. I'm the eternal pessimist. I can see bad in any situation. These Tralfamadorians are just over-developed machines. They have trouble with moral dilemmas. They can trust me to show them the downside of all their schemes. They enjoy learning about the inefficiency of indecision in others.'

Eeyore laughed at his own self-deprecation. The sound was like the bray of a donkey, nothing at all like the soaring, querulous, intertwined hooting of the Tralfamadorians.

'Why do you stay?' asked Yaroslav. 'Why haven't you flown away?'

Eeyore fixed Yaroslav with three of his red and watery eyes.

'You tell me?' he pleaded, emotion in his voice for the first time. 'I'm alone, you realise; no friend or partner like you two. Every time I come up with a new scheme, my natural belief in its failure floods in. Anyone apart from the crocogators can get out of here. That's because those beasts are kept under lock and key. They lie in ambush and have the strongest bite in the universe. Nobody dares turn their back on them.'

'The big question is what do I do when I get outside? I don't know the lie of the land. I don't know where to go. What is there to eat? Even the sky doesn't look real.'

'And the real big one, how do I get to my home, wherever it is?'

There was a pause.

Kempinsky then asked one of those questions which, with hindsight, sound life changing.

'If you're game, no disrespect Eeyore, we could put our heads together and make a plan?'

13
A PLAN OF SORTS

The robots were switched on and deliveries and cleanings restarted. The escape committee met every day. In truth, its hard core consisted of the owl and the humans. Other creatures drifted in and out as the mood took them. The crocogators asked to attend, but were refused. Anytime, the snake, commented on unspoken thoughts which confused almost everyone. The woodlouse turned out to be one of a pair who thoughtfully came to provide an extra seat. Kempinsky was sure they had taken against him for they often brought tardigrades as snacks and sat cracking their shells and spitting them onto the floor. No one was sure why the automatic sloth with the slowly flashing lights occasionally came. It never spoke and usually hung upside down and stayed asleep long after a meeting was over. The gorilla shared their personal frustration. As the sloth never spoke, they had no opportunity to learn its language.

No profound thoughts or sprigs of brilliance bubbled to the surface, although most of the creatures tried in their own way to stay involved and to be creative. Any idea that might lead somewhere had to pass Eeyore's relentless destructive streak. There was no attempt at security. After one particularly dispiriting meeting, Yaroslav shared with Kempinsky that he wouldn't be surprised if a Tralfamadorian or two were hovering quietly unnoticed in the background.

Everyone now slept where they liked. The cosmonauts often stayed with Eeyore, but they looked away when he tucked into his fresh rodents. He didn't go for a direct kill, but liked to toy with his food first, often shaking it ferociously. He shrugged.

'Habit of a lifetime,' he explained. 'More hygienic than dead meat. You never know where it's been and how long it's been there.'

It was only Kempinsky's innate positivity that kept the meetings going. As inaction became the norm, participants talked less and less about escaping and used the togetherness as gatherings to discuss social topics. Racial standing had never been an issue. All those in the room had at least one characteristic in which they were supreme, even over the Tralfamadorians. Conversations meandered into the meanings of equality and diversity and sub-groups were formed to develop working papers. Some creatures discovered they had previously unknown grievances. The first point of discussion was deciding which language should be used for these papers. The gorilla volunteered to produce them in any requested language. This was accepted, but, in practice, it meant that the gorilla took control of the minutes whatever the agenda and no one was any the wiser. The gorilla, especially Ng, particularly enjoyed this new found power. The three heads began to keep information one from another.

The saucers lost their uniqueness so that the excitement which had previously been a hallmark of the visitors from outside decreased. The flashing purple waned and often turned a dull grey. Owl sounds were little heard. The physical charm of defecation was hardly seen. The specimens sat in circles communicating, then slept where they lay, then talked some more.

What pleasure was there in this for forward-looking machines?

The pessimism infected Yaroslav, already a willing recipient. He began to remember Kempinsky's relentless hope and started to dislike him all over again. Most nights, vague dreams of his lost family came to him in vivid colours. The same twist of fate that brought back fuzzy memories of his wife and children had also landed him in these endless, pointless meetings. That human Kempinsky was at the root of all his problems.

Eeyore waddled into one meeting where everyone was dozing.

'I have some news,' he exclaimed in a voice close to carrying a surprising hint of interest.

No one stirred, which met his expectations. He sat, lonely, in a corner exhibiting every indication of uselessness. He dozed himself until he was wakened by Kempinsky.

'Did somebody say something?' the human asked without enthusiasm.

After a while, Eeyore replied, 'It was only me. I was outside walking around wondering what we all could do next so that we could be free. I noticed that there was a sort of a notice outside our main entrance which said the place was closed through lack of visitors. As I came back in, I saw that all the robots had gone and so had the food stations. I just thought that you might be interested, that's all. I didn't mean to bother you. Sorry.'

'That could be a bummer,' offered a woodlouse. 'There's plenty of dead wood around for us, but there's no longer any free fresh food for most of you. I guess you guys will want to have a meeting about it. Some time.'

14

LOSS OF INNOCENCE

Kempinsky sought Yaroslav's attention in a quiet moment towards the end of yet another unending party, or perhaps it was the same party, unending.

'I think we should go outside more, Yari,' he said. 'See what there is to see. Perhaps find out what opportunities we might have by understanding how this planet works, how the Tralfamadorians live. We might see a way to freedom.'

Yaroslav gave a huge sigh and gazed despondently at his companion. Could he bear to spend any time at all with this lump of positivity?

'Miki,' he began, 'what freedom are you looking for? Have you thought about it in practical terms? You are free now to think what you want, to say what you want, to meet who you want and it seems, as far as we know, to go where you want. Nobody is ordering you about. It's freer than ever Russia was, but I would accept even those stupid and demeaning constraints if it meant that I could get my family back.

'Do you want to be free to associate with other humans? Well, as far as we know, there aren't any others and, if there were, how would we find them, get to them?'

Yaroslav gave another great sigh and fixed his eyes on his erstwhile comrade. He could feel his bile rising. He didn't like what he was becoming. Even more, he didn't like that he couldn't control it.

He continued his lesson. 'Or is it that, freedom to you is going to any place without Tralfamadorians which, from what I understand, is no place at all in this universe nor, perhaps, in any other?'

He raised his arms in a futile plea.

'Wherever we went, we would find other species. We have no inalienable rights. We are just flotsam in space that can be extinguished in a blink. We would have to fit in with whatever government already existed. We wouldn't be free unless we captured the place and subjugated its people.

'And then they wouldn't be free, would they?'

Kempinsky slumped onto a woodlouse and seemed to go into a trance.

'It's not very free being used as a seat without being asked,' the woodlouse said. 'But, in truth, I don't mind. I like being useful and having company. And, I can always ask questions.'

Finally, Kempinsky responded. He looked like he had aged since the time of the first party, now more a dried leaf drifting in the wind than a proud branch sprouting green growth and ready to stand its ground. He conceded most of his position.

'You're right, Yuri, of course, but I can't just give up on the way I've always lived my life. It's to do with self worth. I need something to exist for, something to strive for. It's a belief that things can be made better. You think that it's just pointless optimism. I think it's what I am.'

He paused to order his thoughts, not too successfully.

A woodlouse interrupted.

'I mentioned this before, but you both ignored me,' she said. 'Have you ever considered what special characteristic the Tralfamadorians saw in humanoids that made them bring you to this zoo? After all, they suspected that you may be a great danger to them personally. They also had proof that your kind had spent its entire existence destroying itself and its planets.'

Neither Kempinsky nor Yaroslav answered although, on reflection, they both thought it an excellent woodlouse sort of question.

'We're going for a walk, Professor Woodlouse,' said Yaroslav. 'We thought we might witness some Tralfamadorian freedom and see what it tastes like.'

'Dreadful confused metaphors,' said the woodlouse. 'You Russians certainly weren't chosen for your command of language. At least, if you go out, it will be a burden off my back.'

'Anyone else coming?'

An unusual convoy of creatures with superlative characteristics made its way out of the tunnels and into the local thoroughfare. Kempinsky thought one might even describe the gaggle of snake, owl, gorilla, woodlouse, humans and several others as arresting, but none of the Tralfamadorian travellers batted a metaphorical automatic eyelid. However, each of the attendants, skipping along in their wake of their master, did notice. Nothing was said, but significant glances were despatched without any hint at their meaning.

Members of the convoy tended to wander and even linger as they took in the sights. They delighted as they slipped through the opaque walls, but caught glimpses only of characterless buildings, stops for a bullet train and, oddly, a plethora of statues.

'How can you have so many statues when all these machines look the same?' mused Yaroslav.

It was Kempinsky's turn to be glum.

'Not much freedom out here, Yari,' he commented. 'It's even more boring than the inside of the space station.'

It was at this moment that Anytime slithered to a dreamy halt in the middle of the pathway. A hurrying Tralfamadorian, oblivious to this lowly obstruction, lost traction and toppled to the ground. One purpose of the attendants became apparent as they immediately worked hard together to right their master. Long golden cloths carried in their belts were used with care to ensure that during the rescue no part of the sufferer was touched directly. However, damage had been done. A dent in the side of the machine had interfered with its balancing mechanism and it flailed around in a disturbing way; disturbing that is if one had a soft spot for wounded Tralfamadorians.

Several things happened almost at once. All Tralfamadorians disappeared through the gauze. A truck with an efficient lifting device appeared at speed and bore away the wounded citizen, perhaps for repair, perhaps for disposal. A robot dropped from the back of the truck, not unlike a Tralfamadorian, but smaller, less pleasant and coloured red. It raised an arm, pointed it at Anytime, who, after a crack-like noise, disintegrated in a mess of fluids and tissue. Without pause, the arm swung towards the now masterless attendant who likewise died. A few others of his kind scattered in terror through the side walls, but not before another was terminated.

The gorilla, fleetingly a stupefied witness, heard the buzz and crackle of a message sent by the robot and instantly translated their latest language.

'Run. Slither. Fly,' shouted Beri, Ng and Ei. 'That thing plans to kill us all for witnessing the humiliation of a member of the master race.'

All the creatures escaped except for the wisest woodlouse, too slow for its task. She died with a question on her lips. Because of her size, she made the biggest mess of all.

Kempinsky and Yaroslav, falling instantly back on their Earth combat training, flung themselves into the cover of a small building. Within seconds, they were landed on by two attendants who tried to disappear beneath the hard ground, shaking in fear. They were followed by the gorilla who translated their frantic warning.

'Don't speak,' came a hiss. 'Those murderers pick up creature sounds. They will kill anything they find in the next few minutes.'

Everyone lay motionless, eyes cast down in the dirt. A large shadow suddenly blocked the little light and they feared the worst.

'I think they've gone, but you can never be sure,' offered Eeyore looking down at them. 'That didn't go very well, did it?'

The gorilla joined in. 'We have a new feeling. We think that it is called anger. We were fond of that woodlouse. She was a friend.'

'Try turning your anger to some purpose,' said Kempinsky. 'Ask your new acquaintances to tell you something about the Tralfamadorians. We have to find a way of hitting back.'

The first problem was getting the names right. The attendants called themselves 'The Originals' as they believed themselves to be the first inhabitants of the planet. Many aeons ago, machines arrived and colonised the place. The invaders were called 'The Masters'. The name of the planet, if it ever had one, was forgotten. The word 'Tralfamadore' was unknown to them.

The master machines were insensitive to creature sufferings. The Originals were seen as dull and almost useless. They were mocked and came to be used as servants for all menial tasks, especially righting their toppled colonists. They were completely dispensable and were often hunted for pleasure. The slightest infraction was met by annihilation. Accidental contact, particularly, was met by death. At other times, The Masters hardly noticed the existence of their slaves. Their population was kept sufficient through breeding farms of such awful conditions that to be taken into direct service was seen as a benefit.

The Originals hated The Masters with a depth of continuous loathing that over the ages became embedded in their psyche. Had they possessed the skills, the means or the freedom there would have been a total slaughter.

'Ask where The Masters live,' demanded Kempinsky. 'How do they reproduce, repair themselves or keep their numbers at a satisfactory level?'

There was a large building known as 'The Factory' where The Originals assumed these activities took place, but they had no knowledge of what form they took. The Originals were not allowed inside its perimeter; to try to enter meant death. It was assumed that, as no original was allowed to travel without a master and they never went any great distance, there were many factories on the planet and many masters unseen.

The Masters showed no sign of ageing. It was thought each of them went to this building at some time and always if they were damaged. However, The Originals could not be sure because to them all masters were identical. There was no discernible difference between any of the machines.

'So, the answer lies at the factory,' declared Kempinsky to the group. 'We must take it otherwise we will never be free.'

Several originals had joined the survivors of the zoo convoy. They debated, neared conclusions, debated some more and neared the same conclusions again. Affection for the woodlouse motivated those in the gorilla faction. Others, like Yaroslav, Eeyore and most of The Originals saw disaster ahead, but had no answer to dealing with the cruelty of The Masters or Tralfamadorians or whatever. The loudest bloc, but by no means the largest, argued for an all or nothing attack.

To everyone's surprise, not least its own, the automatic sloth suddenly began to flash its lights in a way that demanded attention. It was hanging from a flagpole above their heads as it raised a weary eyebrow.

'When a machine goes bad,' it said, 'there is no saving it. It must be destroyed because it has no conscience. If upset, it will destroy everything in its path. I expect to die in the attempt, but we have no choice.'

With a gentle snore, the sloth then dropped into its natural state.

The group fell silent until Kempinsky said quietly and firmly, 'So, it is settled, then.'

It wasn't a question. Yaroslav felt all his bottled anger and yearning swell. He did not want to be coerced any longer by this man.

15

BLOW FOR FREEDOM

The factory lay in a desert of blue calcite marbles dotted with patches of shiny metal. After a period of intense observation, Kempinsky realised that the patches were discarded shells of Tralfamadorians. So much for the holiness of their skin. About every hour of Earth time, a transport arrived bringing machines for attention, often carried into the building, while others, perhaps the same in number floated out under their own power to be taken back to where they belonged.

It was in the middle of one of these gaps between arrivals that the band of avengers were to attack. Just four of the murderous red guard robots were spotted, one outside each corner of the building. The perimeter was a barrier in name only. Marbles had been pushed together to make a wall that would not seriously impede a woodlouse. Security appeared to be lax, but who knew what waited inside? There were twenty-two attackers spaced evenly around. The only weapons were handy rocks.

It was a suicide mission. Everyone would inch towards the building close to the ground until somebody or something was spotted, then all would rise and rush. Those who made it would use rocks to smash the guards' gun hands and their sensory centres until they were disabled.

Survivors would enter the building and deal with whatever they found. The equivalent of blood lust was in the air. Revenge or individual and differing concepts of freedom were firmly on the agenda.

The faster attackers had reached almost halfway when a robot became suspicious. Eeyore's shape and natural posture were not best designed for the task in hand. Nevertheless, a feathery lump on the marbles was not immediately threatening. A robot floated out to investigate. Eeyore, oblivious to the danger, and naturally expecting the worst, kept his head down and pushed on. Yaroslav, crawling to Eeyore's right saw all that happened in horror and in slow motion. Finally, the guard realised that something was amiss. It was not programmed for moral scruples or excessive caution. The crack was heard across the compound as he fired and the owl became a mass of gore and flying feathers.

Yaroslav, in truth not the bravest of men, was outraged. His only true friend had been killed. With a yell that filled the air, he rose and ran at the killer, who managed just one misplaced shot at the quickly moving target. Yaroslav ignored the gun hand and smashed his rock into the body. He smashed it again and again and again.

Across the marbles, the rush began. Several originals fell and were joined by the sloth and the last woodlouse, neither of whom showed the speed or necessary élan. The remainder used their rocks with purpose and vigour.

When Yaroslav joined Kempinsky at the open door, their number had halved.

Inside was a mass of automation. Some two dozen Tralfamadorian-sized cannisters were filled by masters. The tubes were connected to a central, circular opaque crystal which slowly rose and fell.

It was the life blood of the conquerors.

Around the room, in various stages of disrepair, six Tralfamadorians waited their turn. If it were possible, the machines looked shocked and aimless at the invasion of their sanctuary. What was happening was not possible.

The remaining originals led the charge carrying with them lifetimes of oppression. Their erstwhile masters were easily toppled and pounded. Cannisters were rudely opened and their occupants dragged to the floor and a similar fate. They made no sound.

The victors barely had time for a smile of comradeship and self-congratulation before the counterattack began. A platoon of red robots summoned to the scene began a slow march to the entrance, firing as they went. Pieces of the factory door flew around into the air. The bodies of the fallen guards provided weapons which Kempinsky and the originals found simple to operate. It was a gunfight. The red robots did not hesitate for it was not in their programming. Their numbers dwindled rapidly as they were outside and unprotected.

In the distance, several transports showed further reinforcements would soon arrive.

'We don't have long, Yari,' shouted Kempinsky. 'There are too many of them. Is there anything you can do?'

As he turned his head for an answer, the nearest robot fired without hesitation. Kempinsky was no more.

Yaroslav heard a second call, this one from the gorilla who was inspecting the central crystal for new languages. It had changed to a purple light.

'This power unit is connected to all the others in factories across the planet,' said Ng, the more technically minded of the three. 'It is capable of taking its feed from the other factories in case of failure. By pushing it to its maximum output, and instructing it to receive from all other crystals, it will come to a very messy end.'

'It's quite clear,' added Ei, 'that these conceited and evil things never imagined that anyone else would take control. There are no security or failsafe measures.'

Across the small mound of disintegrated originals laying at the threshold, Yaroslav could see red shapes moving into the building. He could also see clearly for the first time in a long while, the individual faces of his family.

'No choice, really,' he said with a finality he welcomed.

The gorillas kissed each other and moved the levers to full power.

16

THE SECOND LAST SECOND

For the universe, it was a day like any other. Somewhere in the vastness, a planet a few called Tralfamadore crumbled and then expanded in a black cloud. In a second, it was no more.

The event went unnoticed apart from on a far-off major star. Technicians noticed a slight blip on monitors used to track inter-galaxy power fluctuations. The planet was one of a large number of outliers for a machine master race. Its destruction was of no great significance, but its loss did signal one predetermined change of policy, immediately transmitted to the known worlds.

'Conclusion of 'Experiment Earth'. Humanoids are declared an existential danger. Whenever found, all their planets are to be exterminated without referral or hesitation.'

The End

Past, present and future: 'For the universe, it was a day like any other. Somewhere in the vastness, a planet a few called Tralfamadore crumbled and then expanded in a black cloud. In a second, it was no more.'

Ailsa Heal

Suggested reading

Adams, Douglas, *The Hitchhiker's Guide to the Universe* (BBC, 1978; many versions in print and sound)

Baker, David, *International Space Station 1998-2011 (all stages), Owner's Workshop Manual, An insight into the history, development, collaboration, production and role of the permanently manned earth-orbiting complex* (Haynes Publishing, Yeovil revised 2016)

Joyce, James, *Ulysses* (1922; The Bodley Head, London 2008); *Finnegans Wake* (1939; Minerva, London 1992)

Kafka, Franz, translated, Williams, John, '*Metamorphosis: the Transformation of Gregor Samsa*', *The Essential Kafka* (1914; Wordsworth Classics, Ware, 2014)

Perec, Georges, *Life: A User's Manual*, translated Bellos, David (1978; Vintage Books, London 2008)

Proust, Marcel, *In Search of Time*, Vol. 1, 'The Way by Swann's', translated Davis, Lydia (1913; Penguin, London 2003)

Trout, Kilgore, numerous (1956-82)

Vonnegut, Kurt, *The Sirens of Titan* (1959; Millennium, London 1999); *Slaughterhouse 5* (1969; Vintage Books, London 1995); *Armageddon in Retrospect* (posthumous collection; Vintage Books, London 2009)

Chris Heal's books are available through selected Hampshire retailers and major internet booksellers. Find details at www.candspublishing.org.uk.

The Winchester Tales (2022) (*concluding part of the Ridge Trilogy*)

An Anglo-Norman love story set during the invasion of England after 1066.
Gilbert of Bayeux, orphan, linguist and administrator, is brought to Winchester by Bishop Odo in 1067 to mastermind the appropriation of the land of the Saxon thegns fallen at Hastings. For the next forty years in Hampshire, he treads a precarious path through the Norman occupation. His great love, Ailgifu, is an outspoken mead seller from Medstead. His servant, Lēofric, provides challenging and dangerous company.

Ropley's Legacy (2021) (*second part of the Ridge Trilogy*)

The Ridge Enclosures, 1709 to 1850: Chawton, Farringdon, Medstead, Newton Valence and Ropley and the birth of Four Marks.
The very first private parliamentary enclosure in England was in 1709 in Ropley. Driven by the less than saintly bishop of Winchester, it was a highly contested land grab seeking to make money by taking control of the common fields. Over 150 years, the government sanctioned theft spread to all the neighbouring ridge villages.

The Four Marks Murders (2020) (*updated second edition; first part of the Ridge Trilogy*)

In this true-life thriller, Chris Heal investigates deliberate and untimely deaths in what was thought to be one of the quiet backwaters of Hampshire. The twenty murders begin in Roman times with over half since 1900 and three within the last few years. They beg the question, 'Is Four Marks the murder capital of Southern England?'

Reappearing (2020)

The semi-autobiographical sequel to Disappearing. *If an elderly couple save you from a bad death in the Sahara, there's an honest debt to be paid. But this couple have conflicting plans. The only escape is down the River Niger where some unpleasant people await. The hunt is on for an elusive father who fought for the French across the globe in the dog days of empire.*

Disappearing (2019)

A nomad with a violent past, infuriated by petty bureaucracy and the surveillance society, determines to live happily ever after, throwing off identity and leaving no trace. Things go awry: fighting for Biafran successionists, gun running in Morocco, murder in Brussels, terrorists in Nairobi and a deathly Saharan escape. Semi-autobiographical.

The Sound of Hunger (2018)

An acclaimed social biography of two brothers, Erich and Georg Gerth, WW1 u-boat captains, set against Germany's political and militaristic development from Bismarck to Hitler. A fast-paced, true detective story that tracks across archives, places and events in Europe and Africa. A select book in several German universities for its surprising English perspective on this key period.

Milton Keynes UK
Ingram Content Group UK Ltd.
UKHW050323121023
430411UK00002B/4